Praise for *USA TODAY* bestselling author RaeAnne Thayne and the Hope's Crossing series

"Thayne's series starter introduces the Colorado town of Hope's Crossing in what can be described as a cozy romance…[a] gentle, easy read."
—*Publishers Weekly* on *Blackberry Summer*

"Thayne's depiction of a small Colorado mountain town is subtle but evocative. Readers who love romance but not explicit sexual details will delight in this heartfelt tale of healing and hope."
—*Booklist* on *Blackberry Summer*

"Plenty of tenderness and Colorado sunshine flavor this pleasant escape."
—*Publishers Weekly* on *Woodrose Mountain*

"Thayne, once again, delivers a heartfelt story of a caring community and a caring romance between adults who have triumphed over tragedies."
—*Booklist* on *Woodrose Mountain*

"Readers will love this novel for the cast of characters and its endearing plotline… a thoroughly enjoyable read."
—*RT Book Reviews* on *Woodrose Mountain*

Also available from RaeAnne Thayne and Harlequin HQN

Sweet Laurel Falls
Woodrose Mountain
Blackberry Summer

Other titles by this author available in ebook format.

And coming soon
Willowleaf Lane

RaeAnne Thayne

Currant Creek Valley

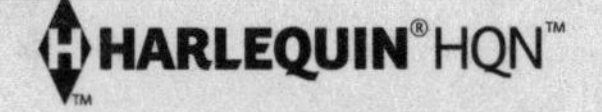

ISBN-13: 978-0-373-77747-1

CURRANT CREEK VALLEY

This edition published by arrangement with Harlequin Books S.A.

For questions and comments about the quality of this book, please contact us at CustomerService@Harlequin.com.

Printed in U.S.A.

To Janice Thayne, whose banana nut bread recipe
I'll never quite be able to replicate, no matter how hard
I try. I love you dearly! Thank you for your
loving example over the years, and especially
for raising your son to be such a wonderful man.

Special thanks to Karen Proudfoot for the delicious
food descriptions that made me so hungry.

Currant Creek Valley

CHAPTER ONE

ALEXANDRA MCKNIGHT opened the door to her dream-come-true restaurant and held her breath.

She loved this place already and she wanted her dearest friends to see beyond the sawhorses and scaffolding and unfinished surfaces to the potential awesomeness of it.

The members of her book club filed in, a little out of breath after walking up the hilly Main Street from her sister Maura's bookstore in downtown Hope's Crossing. At least they had a lovely April day for the walk, sunny and pleasant, with only a few puffy clouds overhead.

Claire McKnight, Alex's best friend and now sister-in-law, was the first one inside. She moved past the new double-sided river-rock fireplace that separated what would be the reception area from the first-floor dining room.

Claire whirled around to take in the walls, peeled back to bare brick, the original wood flooring and the intact fire pole that descended from the second-floor dining area that used to be the sleeping quarters of the old firehouse, back in the days when Hope's Crossing was a rough and rowdy mining town.

"What a fantastic space," Claire exclaimed. "I'll admit, I was more than a little nervous when you told me Brodie and Jack were cooking up this idea. I mean, this old place has been an eyesore in town forever! I thought they should have torn it down years ago. Now that I see the renovations, my mind is racing with possibilities."

"I know, right?" Alex beamed at Claire and her other friends and several family members gathered beside them.

"Pure genius to replace the fire-truck doors with that big sliding wall of windows," Charlotte Caine exclaimed, her pretty features alight. "What an incredible view of Woodrose Mountain and downtown. You can see everything from here."

"I know. And on summer days, we can roll the windows to the side and make the whole thing a big outdoor space.

"Oh, darling. This is fantastic," her mother exclaimed. Mary Ella squeezed her hand, and Alex was so glad she had brought them to the restaurant for the quick tour and an impromptu picnic dinner to take care of the Bites part of their Books and Bites name.

"Brodie is so excited about Brazen." Evie Thorne tucked a strand of long blond hair behind her ear. "I haven't seen him this enthusiastic about a project in a long time."

"Jack really did a fantastic job with the design," Mary Ella said, looking around.

"Of course he did. He's Jackson Lange." The wife of the man in question smiled with a contentment Alex never thought she would see again on her older sister's features, after the hellish time two years ago. She owed Jack so much. The creative architectural genius that had gone into designing this space was the very least of her debts to him.

She smiled at this group of women she loved dearly. "I'm am indeed blessed to have friends and sisters who are not only brilliant and talented in their own rights, but who also have the good taste to marry well…so I don't have to."

As she might have expected, her words earned a laugh from nearly everyone except her mother. Alex didn't miss the spark of worry in her mother's eyes behind their trendy little glasses.

She ignored it, as she customarily did. She wasn't going to let her mother's concern bother her. Not when she was so relieved at their excited reaction to the restaurant, even at this embryonic stage.

"Thank you for walking all the way up the hill for lunch today. As a reward, you get to be the first to enjoy a meal here at Brazen, of sorts. I packed a picnic for us. It seemed appropriate, given the infamous picnic in this month's selection."

"I still say we should have picked *Pride and Prejudice* instead of *Emma.* Mr. Darcy is a much sexier hero than Mr. Knightley," Brodie's mother, Katherine, opined, a distinct gleam in her eyes.

"We read P and P two years ago, remember?" Mary Ella reminded her. "Alex made that fantastic white soup and the trifles."

"I do hope you don't have pigeon pies and cold lamb in that hamper you lugged all the way up here," Alex's oldest sister, Angie, said.

"How do you remember what they ate at the picnic in *Emma?*" Charlotte asked with a laugh.

Angie grinned. "I'm all about the food. You should know that by now."

"No pigeon or lamb. Boring cold fried chicken, potato salad and fruit. But I do have pie. And other things."

She pulled open the large hamper, reached inside for the blanket and spread it out on the wooden floor. "Sorry we don't have tables and chairs yet. They're on order but won't be here for another few weeks. If you prefer not to sit on the floor, you can sit on the stairs. Katherine, Mom, Ruth, you three can sit on the hearth ledge."

"Perfect," Katherine Thorne declared.

Alex set the dishes out in the middle of the blanket, and for the next few moments, everyone in the book club was busy filling plates.

This had been a crazy idea to bring them here for the picnic. They all would have been far more comfortable back at Dog-Eared Books & Brew, Maura's shop, but Alex had been dying to show everyone the progress.

"You must be so excited for the restaurant to open," Janie Hamilton, one of their newer members, said around a mouthful of chicken salad sandwich.

"I can't wait," Alex said, though she declined to add that part of her also quaked with fear, if she let it.

Running her own restaurant had been her dream since she first decided to go to culinary school. Now that the opening date was drawing closer and the dream was quickly on its way to becoming reality, raw anxiety warred with her anticipation, the fear that she didn't really have the necessary skills and creativity to make Brazen shine amid the crowded Hope's Crossing restaurant scene.

"As far as I can tell, only one small detail is missing," Angie said.

"What's that?" Mary Ella asked.

Her sister scanned the open space again. "Maybe I'm missing something but, um, where's the kitchen?"

"Oh, my word, you're right," Janie exclaimed. "There's no kitchen!"

"Where's your brilliant architect of a husband now?" Katherine teased Maura. "He left out the most important part."

"Yeah, yeah," Alex said, though she felt a stab of nerves. She needed a kitchen! "It's coming. Another three weeks, according to Brodie. The contractor who has done most of the rehab work so far had a medical emergency in his family and Brodie had to hire someone else to finish up."

"Sam Delgado," Evie said. "He's worked with Brodie before on some projects closer to Denver. I've met him a few times. He's really nice."

"I don't care how nice he is. I just want him to get his butt in gear and finish the kitchen so I can start stocking it and we can set an opening."

That uncertainty was just one of the worries keeping her up at night. After years of being a sous-chef in someone else's kitchen, she finally had the opportunity to prove herself. As owner and developer of the restaurant, Brodie was giving her this chance, and she couldn't afford to blow it.

She would be fine, she assured herself again. She was hardworking and talented and had years of experience under her white toque. What else did she need?

"I read something once that said nine in ten new restaurants close in the first year," Ruth Tatum said, wiping a napkin daintily at the corners of her mouth.

"Mom." Claire grimaced.

"What? I did."

Alex was quite used to Ruth's pithy comments, since she had practically grown up with Claire, but the words and the pessimism behind them still stung. "That's actually a myth," she was quick to point out. "The actual number is about one in four in the first year. Closer to three in five after about three years."

Yet another worry that kept her up at night. How would she face everyone in town who believed in her if she couldn't make Brazen a success?

"This place is going to be one of the restaurants that makes it," Mary Ella declared loyally. "Assuming you do get a kitchen and don't have to cook everything on a barbecue grill out back."

Alex sighed. "For now, you're going to have to use your imagination about the kitchen. Trust me when I tell you it's going to be fantastic. I've gone over the plans with Jack and Brodie. You've all seen Brodie's other restaurants in town. I'm sure you can guess this one is going to have state-of-the-art everything."

"So when will we actually be able to eat here?" Maura asked.

"You're eating now," she retorted. "A particularly delicious chopped spinach salad, if I do say so myself."

Her sister made a face. "That's not what I meant, Alexandra. When is Brazen supposed to open?"

She firmly ignored the flutters in her stomach. "Near the end of May but before Memorial Day weekend. We wanted to have a few weeks to work out the kinks before the summer tourist season hits."

"That doesn't give you much time, if the contractor still needs three weeks to finish the kitchen," Ruth pointed out, helpful as always.

"Yes, I know. He's supposed to be coming to town this weekend. It won't be soon enough for me."

"He'll be here," Evie assured her. "And I promise, you'll love the job he does."

She still couldn't believe the single most important component of her new restaurant wasn't complete. The previous contractor should have started in the kitchen and worked out from there, as far as she was concerned.

"Don't worry. Everything's going to be fantastic," Claire assured her. "Everyone knows what a brilliant chef you are. You're going to have people lined up from here to Silver Strike Canyon, waiting for your food."

She loved Claire dearly for her unwavering faith but had to take it with more than a grain of salt. Claire would probably bite her own tongue off before she would say anything that might be construed as even a sprinkle or two on Alex's parade.

"Thanks, hon."

To her relief, the conversation shifted away from the restaurant and on to the reason they ostensibly met, the book they had read that month. They discussed the mismatches in the book, Emma's strong and sometimes unlikeable personality, how different she was from many Austen heroines.

By the time the lively discussion trickled out and the conversation shifted again to gossip around town, most of the book club members had moved on to dessert.

"Charlotte, how's your brother?" Mary Ella asked into a rare lull.

Charlotte set down the sugar-free cookie Alex had specially fixed for her. Whenever she fixed a meal for the book club, she tried to remember that the candy-store owner was very aware of each bite after losing nearly eighty pounds over the past year.

"He's coming home, finally."

"Oh, I hadn't heard!" Katherine exclaimed. "That's wonderful news."

Charlotte didn't look as if she completely agreed but she gave a forced-looking smile. "He was officially released from Walter Reed several months ago but he stayed in the area for rehab. Dad will be happy to have him home."

Much to Alex's amusement, Katherine looked a little flustered at the mention of Dermot Caine, who owned the Center of Hope Café in town. The two of them shared a mutual crush but so far neither had done anything about it.

Dermot would certainly take good care of his son's nutrition needs, but Alex still made a mental note to add Dylan Caine to her informal list of food deliveries. The café served good, hearty comfort food, but a war hero like Dylan deserved gourmet fare once in a while.

"We'll have to throw a barbecue for him or something," Mary Ella said.

Charlotte shook her head quickly. "He would hate that. He's very…different from the Dylan you all probably remember. He will barely talk to any of us."

Charlotte came from a family as large as Alex's, though she was the only girl in a household of boys, while Alex had four sisters and only one brother, Claire's husband, Riley.

"I guess I should get back to the bookstore," Maura said. "Jack has Henry this afternoon over at his office and he's probably ready for a nap."

"Who? Jack or Henry?" Mary Ella asked.

"Both. Definitely."

Maura's adopted son was just about the most adorable ten-month-old Alex knew, but he was already turning into a handful.

"I need to go, too," Claire said. "We left Hannah in charge of String Fever while we were gone. She has such a soft heart, she just might give away half my inventory."

Alex had to swallow a laugh at the irony of Claire worrying about anyone else's soft heart when she was renowned for her overwhelming generosity.

"I really do love your place, Alex," she said.

"Same goes," Maura said, kissing her cheek. Alex almost wanted to cry to see her sister's obvious happiness, when she thought Maura would never be able to find joy again.

"We're all coming on opening night. Just try to keep us away," Katherine added.

Her friends gathered up their things, and Alex watched as they all began heading down the hill toward downtown.

Her mother was the last to leave. Mary Ella hugged her hard, surrounding her with the familiar scent of flowers and fabric softener. "I love this place, darling. It's so good to see you happy."

She drew away from her mother's embrace. "What are you talking about? I'm always happy."

"Are you?"

She wasn't in the mood for her mother's concern today. "Yes. I'm so happy, I beam with it. I'm a freaking glow stick. Why wouldn't I be?"

Annoyance flickered in Mary Ella's green eyes that she had passed on to each of her children.

"The restaurant is going to be wonderful. I just… hope it's everything you want."

"It will be," she said firmly.

"You know I worry about you."

"Because I'm not happily married, you mean, like everybody else, and cranking out grandbabies for you."

She meant her tone to sound flippant but she had a strong feeling she sounded prickly and sensitive instead.

Mary Ella stiffened. "That's not what I'm talking about."

She didn't want to get into this right now with her mother, not after their lovely book club meeting. She adored Mary Ella and admired her greatly for pulling the shattered pieces of her life together and moving on so many years ago, but sometimes her mother had very decided tunnel vision on some topics.

"Are you sure? Lila and I are the last ones standing, now that Riley and Maura have taken the leap, and Lila's too far away in California for you to meddle with."

"Do I meddle?" Mary Ella asked, her tone mild but her eyes flashing.

That wasn't fair to her mother, she knew. "No," she admitted. "But I know you would like to see me settled in a relationship like everybody else."

"Only if that's what you want. I don't care if you never marry, Alex. I've spent the last twenty years of my life single and thought I would remain that way for the rest of it. I certainly never expected Harry Lange to come blustering in."

She was glad Harry made Mary Ella happy, for reasons she still didn't understand, but that didn't mean she wanted to discuss her mother's love life.

"You can stop worrying about me, Mom. I have nearly everything I want."

"Nearly?"

She gestured around to the empty, echoing space. "I just need Brazen to catch fire on the local restaurant scene, so to speak."

Mary Ella didn't look convinced but she said nothing as she slipped her arms through the sleeves of the jacket she had shed during the picnic.

"I just hate to see you so…restless."

The term was painfully apt. She couldn't focus on anything, she was cooking up a storm trying out new recipes, she wasn't sleeping well.

Alex wanted to think her trouble was only jagged nerves prior to the restaurant opening, but she had a deep-seated fear the root was something else.

She had been looking for something for a long time since she had returned to the States. She had convinced herself it was only anticipation for this time in her life, when she was finally in control of her own restaurant, but what if Brazen still didn't fill that emptiness inside?

"I'm perfectly content with my life. Everything is just the way I want it."

Mary Ella stepped in to brush her lips to Alex's cheek. "If that's truly the case, then I'll try to stop worrying."

"I do believe you could survive without air and water longer than you could go without fretting over one of your children."

Her mother smiled, as she had intended. "It's a good thing I have so many of you to spread the love, then, isn't it? Imagine if you were an only child."

"The mind boggles."

Her mother's laugh trailed behind her as she headed out into the April afternoon.

She closed the door behind Mary Ella and twisted the lock then returned to stand in the empty space that would shortly—she hoped—hold her dream kitchen.

Though the kitchen faced away from the street, leaving the prime views for the diners, Jack had still designed this space with a few well-situated windows that offered lovely views of some of the older homes in Hope's Crossing that climbed the hillside and then the mountains beyond.

This was hers. She loved it already.

All the years of planning, working, dreaming, and in a few more weeks, that dream would be real.

She had worked as a sous-chef in other restaurants for years, since she had returned from Europe. She had been offered opportunities in the past to take over as executive chef but none of those situations had ever felt quite right. Either she had always told herself she wasn't ready or she didn't like the restaurant owners enough to work that closely with them or she had just plain been afraid.

When Brodie Thorne approached her with his plans for this old firehouse, she had instinctively recognized this was her time. She had known Brodie her whole life and she trusted him completely, both as a savvy businessman with a well-established track record of running restaurants and, more importantly, as a person.

The stars had aligned and she couldn't make any more excuses.

She closed her eyes for a moment and imagined this place crowded with customers, standing in the middle of a gleaming kitchen giving orders to her own sous-chefs, smelling delicious things cooking, listening to the clink of glasses and contented conversation.

And a string of colorful words coming from the back entrance.

She jerked her eyes open as the words pierced the last of her hazy fantasy and sent it whooshing away.

A man was here, in her restaurant. An unhappy man, by the sound of it. Seriously? Somebody really thought they could break into her restaurant in broad daylight, probably hoping to steal construction tools left on the site?

Guess again, asshole, she thought.

She reached for the closest weapon she could lay her hands on, a two-by-four about the length of her torso, and edged around the corner.

A hallway led off the main dining room toward the restroom facilities, as well as a space she intended to make a separate dining room for private parties.

With her heart pounding, she peeked around the corner, two-by-four at the ready. Afternoon sunlight filtered in through the windows and she registered only a few quick impressions of height and muscled bulk, dark short-cropped hair and an unmistakable air of menace.

The man had already pilfered a reciprocating saw in one hand and had a tool belt dangling from the other. Thieving bastard. No way was she going to let him get away with robbing her place, even if the stuff belonged to the contractor responsible for these knuckle-gnawing delays.

She was too angry to think about the wisdom of taking on a very large man presently armed with power tools. This was her restaurant and she had worked too blasted hard for it to let some jerk think he could march in here and loot the place.

Gripping the two-by-far in suddenly damp hands, she stepped forward. "Don't even think about it."

He whirled around, even tougher and scarier than she had first thought. He was also surprisingly clean-cut for someone up to no good.

"Don't think about what?" he growled, his voice as hard as his features.

"You picked the wrong place to rob, buster. My brother just happens to be the chief of police."

He cocked his head, one eyebrow lifted. "Is that right?"

"You better believe it. Now put down the tools and get out of here before I call him."

"Trust me, you don't want to do that."

Her anger kicked up a notch at his tone. As a sous-chef, she had spent more than a few years in the kitchen with temperamental, patronizing little men who thought they could intimidate her with their bluster and bluff. She was tired of it, yet another reason she couldn't wait to open her own restaurant.

She refused to acknowledge the grim truth of his words. She absolutely *didn't* want to call in Riley to help her deal with this. As a general rule, she had always tried to take care of herself, not drag her family into her problems.

She wasn't about to tell *him* that. Instead, she shifted the board—now growing increasingly heavy—and whipped out her cell phone. In this case, she would do whatever was necessary. Even if that meant turning to her brother. She scrolled through her address book and found Riley's number but paused, her thumb hovering over the name.

"You've got until the count of three to clear out," she said, aware she sounded perilously close to something out of a spaghetti Western.

He apparently agreed. "You're going to feel really stupid if you call in the cavalry right now. I'm not doing anything wrong."

She sniffed. "Funny, that's exactly what I would expect a criminal to say."

"I'm not a criminal."

"Again, I would have *totally* expected you to say that."

He gave a rough laugh that seemed to sizzle through her. Just nerves, she told herself. To fight them, she gripped the board more tightly and stared him down.

He looked a little bit old to be doing the smash-and-grab thing, maybe her age or slightly older, but he did have a biceps tattoo dripping beneath the short sleeve of a worn T-shirt that showed off every hard muscle.

All in all, he was really quite gorgeous, for a criminal, even if he didn't seem in the least threatened by a woman holding a two-by-four and a cell phone.

"Can I ask who you are and what you're doing here?" he actually had the effrontery to say.

She gaped at him. "None of your business! *You're* the one who's trespassing."

"Really? You think? Then why would I have this?"

He reached into the pocket of his jeans and pulled out a key that looked remarkably similar to the one she had used to unlock the door for her book club over an hour ago.

"You think I'm stupid enough to fall for that? For all

I know, that could be a key to the storage shed where you hide your victims in barrels full of acid."

He blinked a few times but didn't lose his amused half smile. "Wow. Been watching a few too many horror movies, have we?"

Okay, maybe it was a bit of an overreaction to accuse him of being a serial killer, but she wasn't about to back down now. "My point is I don't know who *you* are or why you're breaking into my restaurant."

"Your restaurant? Wrong. This is Brodie Thorne's restaurant."

The board slid a little in her hand and she finally set it down to rest one end on the ground, wondering uneasily if she might have made a teensy little mistake here.

"Okay, technically, yes." The restaurant was Brodie's, if one considered that he was the person who took all the risks and paid all the bills. "But I'm his chef."

The guy's half smile turned into a full-fledged one and her stomach fluttered at the impact of it. *Oh, my.*

"We appear to have a little misunderstanding here. You must be Alexandra McKnight."

She squinted at him. "Maybe."

"Brodie told me about you, but for some reason I thought you would be older."

She made a face. She would be thirty-seven this year, which felt ancient sometimes. "Okay, so we've established who I am. Now who the hell are you?"

"Oh, sorry." Coming out of that rough-edged, dangerous-looking face, the charm of his friendly smile caught her off guard.

"I'm Sam Delgado. I'm going to be finishing up your kitchen."

His words finally penetrated her thick skull and she

wanted to throw her face in her hands. She was an idiot who shouldn't be let out in public.

This man was charged with building her kitchen in an insane handful of weeks and the first thing she did to welcome him aboard the project was accuse him of stealing what were probably his own tools.

If she wanted this kitchen to provide ideal working conditions, she had to work closely with the contractor Brodie had picked. How would she be able to do that now, with this inauspicious beginning?

She propped the board against the wall and faced him with what she hoped was an apologetic look. "Oops."

To her relief, he didn't seem upset, even though a little annoyance would be completely justified. "Now aren't you glad you didn't call the police?"

"It was an honest mistake. You have to admit, you're a scary-looking dude, Sam Delgado. It must be the ink."

"I'm a pussycat when you get to know me."

"I doubt that."

"Just wait."

She knew perfectly well the words shouldn't send this little tingle of awareness zinging through her.

At least he was being decent about her almost beaning him with a board. She had to give him points for that. "I wasn't expecting you until the weekend. Brodie said you couldn't start until then."

"I wrapped up some other projects in Denver ahead of schedule and was able to break away a few days early. Figured I would come to town and do a little recon of the situation before my crew comes up tomorrow."

The way he spoke, the short haircut and what she glimpsed of his tattoo—which she could now see looked vaguely military-like—reminded her that Brodie had told her the guy was ex-army Special Forces, like Charlotte's brother, Dylan.

She figured it was safe to move closer to him. "Well, welcome to Hope's Crossing, Sam Delgado. I can promise you, not everyone in town will greet you with a two-by-four."

He smelled good, she couldn't help noticing. Like wind and sunshine and really sexy male. She really *was* an idiot to even notice.

"I don't blame you for being cautious. Any woman would have to be a little wary to find a stranger invading her space. No harm done." He set the reciprocating saw down on the floor and the belt with it.

"Brodie tells me you have definite ideas for your kitchen. I'm glad you're here, actually, so we can go over what you want. Care to fill me in?"

"Now?"

He shrugged. "Sure. Why not?"

She could think of several reasons, beginning with her heart rate, which still hadn't quite settled back down to normal. "Um, sure. Come on through to where the kitchen should be and we can talk."

"Let me grab your plans," he said, pointing to the back door.

When he returned, he unrolled the blueprints and she spent the next few moments detailing what she wanted in the kitchen, and the design she and Brodie had already come up with. Much to her delight, Sam had a few suggestions that would actually improve the work flow and traffic patterns.

"Are you sure you can bring us in with only a month before our projected opening?" she asked.

"It will be a push, I'm not going to lie to you, but my

guys are up to the challenge. I wouldn't have taken the job if I didn't think we could do it."

"I admire confidence in a man," she said. That wasn't the only thing she was admiring about Sam Delgado, but she ordered herself to settle down. For all she knew, he might indeed have a storage unit full of severed heads.

On the other hand, Brodie trusted him, and that carried a great deal of weight, as far as she was concerned. He wouldn't have brought Sam in on the project unless he had vetted him fully.

Even if Brodie weren't giving her this unbelievable chance at her own restaurant, he was also the husband and son of two of her dearest friends.

What was wrong with a little harmless flirtation? In fact, Sam Delgado might just be the cure to the restlessness her mother was talking about. She hadn't dated anybody in months, not since Oliver, the very funny Swiss ski instructor who had returned to the Alps midseason.

Sam was actually just her type—big, gorgeous and only in town for a few weeks. He would be leaving Hope's Crossing as soon as he wrapped up work on the restaurant. Why couldn't she spend some enjoyable leisure time with him while he was here, as long as he still had plenty of time to finish the project?

"Looks clear enough," Sam said, rolling up the blueprints he had pulled out of his pickup truck. "Since all the appliances and shelving and counters are already here, it's only a matter of putting everything in place. You should still be able to have your mid-May opening."

"I'm going to hold you to that, Mr. Delgado," she said. "Once my crew comes tomorrow, we can dig in."

"How many guys will you have?"

"Three others, besides me. We've all worked together a long time."

"Does everybody have a place to stay?"

"Brodie has made reservations at a hotel on the edge of town. Nothing fancy but it will do for now."

"Good. Good." She smiled. "Well, let me know if you need anything."

"I'll do that."

It was now or never, she thought, and plunged forward. "So I don't see a ring. Is there a Mrs. Delgado?"

Plenty of men didn't care to wear a wedding ring, either out of personal preference or deliberate obfuscation. When she was interested in a man, she was scrupulously careful about double-checking that particular point.

Some hard-earned lessons tended to stick with a woman.

Sam Delgado blinked, obviously a little bemused by the question. If she hadn't been watching him carefully for some sign of deceit, she might have missed the tangle of emotion in his gaze.

"As a matter of fact, there is. My brother's wife."

"But you don't have one of your own?" she pressed.

"Not currently."

His guarded reaction didn't seem particularly encouraging. He could be engaged—another hot button of hers because of family history—but she hadn't missed that sadness in his eyes and sensed he was telling the truth.

"Do you anticipate that changing anytime in the near future?"

"Not that I'm aware of, no. Why are you so curious?"

She shrugged. "Personal rule. I don't date men who are married, engaged or otherwise involved in a long-term relationship."

A corner of his mouth danced up. "I didn't realize we were planning on dating."

"Planning on it? No. But if the opportunity arose, I like to be certain ahead of time that both parties are… unentangled. Poachers bug the hell out of me. And men who allow themselves to be poached are even worse."

He gazed at her for a long moment as if he wasn't quite sure how to answer. "You don't have any problem speaking your mind, Ms. McKnight, do you?"

"Please. Call me Alex. Especially considering we might be planning on dating at some point in the foreseeable future."

He laughed as he shook his head. "Here's something you should know about me then. Call me old-fashioned, but I like to be in the driver's seat in these sorts of things."

She gave him a sultry smile over her shoulder. "Oh, you foolish, foolish man. You might *think* you're behind the wheel when it comes to most women, but that's only because we've decided to hand over the keys."

He chuckled that rough, sexy laugh that sent shivers down her spine again. "I don't know what sort of p—er, pansies—you traditionally date, Alex McKnight, but I'm a former Army Ranger. Know what our motto is? Rangers lead the way. And we don't just mean into enemy territory."

She hadn't been this attracted to a man in ages. She generally didn't go further than second base with the guys she dated, but something about Sam Delgado made her suspect he was just the sort of guy to tempt her into changing her mind.

"I'll keep that in mind. I guess I'll see you around, then."

She gave him a smile and a wave, tucking a strand of flyaway hair behind her ear as she picked up the basket of picnic supplies and headed for the door.

"Wait a minute," he called out. "You can't just leave. We were having a conversation here."

Was that what he called it? She smiled. "I thought we were done."

"What time am I picking you up tomorrow night?"

Oh, she really, really liked a man who took the initiative.

"I'm working tomorrow night until nine."

"Perfect. I'll probably be busy here until late and will need to unwind a little before I head to the hotel."

"Do you play pool, Army Ranger Delgado?"

"I've been known to chalk a few cues in my time."

"Great. Why don't I meet you at The Speckled Lizard? It's on Front Street, two blocks west of the center block of Main Street. It's one of the few places that stays open late on a Thursday night during the off-season."

"I'll see you then. Tomorrow, twenty-two hundred, Speckled Lizard. It's a date."

She smiled and headed out the door, anticipation winging through her.

All in all, she was very glad she hadn't hit him with a two-by-four.

CHAPTER TWO

SAM WATCHED BRODIE'S CHEF walk down the hill toward town swinging a picnic basket at her side, her blond curls bouncing behind her as she walked.

His heartbeat was still racing and he didn't know what the hell just happened there. Right now, he felt as if he'd just spent the past thirty minutes tumbling around in a cement mixer.

This surge of adrenaline and anticipation and *life* churning inside him was unfamiliar, uncharted territory.

When he walked into this old firehouse, he certainly never expected to stumble across a woman like her, brash, funny, brimming with energy.

What was it about her? She was beautiful, yes, with those huge green eyes and the endless spill of hair, but he knew plenty of beautiful women.

Though he continued to insist it wasn't necessary, Nicky's wife, Cheri, was always trying to hook him up with some friend of hers or other. For a stay-at-home mother, his sister-in-law seemed to know an unusually large number of lovely women, many from her previous job as a public-relations executive.

While he might have been attracted to a few of those women Cheri had found for him, none of them had ignited these wild sparks that still snapped and buzzed through him, even after Alex McKnight had turned down a side street and disappeared from view.

He would have to tread carefully here. The situation had the potential to spawn a whole morass of complications.

For the next month, he would have to work closely with her on the Brazen project. She was the chef, after all. Not only that, he knew from conversations with Brodie that Alex was good friends with Brodie's wife, Evie.

His whole life hinged on making a success of this project, on finishing the work on budget and on time and on doing a good enough job that Brodie would continue to contract with him and would recommend him to his friends around Hope's Crossing.

Sam couldn't afford to screw things up.

He looked at the scene below him, the neatly quaint downtown with its wide streets and graceful old historic buildings, the rows of established clapboard houses mingling with higher-end log homes.

Colorful spring blooms already burst out in patches, and the trees leading down the street had new pale green buds on them. He could imagine the place would be spectacular in the summer, with those raw, rugged mountains looming as a backdrop.

He breathed in the high mountain air. It seemed sweeter here, though he knew that was probably just the abundance of pine and fir trees around, sending out their citrusy fragrance.

This was the new start he wanted, that he needed, and he couldn't afford to screw up his chances of making a life here.

A couple kids rode down the hill on bicycles, legs

sticking out as they let gravity take over and flew past him, their laughter ringing loudly.

Across the street, an older lady with snow-white hair tended to flowers in a box hanging from her porch railing, and farther down from that, a couple people stood talking beside a mailbox.

It looked peaceful, comfortable. Perfect.

A few weeks ago, he had come up from Denver to check things out. From the moment he had driven into the city limits, he had felt the tension in his shoulders relax, the dark edges retreat.

He wasn't naive enough to think trouble couldn't find him here. While the surface of Hope's Crossing might look like something out of a Norman Rockwell illustration, the reality was never as ideal.

After all, he had met Brodie at the Denver Children's Hospital when Sam had been working on renovations to an office suite there at the same time Brodie's teenage daughter was a patient, after she had suffered a terrible accident here in Hope's Crossing.

Bad things happened in small towns just as easily as big cities like Denver. Marriages still fell apart, plenty of kids dabbled in drugs and alcohol, people still got cancer and died.

He grimaced at that thought and turned around to head back into the restaurant just as his cell phone rang. After a quick glance at the caller ID, his frown disappeared.

"Why, hello," he answered. "If it isn't my favorite son."

"Favorite and only," Ethan said primly.

Sam smiled, picturing his nearly seven-year-old's dark curls and the blue, blue eyes he had shared with his mother. "Maybe so. But even if you had a half-dozen siblings, you'd still probably be my favorite."

"That's hypothetical, though. We can't really know that for sure, can we?"

Hypothetical was apparently the word of the week. Last week it had been *enumerate* and the week before *precocious*. Spoken in that sweet young voice that still had a trace of a lisp, the hundred-dollar words always made Sam smile.

Love for his terrifyingly brilliant son was a sweet ache in his chest. "How is everything at Uncle Nick and Aunt Cheri's?"

Ethan's sigh was heavy and put-upon. "All right, I guess. I had to play Barbie dolls today with Amanda. I was Malibu Ken and she had Hula Barbie and they were supposed to be going on a date. I decided they should go on a date to the beach and we had them go surfing down the rain gutter in front of the house. How was I supposed to know Malibu Ken would fit down the sewer grate?"

"I bet that went over real well with your cousin."

"Aunt Cheri made me stay in my room for an entire half hour. I don't see why I had to be punished when it was simply an estimating error."

"Life isn't fair, is it?"

"Rarely, in my experience," Ethan said glumly.

His son was six for a few more weeks but acted as if he was thirty-six most of the time.

"When can I come see Hope's Crossing again, Dad?"

He grimaced, though there was no one but the lady across the street with her flowers to see. He missed his son already. "I'll bring you up first chance I get, I promise."

"I want to live with you for good in our own house, where I don't have to play Barbies or share a room with somebody who still watches Barney."

"I want that, too, more than anything. I'm working on it, I swear. Soon, okay? Six weeks. You have to finish the school year first and I need to find a decent place for us to live."

"Six weeks seems like *forever.*"

"I know. To me, too. But we'll spend every weekend together and before you know it, school will be out and you can come here for the summer when Uncle Nick and Aunt Cheri take off to Belgium. Then next fall you'll have a whole new school and new friends."

"I don't want to go to a new school," Ethan said, that stubbornness creeping into his voice.

"I know you don't, son. But Hope's Crossing is too far for us to drive to St. Augustine's every day. If we're going to live here, we'll have to find a school here, too. Don't worry. I've heard this one is terrific. You'll see."

Beyond the two-hour distance involved, Ethan attended a very elite private school. He had thrived at St. Augustine's, where they celebrated his brain and had spent the past two years trying to stimulate it.

Move or not, he couldn't continue there now. For one thing, Sam's former in-laws had insisted on paying the hefty private school tuition but those funds had dried up a year ago.

They loathed Sam now. While they claimed they wanted to continue a relationship with Ethan, he couldn't allow it, not when they filled his son's head with lies and vitriol.

The whole thing was such a mess. When his late wife's father had been arrested, the tuition payments stopped. Sam had managed to scrape together enough to keep Ethan at St. Augustine's this year but he certainly couldn't continue paying that much unless he wanted to deplete Kelli's entire life insurance policy before Ethan even reached college age.

"You were going to have to go to a new school either way, kid. You know that. You couldn't stay at St. Augustine's. The schools here in Hope's Crossing are supposed to be excellent. We'll have all summer together to get ready for second grade."

"I miss you," Ethan said, his voice small.

"Oh, son. I miss you, too. It's only a few weeks and then things will be better. You'll see."

"I guess."

"Hang in there and be good for Uncle Nick and Aunt Cheri. I'll call you every night to check on your homework and I'll come home next weekend, okay?"

After a few more moments, he hung up with his son. As he gazed down at the picturesque little town, he decided he could use some of the town's eponymous Hope.

He sincerely hoped he was making the right move here. He had to make a living and that was becoming increasingly difficult in Denver. His reputation in Denver construction circles suffered coming and going.

From J.T.'s friends, he was considered a traitor for whistle-blowing on his own father-in-law and starting the chain of events that had led to J.T.'s conviction. Sam still didn't know what else he could have done except go to authorities in Denver with his suspicions about his father-in-law. After all, Sam had first given J.T. the chance to make things right when he had discovered Tanner and Sons Construction was dangerously cutting corners—and using shoddy imported materials—but billing full price on government contracts.

From the honorable contractors left, Sam was painted with the same ugly brush as his father-in-law because he had been J.T.'s second-in-command for the last three years and should have known what was happening under his nose at the company. They didn't seem to make allowances for a floundering man who had been helping his wife fight cancer and then grieving when she lost the battle.

Hope's Crossing offered a chance to make a new start, away from all that ugliness. Thanks to Brodie and a few of his contacts, he had jobs lined up for several months. He had no doubt he could keep them coming, as long as he focused on the work at hand.

That was all the more reason to keep things casual and friendly with Alex McKnight. He couldn't afford the distraction and the complication of a woman like her. He would meet her the next night for a game of pool and some friendly conversation, but that was as far as he would let things go.

His future—and, more importantly, his son's—depended on it.

CHAPTER THREE

THE NEXT NIGHT, THURSDAY, Alex escaped to the employee restroom after her shift and quickly changed out of her white jacket and black slacks to jeans and a tailored soft green shirt. She added a chunky hammered silver necklace she had made a few months ago and a matching pair of earrings and bracelet.

Much to her dismay, she had spent hours before her shift trying to figure out what to wear for her little outing with Sam. Discarded clothes were still strewn all over every flat surface of her bedroom.

She wanted to set just the right tone for the way she had decided the evening should proceed. She would be friendly and fun but completely casual. No more of that high-octane flirting from the other day.

She couldn't deny she was fiercely attracted to Sam. He was big, gorgeous, tough…but he was also building the kitchen of her dreams. She couldn't afford to screw this up.

Earlier that day she had stopped in at Brazen to check things out and had been astonished at the progress he and his crew had made in just a single morning of work. They already had one whole section of cabinets installed and had been close to finishing another.

A gruff guy named Joe—who hadn't met her gaze more than a millisecond when she talked to him, and who had only said three or four words at a time—told her Sam had been out picking up a few things at the building supply store.

She tried to convince herself she wasn't at all disappointed to miss him but she recognized that for a lie. She *had* been disappointed, seriously bummed, which was when she had decided she needed to think twice about entangling herself with him.

Any man who could make her react like a teenager driving by her crush's house a half-dozen times a day spelled trouble.

The door opened and Lucy Martineau, the pastry chef, walked in and headed for the open stall. "You look great. Hot date?"

"No. Not a date," she was quick to assure her friend. "I'm just meeting somebody at the Lizard for drinks and some pool."

"Anybody I know?" Lucy asked. "Stupid question. Of course he wouldn't be. Let me guess. Is he in town on business or fun?"

Mascara wand in hand, she paused her quick makeup job long enough to make a face in the mirror at Lucy, who was washing her hands at the other sink.

"Very funny."

"Which is it? You know you never date anybody longer than a few weeks, Alex."

"Not true," she protested.

"Isn't it?"

"I went out with that musician for nearly a month, until his gig up at the lodge ended."

"I forgot about him."

So had Alex, but she wasn't about to admit that to Lucy. "It's easier to date somebody who's moving on anyway. We both know where things stand from the outset and nobody develops unrealistic expectations. It's cleaner, all the way around."

"If you say so." Lucy looked doubtful, but then, she had been married for a decade. "So who's the guy?"

She didn't want to answer but since others would probably see them together at The Speckled Lizard, she didn't see any reason to lie. "He's the contractor finishing up the remodel at Brazen. Our relationship is strictly professional. I figured I would introduce him around, help him feel welcome here, that sort of thing. I figure if he's happy during his stay in Hope's Crossing, he'll be more motivated to make sure he does a good job on my kitchen."

Lucy didn't lose her skeptical expression. Alex couldn't really blame her since it all sounded like a load of manure to her, as well.

"Well, have a good time."

"I intend to." Even if that meant backing away from the flirty fun of the day before, she thought with a sigh.

To her amazement, she quickly found a parking place right by The Speckled Lizard. This was a happening spot from December to March, jam-packed with skiers and boarders looking for somewhere to relax after a hard day on the slopes. The bar served generous drinks and usually had live music on the weekends.

During the summer months, it wasn't quite as busy but still did a lively business, both tourists and regulars. They grilled a mean burger out on the patio in warm weather and it was always a fun place to meet up with friends.

Like many establishments in town, the shoulder

seasons—April to early June and then September to mid-November—belonged to the locals.

She was early and didn't see any sign of Sam Delgado, of the broad shoulders and warm dark eyes. She waved to Mike from the bike shop in town, who was sitting with Cathy and Jonah Kent, both paramedics.

She always hated sitting by herself at the bar and was about to ask if they minded if she joined them while she waited when someone walked right in her path.

"Hey, there, Alex."

She gave a mental cringe. "Hi, Corey."

He had a tumbler of what looked like whiskey in his hand and a bleary-eyed look that indicated it wasn't his first of the night. No surprise there.

"You look fantastic," he said, stumbling a little over the adjective as he threw an arm around her shoulder.

Her mental cringe turned into an actual one but Corey Johnson didn't seem to notice. He never did. To Corey, the three dates they went on in high school twenty years ago apparently left him feeling entitled to paw at her whenever he wanted.

"Pat, bring the lady a drink. My treat." He beamed at her as if he were bestowing a huge honor and she squirmed a little more.

How was she going to play this? Being firm was generally not a problem for her but she had to admit, she felt a little sorry for Corey. About six months ago, he had lost his job as a mortgage loan officer because of the struggling economy and hadn't been able to find anything since.

Though he'd been scrambling to make ends meet and the family had even had a few visits from the Angel of Hope—the mysterious anonymous benefactor who went around town doing good deeds—his wife had finally tired of their ride to Nowheresville and had taken their kids to Grand Junction to stay with her mother.

Things weren't going all that great for old Corey, but that didn't mean she was willing to be his consolation prize. He was still married. Even if he wasn't, she hadn't been interested enough in anything but a handful of dates in high school and she was less interested now.

"I'm good, Pat. I'm just having mineral water tonight," she told the bartender, who lived down the road from her.

"Oh, come on." Corey leaned in close and the blast of liquor on his breath seared her nasal passages. "You need something more than that after a hard day."

"No, really. Mineral water is enough."

"You're no fun anymore, Al. You used to be fun."

"I'm still fun. I've just never needed alcohol to get me there." She forced a smile, which in retrospect was a bad idea. Corey took that as encouragement.

"What do you say you and me go out back and see just how much fun we can have together?"

Eww. Seriously? She tried to edge away but Corey had won second place in the state wrestling championship for his weight class their senior year and still had a pretty darn good half nelson.

"Yeah, I'm going to have to pass on that charming offer," she said firmly.

"Come on. We can just make out, if you want."

The very thought made her glad she hadn't eaten anything since lunchtime. "No, thanks. Let go, Core."

Instead, he tightened his grip and leaned his head down to her ear and whispered a filthy suggestion. She decided she didn't have any sympathy left for Corey and hoped like hell his wife had taken every penny of whatever the Angel of Hope had given the family when she made her way out of Dodge.

"Let go. Now," she said firmly but Corey ignored her.

Nobody else at the bar seemed to have noticed her predicament, probably assuming it was just a warm chat between old friends. She was trying to figure out whether he would even feel a sharp elbow shoved into his slight beer belly or if she would have to knee him hard where it counted when another voice intruded.

"The lady said no, I believe."

She shifted her gaze and knew she shouldn't be so glad to see Sam Delgado standing next to them in all his rough-edged, ex-Army Ranger glory.

She totally had this and didn't need rescuing, but it was still really, really nice of Sam to step in.

Corey turned his red-rimmed eyes in Sam's direction. "Mind your own business, asshole," he slurred.

Sam's expression didn't change. She might have thought it almost apologetic, if she didn't glimpse the hard steel in those dark eyes.

"Technically, this is my business. I'm afraid Ms. McKnight is my date."

Something in Sam's tone, his massive size or his deceptively casual stance seemed to pierce Corey's alcoholic stupor. It was fascinating to watch his bluster trickle away like beer out of a cracked bottle.

He pulled his arm away. "Sorry," he mumbled. "I didn't mean anything. Alex and I are old friends, aren't we, Al?"

She said nothing but Corey didn't seem to need a response—or maybe was grateful she didn't offer one.

"Talk to you later," he mumbled and ambled away with his drink.

Not the most auspicious beginning for their evening together. How was she supposed to put things back on a fun, casual footing now after he rescued her from being pawed by a drunk and disorderly high school classmate?

"Sorry I'm late," Sam said. He didn't offer any explanation other than that and she had the odd feeling he was troubled about something.

"No problem. You're here now. That's the important thing."

Oops. That came out more flirtatious than she intended. Apparently it was a hard habit to break.

He looked around The Speckled Lizard, with its high tin-stamped ceilings, the long, gleaming bar and the dark-paneled woodwork carved in elaborate designs.

"Any chance the grill is still open? I haven't had time for dinner."

The nurturer in her wanted to take him home and cook something delicious for him, but that sort of offer would almost certainly be misconstrued.

She was hungry, too, she suddenly realized. One of life's little ironies, that she spent all night cooking for others and sometimes didn't take time to eat, herself.

She glanced at the clock. "The grill here stays open for ten more minutes. I happen to know the cook, though, and I bet we can persuade her to keep it warm a bit longer. They have really excellent burgers. You can have beef, bison or beefalo if you want."

"Beefalo? Is that anything like a jackalope?"

She laughed. "Nope. Cross between bison and beef. It's actually quite good."

"Think I'll stick with beef, if it's all the same to you."

"Give me a couple minutes and I'll get you fixed up."

She headed back to the kitchen, waving to Pat as she went, then found the irascible Francesca Beltran in the small galley kitchen, all three-hundred pounds of her.

"Hey, Frankie."

"What you doing in my kitchen, baby girl?" She was so round, her only wrinkles were around her eyes.

Alex grinned. "Got me a friend who's hungry. I know you're probably ready to wrap things up. Any chance you'd let me throw on an apron and burn us up a couple burgers?"

She narrowed raisin-black eyes. "I was just about to clean the grill."

"He's really hungry, Frank. Come on. Please? He's been working hard all day building my kitchen at the new restaurant. If I can't cook for him here, I'll have to take him to my place to feed him and who knows what will happen then? I can't do that. You know I'm a nice girl."

Frankie's deep, full-bodied laugh always made her smile.

"Yeah, yeah. Okay. Make it fast."

She grinned and kissed the woman's cheek, threw a spare apron over her clothes, washed her hands and went to work.

Ten minutes later, the result was two perfectly cooked burgers, spiced just right and the buns toasted. Frankie deigned to drag them through the garden for her—one of her favorite diner slang terms for topping it with condiments—and even added some of The Speckled Lizard's signature crisp, fresh-cut fries.

She carried them out and found Sam sitting at a quiet

booth, a bottle of one of the local brews open in front of him.

"Sorry about the wait. I had to sweet-talk the cook. She can be a little territorial about her grill."

"You cooked this?"

She knew she shouldn't find such satisfaction from the surprise and, yes, delight in his eyes. "Frankie's great, don't get me wrong, but I have my own preference when it comes to my burgers."

"I really didn't mean to put you to work."

She slid into the booth across from him and picked up her napkin. "I was hungry, too, as you can see. Anyway, I like to feed people. It's kind of a thing with me."

As a relatively self-aware woman, she didn't need months of psychotherapy to explore the reason. When she was a girl, she had loved cooking for her whole family but especially for her dad. As the youngest girl, she had been the proverbial apple of her father's eye. They had bonded over grilled cheese sandwiches and pancakes at first and as she'd gotten older, she had expanded her repertoire and tried new things, always to gratifying raves from her father.

She had figured out a long time ago that she was compelled to feed people in some vain hope of making them love her enough to stay this time.

Not that she wanted Sam Delgado to stay anywhere. Sometimes a meal was simply a meal, right?

He took a bite of the burger and an expression of pure bliss crossed those rugged features. "I do believe that just might be the most delicious thing I've ever tasted."

She laughed, pushing away all thoughts of her childhood. "Oh, you poor man. If that's the case, I have so much to teach you."

The burger *was* good, she had to admit, with the bun toasted just right, the flavors of meat and good sauce harmonizing together perfectly.

He took a few more bites, concentrating all his attention to the meal. She didn't mind. She did love a man who knew how to enjoy his food.

Finally he set the second half of the burger down as if he wanted to prolong the pleasure and wiped at his mouth. "So, Alexandra, what do you do in Hope's Crossing besides cook very delicious burgers?"

Very few people called her *Alexandra* anymore. In school, all her teachers had used the full version of her name, as well as the principal, with whom she had been entirely too well acquainted.

Then later Marco had also used her given name, during their time together. In his heavily accented English, her name had sounded exotic and extravagant.

To everyone else, from her family to her wide circle of friends to the men she dated, she had been just plain *Alex* as long as she could remember, though her mother still sometimes went for Alexandra Renee when she was exasperated with her.

She liked the way Sam said her name and decided not to correct him.

Cooking was who she was, what she did, so it took her a moment to figure out how to answer him.

"I like to cross-country ski and snowboard," she finally said. "I just bought my first house a few months ago and I've been fixing it up the way I like it. Nothing of the scale you do, of course, just new paint, furniture, that kind of thing."

"What about in the summer?"

Did he really want to know about her or was he

simply being polite, laying the groundwork for what he hoped might eventually be a seduction? It was always a hard call on a first date. Not that this was a date, she reminded herself firmly.

"I hike. Mountain bike. Garden. Hang out with my family and friends."

"Your family lives close, then?"

"Just about all of them. I come from a pretty big family. Six kids. My mother and four of us children still live here in Hope's Crossing. Two of my sisters live out of state, one in California and one in Utah."

"Wow. Six kids. Seriously? That must have been crazy. I can't even imagine having that kind of family."

"It has its moments. Some bad but most of them good. We McKnights are all pretty close. Amazingly, we all get along. Except Riley, the only brother. He can still be a pest sometimes. It doesn't help that now he's a pest with a badge."

"Right. You mentioned he was the police chief."

It took her a minute to remember she had threatened him with calling her brother when she thought Sam was breaking into the restaurant the day before. Heat soaked her cheeks and she really hoped she wasn't blushing. She never blushed.

"What about you?" she asked, to distract him from remembering what an idiot she had been. "Do you come from a big family?"

"One brother, that's it. He lives in Denver with his wife and kids. That's where my s…" His voice trailed off. "My stuff is. I'm between places."

She had the distinct impression he meant to say something else. What? She had a zero-tolerance policy for deception in a man.

"So how long have you been out of the Rangers?"

"Three years."

Now, *there* was a verbose answer. Did his clipped tone indicate a hot button?

"What did you do for the Rangers?"

He took another bite of the burger and a drink of beer before answering. "Oh, the usual. Kick butt, take names, general mayhem."

He spoke in that same clipped tone, but she saw a little muscle quirk at the edge of his mouth as if he were working to hold back a smile.

She really liked Sam Delgado.

Too bad.

"General mayhem, hmm. I imagine building my kitchen must seem fairly tame to a guy like you, then."

"Not really. You'd be surprised how satisfying it can be to set those stainless-steel countertops exactly how the customer, in this case *you,* envisioned."

No trace of sarcasm or irony there. He was dead serious, she realized. She very much respected a man who enjoyed his work.

"Why did you leave the Rangers?" she persisted. The routes people took in their lives to bring them to a certain point in time endlessly fascinated her.

"Didn't really have a choice at the time." Again, the clipped tone.

"Conscientious objector or dishonorable discharge?"

He laughed roughly. "Anybody ever tell you you've got some cheek?"

"So my family says." She had always been the sassy, smart-mouthed sister. Since she didn't feel as if she could compete in looks or brains with four older sisters, she had found her own way to stand out.

After their father left, that had been one more way to manage the pain.

"So why *did* you leave the Rangers? Judging by your ink, you were a loyal soldier. I figure somebody who cares enough about a particular branch of the military to make it a permanent part of his body ought to stick with it as long as he can."

He sighed. "You're not going to let up, are you?"

"Would you like me to?"

He gave her a long look and appeared to be choosing his words as carefully as she picked over the fresh fish selection from her suppliers.

"I left the Rangers after my wife was diagnosed with stage-four breast cancer."

And *there* was the problem with being a smart-mouth. Sometimes you missed important signals and ended up feeling like a jerk.

She remembered him telling her the only Mrs. Delgado was his brother's wife. She believed him, so either his wife had gone into remission and divorced him or she had lost her battle. Alex was afraid it was the latter.

"I'm sorry."

He shoved away from the table, long fingers loosely clasped around the neck of his brew. "That was delicious. Let's go play some pool."

He obviously didn't want to talk about his late wife. It was one thing to flirt with a player who had no more interest in anything long-term than she did. It was something else entirely when the man was a grieving widower whose pain was so raw he couldn't even talk about it.

She grabbed her mineral water and followed him to

an empty pool table. The Lizard had four billiard tables, two of them currently in use.

To reach the table where Sam was now setting up, she had to pass a group of college-age guys—mountain biking tourists, if she had to guess. With them was one woman wearing a skintight pair of pegged jeans and a white halter top that was completely inappropriate for a Rocky Mountain spring night.

She laughed suddenly, overloud and overfriendly, and playfully punched one of the young studs on the shoulder.

Only when Alex had nearly reached Sam's table did she happen to glance at the woman from an angle where she could see her face, and a shock of recognition just about made her stumble.

Of all the people in town she might have expected to find flirting and half-drunk at The Speckled Lizard, Genevieve Beaumont would have come in dead last. Even behind Katherine Thorne.

"Hey, Genevieve."

The younger woman shifted her gaze, and her eyes widened. "Alex." She gave a noticeable sniff and turned back to her boy toys.

Bitch.

On some level she had sympathy for Gen Beaumont, who had been through some definite emotional turmoil the past year. She also would freely admit to a healthy degree of respect for at least one of Gen's decisions to break off her engagement a year ago when she found out her fiancé impregnated Alex's niece Sage.

But Gen had taken her anger at her fiancé and turned it into definite antipathy toward all things McKnight, as if the whole family was responsible for the man's decision to screw around with a vulnerable young woman.

Sage was doing well now, busy at school studying to be an architect like her father, Jack, but Alex had deep sympathy for what she had endured with her unexpected pregnancy. She had planned to put the baby up for adoption but, in the end, Maura and Jack had adopted the baby and were raising Henry as their own son instead of their grandson. On the surface, it might look as if everything had worked out for all parties concerned. That pretty picture tended to gloss over all the complicated snarls of emotions.

She pushed away her family dramas and any concern for Genevieve Beaumont and the old tendrils of pain, and grabbed a cue off the rack on the wall.

"You want to break?" Sam asked her.

"Sure. I'll warn you, I haven't played in a long time. I'm afraid I won't be able to give you much of a game."

"Don't worry about it. I'm pretty rusty, too."

An hour and three games later, he won two out of three, but just barely.

"Not much of a game." He snorted. "I haven't had to work that hard for a win since basic training, when I came up against a guy who hustled new recruits for fun."

She smiled. "We had a pool table in the basement when I was growing up. My dad, brother and I used to play for matchsticks. At last count, I think Riley owed me about eight hundred thousand. One of these days, I might have to collect."

"Why do I feel like I've just been scammed?"

She smiled. "You won, didn't you?"

"Barely."

"I wasn't lying when I said I hadn't played in a while. But I guess it's like so many other things. Once you take those first strokes, it all comes flowing back."

He cleared his throat and she couldn't hold in a smile at the sudden glazed look in his eyes. Was he, like her, thinking about something else completely? "Do you want to go for best of five?"

A loud burst of laughter from Genevieve's group drew both their attention. While she and Sam had been playing, a couple others had joined Gen's crowd. On the other occupied table, two rough-edged guys were arguing heatedly about a move. A couple danced nearby to an up-tempo country song playing on the jukebox.

Sometimes the loud, hard-partying scene at The Speckled Lizard grated on her nerves, especially after a long night at the restaurant. The only problem was, during the off-season, the after-hours nightlife in Hope's Crossing was basically nonexistent, other than a few fast-food joints that stayed open 24/7.

She could always call it a night but she selfishly didn't want to. She liked Sam. The way he moved, the way he smelled, the way he played pool. It had been a long time since she had met someone so intriguing.

"How do you feel about taking a little walk?" she asked on impulse.

He blinked at her, cue in hand. "Now? It's past eleven. The whole town is closed down, in case you didn't notice."

"Why not? It's a beautiful evening. These kind of mild spring nights are something of a miracle here in the high mountains."

Don't say no, she thought. The idea of going back to her house by herself tonight depressed her more than it should. Not that she had any intention of taking Sam there, but she definitely wanted to spend a little more time with him. This was a nice compromise.

"We don't have to," she added. "I only thought maybe you might like a quick guided tour of Hope's Crossing, being new in town and all."

He leaned a hip against the edge of the pool table, all those rangy ex-army muscles in delectable view.

Maybe inviting him out for a walk wasn't the smartest idea she'd ever had, when she had to keep reminding herself he was the contractor at the restaurant and she couldn't afford to mess things up now that her dream was within reach.

"A walk could be…interesting."

"Great. Let's go." She ignored the flurry of nerves in her stomach as they hung up the cues and settled their tab with Pat at the bar.

He helped her into her jacket and then pulled on his own—a soft, thin leather jacket that made her think of motorcycles and bad boys—and then they walked out into the sweetly scented spring night.

CHAPTER FOUR

THE NIGHT WAS RELATIVELY WARM for mid-April with a southerly breeze that smelled moist and earthy. She wouldn't be surprised if Hope's Crossing saw rain before daybreak, the kind of sweet and cleansing storm that blew through quickly and left everything fresh and clean, saturated with color.

She loved walking on these kinds of nights, when the rest of the world seemed huddled in for the dark hours but she was alone with the rustling music of the breeze in new leaves.

Except this time she wasn't alone. She was accompanied by a big, tough-looking man who had secrets she hadn't begun to guess.

"Let's walk up to the fire station and I'll give you the high points of Main Street along the way."

"You're the tour guide." He flashed a lopsided smile, looking sexy and almost rakish, and she had to remind her hormones to settle down.

She adopted a deliberately casual tone, her best officious voice. Maybe if the restaurant thing didn't work out, she could get a job at the tourist welcome center. "You probably already know this but Hope's Crossing was once a wild and woolly mining town, with more brothels and saloons than houses."

"I'd heard that, yes. Tell me this. Don't you think

it's odd that even with that sort of start, the town was still named a sweet, flowery name like Hope's Crossing instead of, oh, I don't know. Something like Hell's Armpit."

She laughed. "While both names are equally appealing, of course, I'm guessing Hope's Crossing might be a bit more of a tourist draw than anything with the word *armpit* in it. But what do I know?"

His smile gleamed in the night and she fought down another shiver of awareness.

"My friend Claire is a lot better at recounting history, but from what I understand, the miners originally called the town Silver Strike after the first mine to produce anything worthwhile up in the canyon. One of the mine owners, Silas Van Duran, happened to fall in love with the only schoolteacher in town, a woman named Hope Goodwin. When it came time to officially name the town, he insisted on Hope's Crossing. Since he had the money, I guess, he also had the power to push through what he wanted."

"A little on the cheesy side, don't you think? Most women I know would prefer a share in the silver mine instead of the rather dubious privilege of having a town named for them."

"Aren't you cynical? You're not a romantic, then. Good to know."

"Hey, I can be romantic when the mood strikes."

"You do know there's a difference between romantic and horny, right?"

He laughed and warmth sizzled through her. He had a really sexy laugh, low and full-throated, with just a hint of surprise to it, as if he didn't do it that often. She wanted him to do it again.

"I've heard that, yes," he said. "Thanks for the reminder. Though in my experience, they're not mutually exclusive emotions."

She was really going to have to settle down here. She drew in a breath and forced herself to return to tour-guide mood as they walked past her favorite boutique.

When they passed String Fever, she paused in front of the lighted display, a combination of ready-made items and a brilliant scatter of loose beads.

"Ooh, looks like Claire is carrying a new line of hand-painted beads. She didn't tell me. The woman is evil. I spend half my paycheck inside String Fever."

He gazed at the necklace that had caught her attention and then back at her. "Somehow I wouldn't have pegged you for a crafter."

"Beading is an art form and I've got serious skills. I made this." She pulled out the hammered-silver necklace. He had obviously once been someone's husband because he was smart enough to dutifully admire it.

"Nice."

"I know," she said smugly. "And it's not even my best work. Claire, the owner, has been my BFF since we were in first grade. She's actually married to my brother now. They're having a baby in a few months."

Why was she compelled to add that last part? She wasn't quite sure. Her own emotions about Riley and Claire combining DNA to bring a new life into the world were as tangled as her jewelry drawer.

She had mostly come to terms with the fact that her best friend and the person she still considered her pesky little brother were head-over-heels crazy about each other. She would never tell either of them this, but she even thought it was kind of sweet the way they couldn't seem to keep their gazes off each other in a crowd, the way they touched whenever they were close, the happiness that just seemed to surround the two of them like a big, puffy cloud.

Even so, it still sometimes freaked her out.

Then there was the issue of the upcoming birth, something that left her both thrilled for them and aching for…something.

Throw in her mother's relationship with Harry Lange and she was probably due for some serious therapy anytime now.

She didn't want to talk about any of it. What she really wanted to do was kiss this big, sexy construction foreman. Too bad things were so complicated.

"This is the Center of Hope Café, a fabulous place for breakfast and lunch. Basically anything on the menu is good. You can't go wrong. I don't know what magic Dermot Caine possesses but he also makes these turkey wraps that always hit the spot."

"Seems like a bad policy, to endorse the competition."

She sniffed. "We're not in competition. Apples to oranges. You want gourmet cuisine, come to my restaurant. You want good, honest comfort food, Dermot's your man."

"Is that right?"

"The French toast alone will make you weep tears of gratitude."

He laughed, assuming she was speaking in hyperbole. Foolish man. After he tried it, he would know she spoke only truth.

"Around the corner there is Dermot's daughter Charlotte's candy store. Sugar Rush. Best place in town for flavored fudge. Blackberry, almond, cashew. She does it all. And she's one of my good friends, too."

"Is everyone in town your friend?"

She shrugged. "Basically. What can I say? It's a friendly town. Why don't we cross the street here?"

He eyed the crosswalk, thirty feet farther up the street. "A rule breaker. I like that in a woman."

"It's nearly midnight," she pointed out. "The streets are pretty deserted right now. I think we'll be safe unless we get rogue moose coming through town. Hope's Crossing doesn't have much of a nightlife this time of year, I'm afraid."

"Not a problem for me. I'm not coming to town to party."

Despite the dearth of traffic, he grabbed her elbow when they crossed the street. She found it incredibly sweet and wanted to lean into the strength of his firm hand touching her, even through the layers of her coat and shirt.

They were only taking fifteen steps across pavement, not fording Currant Creek during runoff, but she still enjoyed that little touch of courtesy.

"This is my sister's shop," she said, when they reached the other side. "Dog-Eared Books & Brew is absolutely the best place in town to get good coffee."

"I'll keep that in mind."

On the other side of the street, she pointed out several of the old buildings in town and the efforts that had been made to keep the town's historic flavor.

Hope's Crossing was always so peaceful late at night when most of the residents slept. Instead of going all the way up to the restaurant, the one place in town she knew he had been, she turned them down Glacier Lily

Drive, intending to make a loop back to The Speckled Lizard. They had only walked about ten feet when something large and dark came toward them out of the alley behind the fabric store.

Alex jumped and gave a little scream at the same moment, her mind on that moose she had joked about earlier. Moose scared her to death ever since just about being charged by one when she had caught it unawares while out mountain biking one day a few years ago.

She felt extremely foolish when she realized the menacing shape was only an off-leash dog who had apparently wandered away from home.

"Sorry. Sorry. That startled me."

He didn't laugh, which was more than most men she knew would have done.

"It startled me, too. We former Army Rangers try to be a little more manly and do our girly screaming on the inside."

"We should probably find where he belongs. Come here, boy."

In the small circle of light from the reproduction streetlamp, the dog looked to be a chocolate Lab. He had a frayed collar but no tags. "Oh, dear. Where did you come from?"

The dog licked her, tongue lolling and tail wagging. He smelled like wet dog, sharply pungent.

"I'm not exactly a dog expert but he looks like a purebred," Sam said.

She had to agree. He had very elegant lines and beautiful hazel eyes that glowed in his dark face in the starlight. "I can't imagine he's a stray, even though that collar looks pretty mangy."

"How do you expect to find his home tonight?"

"Good question, especially without tags. I'm trying to think if I know anybody with a chocolate Lab. Nobody comes to mind. He doesn't look familiar."

"You can't know every dog in town."

"Not *every* dog, no," she admitted. "But I'm sure I would remember a good-looking guy like this one."

The dog licked at her hand again and she rubbed his ears. She loved dogs. Claire and Riley's morosely adorable basset hound, Chester, was one of her favorite creatures on earth. If her life weren't so chaotic, she would definitely have one of her own.

"Any suggestions?" Sam asked. "Is there an animal shelter in town where we can take him for now?"

"There is, but they're usually pretty packed."

She considered her options and came up with only one viable possibility. "Looks like I'm going to have company for the night."

"You're really going to take him home with you? What if he's rabid?"

"He's not. Look at how sweet he is. I can't just leave him to run wild on the streets. He could be hit by a car or even attacked by a mountain lion. I can call the shelter in the morning and see if they've had any missing pooch reports that match his description."

"What if they haven't?"

"I'm pretty connected," she said modestly. "I can get the word out through the police department and even put a few posters up at the bookstore and Claire's place. The owner will probably hear through the grapevine that I found a chocolate Lab. I should only have him for a day or two. It will be fun to have company, won't it, bud?"

The dog woofed at her and licked her hand a third time, almost as if he understood.

"Take off your belt," she ordered.

Sam angled a sidelong look at her. "I do believe that's the first time I've been propositioned on a public sidewalk."

She snorted. "That you've heard out loud, anyway. I'm sure plenty of women have *wanted* to proposition you, public sidewalk or not. Seriously, I need a leash and I'm not wearing a belt. I need yours. Don't worry, you'll get it back."

He shook his head. "This is the most interesting evening I've had in a very long time."

"Don't get out much, then, do you?"

She tried not to ogle as he unfastened his belt and slipped it out of the loops. As he handed it over, his finger brushed hers with a shock of warmth against the chilling night temperature. With one hand, she pulled the belt through the dog's collar and drew the end through the metal loop.

"There. Now I just need to hope it doesn't slip through my fingers, but you're not going anywhere, are you, bud?"

The dog wagged his tail, his haunches firmly planted on the sidewalk.

"Clever." Sam looked amused.

"I can be. Your pants aren't going to fall down now, are they?"

"I believe I can manage to avoid that horrifying eventuality for the few minutes it will take me to walk you to your car."

Oh, she liked Sam. It was really a cruel twist of fate that the planets were so far out of alignment for them.

They walked through the quiet streets of town in a companionable silence, broken only by the dog's snuffling as he investigated each crack in the sidewalk, the spring flowers blooming in baskets outside the storefronts, each streetlamp, signpost and fire hydrant.

"What's your name? Hmm?"

The dog gave her a goofy grin in response.

"I think I'll just call you Dude for tonight."

"Oh, please," Sam protested. "Leave the poor guy a little dignity."

"Okay, okay."

She considered ideas as they crossed the street again and headed back to The Speckled Lizard. The perfect name came to her when they were almost to the bar. "I've got it. I think I'll call him Leo. He's exactly the color of my favorite Leonidas Belgian chocolates."

"Sure. That was going to be my choice, too."

She couldn't see Sam roll his eyes in the dark but his dry tone conveyed the same sentiment.

She laughed and squeezed his arm. What a wonderful night. Walking the quiet streets of Hope's Crossing on a lovely April evening that smelled like spring with a gorgeous man at her side—and now a very adorable dog. What woman wouldn't have this little bird of happiness fluttering through her?

Soon enough, though, they reached her little SUV and she opened the back door.

"Come on, Leo. Let's get you inside."

The dog didn't hesitate, just jumped right into the backseat as if they had been practicing this routine for years. Her seats were probably going to stink for weeks. First order of business for Leo was a bath, even though it was nearly midnight. Both of them would sleep better for it.

She reached inside and pulled the belt end through

the buckle and handed it back to Sam. "Thanks for loaning your belt. And for the evening. I had a really great time."

She had said those words often on dates but had never meant them as much as she did in that moment.

"I did, too." His voice held a slight note of surprise, as if he hadn't been expecting to enjoy himself. "I would like to do it again. Soon."

Okay, here was the awkward part of the evening. She couldn't encourage him, not with all the complications, but she liked him far too much to turn him down flat. "Sure," she finally said. "I'm pretty busy right now, between preparing for the new restaurant and wrapping things up at my current job, but sure. It was fun."

"You're an intriguing woman, Alexandra McKnight. I don't meet very many of those."

She tried to come up with something flippant in response, but before she could make her brain work, he stepped forward, leaned down and kissed her.

It started as just a brush of his mouth against hers, a simple "thanks for a fun night" sort of kiss. She should have let it stand there but he smelled so delicious, like sunshine and warm male, and he kissed with just the right amount of pressure, not too soft, not too hard, and she hadn't been kissed in *forever.*

She moved her mouth slightly under his, just a taste, and was vaguely aware of her hands moving to his hard, slim waist. He made a sound low in his throat that seemed to shiver down her nerve endings, one hand tangled in her hair, the other resting on the small of her back, and deepened the kiss.

One minute the kiss was sweet and easy, almost innocent, the next was heat and fire and the hard churn of her heartbeat.

He could build things, he was kind to stray dogs and he was a fantastic kisser, too. Um. Yes. She wanted to grab hold of those big, gorgeous shoulders, shove him into her car and take him home with her....

Something cold pressed against her back—the metal side of her car, she realized, vaguely aware that he had her caged in by all those muscles against her SUV and was kissing her as if his next mission depended on it.

She couldn't seem to catch her breath and felt as if she'd just leaped off the highest point of the mountain and was soaring, soaring out into space.

Reality intruded in the form of a stray dog, who poked his head out the driver's side door where they stood, with a curious sniff. At the feel of that nose nudging at her, Alex realized she was wrapped around a man she had only met a few hours ago while heat coursed through her like the propane torch she used to caramelize sugar for crème brûlée.

"Wow. Okay. Um. Wow." She drew in a ragged breath and then another one. So much for casual, flirty fun. She couldn't remember *ever* igniting so instantaneously, not even back with...

Out of habit, she jerked her mind away from even thinking about the past, from that long-ago girl she had been who had given her heart so freely and so foolishly.

"Yeah. *Wow.* Funny, that's just what I was thinking."

She leaned a hip against the door of her SUV, fighting the urge to step back into his arms and stand here kissing him for a few more hours.

Hadn't she spent all evening reminding herself of all

the reasons why she couldn't afford this complication with him, no matter how tempting?

She was apparently a weak-willed woman.

"I should go. It's late and I probably need to get Leo settled in for the night."

"And I've got to be at the work site bright and early in the morning. You never did give me a direct answer. When do you think we can do this again?"

How about now? And then five minutes from now? And then ten minutes after that?

"I didn't, did I?"

Despising herself for the cowardice, she gave him a quick smile and slid into the driver's seat of her vehicle then quickly closed the door. Before he could protest or she could do something completely stupid like make another date with him, she yanked the gear shift into Drive and took off, leaving him standing on the sidewalk, looking just as dazed as she felt.

WITH DESIRE STILL PULSING through him, Sam watched her drive off in a sporty little SUV that probably came in handy during the cold high-mountain winters.

He hadn't intended anything more than a fast, polite kiss but then she had moved her mouth against his and heat had rushed in on a relentless tide, blasting away any chance he had of hanging on to his sanity or control.

Alexandra McKnight, with her blond curls and those incredible green eyes and that smart, delectable mouth, was a dangerous woman. He couldn't remember when he had smiled so much in an evening or known this effervescent sense of anticipation and sheer fun.

He shook his head. This was *not* why he had come to Hope's Crossing. A relationship was the *last* thing on his mind as he considered uprooting his son and setting up shop in a new town, away from his entire support system.

The timing couldn't be worse. He had more than enough on his plate right now, trying to build a new life here.

The two of them stirred up enough sparks to burn down the whole town. Chemistry wasn't everything, he reminded himself. The trouble was, he genuinely liked her, too. She was funny but not at the expense of other people. She had to be a kind, compassionate woman to pick up a stray dog and take him home with her.

With a sigh, he headed for his pickup truck. He had to tread carefully here. She was obviously well-known in town. The short tour she had taken him on had illustrated clearly that every store in town had some link to her. Sisters, best friends, neighbors. Everyone here was interconnected.

If he started something with the very appealing Alexandra McKnight and it went south, he had a strong suspicion he would automatically be blamed, by default. He was an outsider and in small towns like Hope's Crossing, people tended to be quick to circle the wagons around one of their own.

He wanted to build a life here, to start a business. How could he hope to do that if he managed to piss off half the town before he even had a chance to settle in?

He would be smarter to take things slow, he decided. Back off, use his head. He would focus on keeping Alexandra happy with the work he did for her and avoid any more intimate evenings that reminded him just how very long he had been alone.

CHAPTER FIVE

"YOU CAN COME with me, but only if you behave," Alex said sternly to Leo early the next afternoon.

The dog gave her what looked uncannily like a grin and planted his haunches by the front door, waiting for her to hook up the extra leash she kept around the house for the times she doggie-sat Chester.

She clipped it on him then juggled the leash while she picked up a heavy cooler and headed out.

"I mean it," she went on as she carried the cooler down the steps of her garage to the open hatch of her SUV. "Caroline loves her flowers. It breaks her heart right in half that she can't tend them as she likes anymore. I won't have you digging up any of her few perennials she has left, understood?"

The dog gave one well-mannered bark, smart as a whip, and she smiled. He was good company, this unexpected guest. He had been docile and easygoing when she had bathed him the night before and hadn't even soaked her much.

Last night, he had politely eaten Chester's leftover dog food and then had trotted out in the yard for his business before coming back and waiting with surprising patience by the door to be let back inside.

She had settled him for the night on some old blankets in a corner of her laundry room and he hadn't made a sound all night long, until she had checked on him after she awoke. She could only wish all her houseguests were so trouble free.

Leo settled in the backseat of her SUV and lolled his tongue, overcome with joy when she rolled the window down.

As they pulled away from her house, she could see it in the rear windshield, the hewn logs gleaming in the afternoon sun. With two gables and a wide front porch that looked out on the mountains, the house looked warm and lovely, though she still tended to see all the work she needed to do.

After years of neglect, first as a vacation house with mostly absentee owners and then in foreclosure when the owners had walked away from the mortgage, the house was a work in progress. The window boxes in the upper window and along the porch railing that ran the length of the house were still empty and the garden was a wild tangle.

She was working on it slowly, determined that by summer's end, the house and yard would glow once more.

The house was a labor of love, just like the restaurant. She loved this place, had since she was a girl. She could remember riding her bike on this road to visit a friend who grew up on the next development over.

All the houses in this area were lovely, mostly log, stone and cedar that had been constructed to meld with the mountain setting and separated from each other by tall stands of pine, fir and aspen.

She had always loved the serenity she found here as she passed fields of wildflowers and that musically rippling creek bordered by wild red- and black-currant bushes that had given the neighborhood its name. This specific little cottage, though, had always called to her.

Maybe it was the decorative shutters or the scroll-work gingerbread trim on the gables that always made the house seem charmed to her, like something out of a fairy tale.

She remembered telling Claire from the time they were young that someday she would live here. Of course, back then she had dreamed of a husband and a house full of children, just like the big family she had known growing up.

Funny how a person's life journey could sometimes meander off in completely unexpected directions. Here she was, without the husband and without the passel of kids, but in the house she had wanted forever.

The dog in the backseat barked as she pulled away from the house and now she glanced in the rearview mirror at him.

"Don't worry. I have a feeling you'll be back."

First thing that morning, she had called the animal shelter and the two veterinarians' offices in town but had come up empty. None of her sources had heard anything about a missing chocolate Labrador retriever.

She had shot a picture of Leo with her phone, uploaded it to her computer and then used her limited design skills to come up with a flyer. It was quite creative, if she did say so herself, and she had promptly emailed a copy to several business owners around town, including Claire for String Fever and Maura for Books & Brew.

She needed to find the dog's owner before she became too attached to the undeniable comfort of having another creature in the house with her.

He had been the perfect companion while she cooked

up a storm that morning. He didn't seem to mind her steady, rather aimless conversation and he even helped clean up the kitchen by snagging a few items she accidentally dropped on the floor while slicing and dicing and sautéing far too much food.

Okay, yes, she had gone a little crazy. She would freely admit it to herself and to any canines within earshot. She had woken after a fractured night's sleep with vast quantities of restless energy. Naturally, she had turned to the kitchen to expend some of it doing what she did best, cooking.

In her burst of energy, she had made spring soups and casseroles, pastas and chicken dishes.

The marathon cooking session had yielded some very nice results and she couldn't wait to share the bounty.

She knew exactly what had generated this burst of energy. That kiss. All through those short few hours of sleep, she had dreamed of entwined breaths, of solid, warm arms around her, and had awakened with tousled sheets and this seething, writhing force to do *something* with her day.

Sam Delgado was an amazing kisser.

She should have guessed he would be from the preliminary work she had seen him do at Brazen. A man who gave such scrupulous attention to detail, such loving care, in one area of his life, likely tended to bring the same concentration and focus to others. When he kissed her, she felt as if nothing else in the world mattered to him but that moment and her mouth and making sure they both took away what they needed.

She blew out a breath as she turned off Currant Creek Valley Road and headed toward the old section of town.

If it were only a kiss, she wouldn't also have this

vague sense of unease, rather like she had when she was a kid and she was about to take on a ski run that was slightly above her capabilities.

She really liked him, that kiss notwithstanding. She hadn't enjoyed an evening that much in…well, she couldn't remember when. Sam had been great company, clever and sexy, with a finely wrought sense of humor.

All morning, she had been fighting the temptation to take a quick little drive up the hill to the old fire station on some flimsy excuse, just to see him again.

She imagined him building her kitchen right now, sweaty and hard muscled, that tattoo flexing while he used some scary-looking power tool. Her toes tingled as if she had missed a step racing down for breakfast, as if she stood on the brink of the high dive, prepared to take a plunge into unexplored waters, but she did her best to ignore her purely physical reaction.

She wasn't about to go to Brazen, no matter how tempting that image…or the man. Instead, she had spent the morning cooking up a storm with a funny dog at her side and now had three dozen meals to show for it. That was certainly a much more constructive outcome than if she had wandered to the restaurant site to moon over something she couldn't have and shouldn't want.

The first stop of the day was a small, neat residence around the corner from the house where she had grown up. She pulled into the driveway, where a sweeping, low-hanging branch of the Japanese maple along the drive scraped the top of her SUV. She made a mental note to ask Riley if he could bring his chainsaw over and cut back some of the trees. Pruning should have been done in March but Caroline's health had been fragile for months and many things slipped off the priority list.

Though the Hope's Crossing growing season was only just beginning, the gardens Caroline tended with great love and care already looked weedy and overgrown. Her friend would hate that. She probably looked out the window and cringed when she saw the perennials that hadn't been cut back properly in the fall, the bare spots where she hadn't planted bulbs.

She would have to ask Claire to add Caroline's yard to the Hope's Crossing Giving Hope Day, when the town residents gathered together to help their neighbors in multiple ways. The event was still several weeks away, though. Maybe she could grab her mother, Evie and Claire before then and have a work party to handle some of the more pressing needs.

In the meantime, she had deliveries to make. She opened the back hatch of her SUV and pulled out the first dozen of the meals she had fixed. Leo thrust his brown nose between the seats to watch her out of big, curious eyes.

"Do you want to come?"

He actually moved his head as if nodding, though she knew no dog could be that smart. Her mother would probably consider taking a strange dog into someone else's home rude but she happened to know Caroline loved dogs. Her own beagle-cross mutt had gone to doggie heaven about four years ago, but Alex had vivid memories of Caroline in overalls and floppy straw hat, working in the garden while her dog looked on.

Cancer could be a bitch. In Caroline's case, the chemotherapy had messed with her brain chemistry and a series of resulting strokes had left her clinging to her remaining independence with both hands.

She rang the doorbell and waited several long moments. Finally, after knocking again, she tried the knob. It turned in her hand and she pushed open the door.

"Caroline? It's Alex. Are you home?"

A moment later, she heard a shuffle-shuffle-thud and Caroline's walker came into view.

"I'm here. Hello, my dear." Caroline's voice was a little garbled, as if she spoke through a mouthful of the smooth, shiny stones at the bottom of her goldfish pond.

"Sorry. I was…in the laundry room…moving a load from washer to dryer."

Every time Alex visited, Caroline's once-strong frame seemed to have dwindled a little more. She only weighed about eighty-five pounds, her wrists so thin a child could probably circle them with thumb and forefinger.

"I told you I was coming this morning. Why didn't you wait and let me help you?"

Despite the fact that she could only get around with her walker, had little energy and fought steady pain, Caroline hated to be a bother to anyone.

"It's enough…that you come to visit. I don't need you to do for me, too."

Leo chose that moment to move into the room, sniffing at the legs of one of the stately Queen Anne recliners Caroline favored.

The left side of Caroline's face lifted in a smile while the right remained immobile. "A dog! I didn't know… you had a dog!"

"I don't. Not officially, anyway. I found him running loose downtown last night. I'm just keeping him company until we find his owners."

"You're a beauty. Yes, you are." Leo stood with

touching docility as Caroline rubbed his head with one gnarled hand.

For just a moment, she had the crazy idea of leaving the dog with her friend, but reality quickly intruded. That would never work. Caroline could barely take care of herself, try as she might. She couldn't handle the needs of another living creature right now, though Alex was convinced she was getting better every day.

But if she was going to respond with such enthusiasm, Alex could certainly bring the dog around to visit while he was staying with her.

"You're a good boy, aren't you? What's your name?" Caroline murmured.

"I've been calling him Leo. He doesn't seem to mind it."

"Why should he? It's a good name. I had a beau once…named Leo. He ended up marrying my best friend's little sister and moving to…Grand Junction."

She kissed her friend's papery cheek. "Idiot. He didn't know what he had."

"Oh, he knew." Her half smile was mischievous. "I dumped him…long before then. Broke his heart, too, I did."

"I'll bet you did, along with dozens of others."

"Not that many…but a few." It might have been the way her mouth could only lift partway, but her expression suddenly seemed pensive and almost sad.

Alex couldn't allow that. "I've brought you a few meals for your freezer," she said, quick to change the subject. "All of them have instructions, as usual, and they're in individual portion sizes. All you have to do is thaw them first, either in your refrigerator or the microwave, and then heat and eat."

"You need…to stop doing that."

"If I don't do it, my mom will, and we both know I'm a much better cook."

That wasn't strictly true, as Mary Ella had fine skills in a kitchen, but it still made Caroline smile, just as Alex had hoped. That shadow of regret and sorrow was gone.

"Besides, you're the closest thing to a grandmother I have, you know," Alex said. "My dad's parents both died before I was born, and my mom's mother was a cranky old biddy who thought we McKnight kids were hooligans, every one."

"Weren't you?" Caroline asked with that mischievous smile again.

"True enough."

Despite that, Caroline had always welcomed Alex and her siblings to her home. Her first memory of the woman had been probably around kindergarten age, when she had sneaked through Caroline's garden gate to pick some flowers to give to her mother. If she remembered correctly, she was in trouble with Mary Ella for something or other—nothing new there—and thought the flowers might help smooth things over.

Like most kids, she'd had no concept of abstract things like ownership and had picked indiscriminately until Caroline had finally noticed her and come out to put a stop to her thievery.

Most of the details of that encounter were hazy but she could still remember Caroline's kindness as the woman had taken the mangled flowers from Alex's hand, patiently trimmed off the root ends she had tugged up and arranged them into a passably pretty bouquet.

Alex had loved her ever since, stubborn independence aside.

When Alex had returned to Hope's Crossing bruised and broken and full of secrets, she hadn't been able to face living at home among the questions. Instead, she had rented Caroline's now-empty basement apartment at a rock-bottom price. Caroline hadn't asked questions, she had only offered quiet acceptance, steady love and that riotously beautiful garden that had provided peace and comfort—along with fresh-cut flowers and a seemingly endless supply of fresh-baked banana nut bread.

Over the weeks and months that followed, Alex had found the time and space to begin gathering up the shattered pieces of herself and forming them back together—and she could never repay Caroline enough for giving her that place to heal. What were a few paltry meals compared to that?

"You don't have to do for me," Caroline repeated. "I can…take care of myself. Things take longer…but I still get them done."

"I know you can. Look at it this way. If you don't have to worry about what you're going to fix for dinner every night, you have more time to read."

"There is…that."

Caroline was a member of the Books and Bites book club, though she hadn't been to one of their get-togethers for a long time. She still read all the assigned books and sent a carefully typed email with her insightful analysis to either Maura or Mary Ella.

"Have you had lunch yet? I brought some fresh grapes and melon, some vegetable root chips and the makings for chicken salad sandwiches."

"Oh, that sounds delicious. Is it nice enough…to eat on the patio, do you think?"

The unseasonable warmth of the day before had been blown away with a morning rain but it was still relatively pleasant. "Yes," she answered. "Let's find you a sweater."

She helped Caroline into a cardigan as well as a blanket for good measure and tucked her in at the bistro set that overlooked her pond and the waterfall that was silent now.

"I'll stay while you eat, then I'm afraid I have to run. I've got a couple other stops to make before I head into the restaurant for the dinner shift."

She wasn't hungry after a morning full of noshing while she tried things out, but she managed to eat half a sandwich and a couple of the chips, especially the purple potatoes, always a favorite. To her immense satisfaction, Caroline polished off her plate, leaving only a few edges of the ciabatta bread.

"That was…delicious," Caroline said forty minutes later after their visit. "Oh, I wish you could stay longer."

Alex smiled and kissed her friend's cheek. "I'll be back. You know I will."

"You're so…good to me," Caroline said with a soft smile. "I don't know…what I would eat if not for your delicious meals."

Neither did Alex. Worry pressed down on her shoulders as she said her final goodbye, gathered Leo from a patch of sunshine in the yard and headed back to her SUV. Once the restaurant opened, she didn't know how much time—or energy—she would have for these impromptu cooking sessions to fill the freezers of several of the older people she loved.

She would just have to make time, no matter how hard. People counted on her and she couldn't let them down.

Her second stop was more brief. Two streets over from Caroline's house, she pulled up to a small clapboard house squeezed in between a couple rehabbed four-unit condominiums. Wally Hicks used to be her family's mailman, and his wife, Donna, taught her and Claire's Sunday-school class for years. Donna had early-stage Alzheimer's and failing vision, while Wally could barely hear and had a bad heart. Between the two of them, they could almost manage to take care of each other and they were always so thrilled when she dropped off a few meals for them and a special treat for their bad-tempered bulldog, Clyde.

The third stop was the shortest of all—and she definitely left Leo in the car for this one.

Frances Redmond lived next door to Claire and Riley and she didn't care for dogs. Or most people, for that matter.

Claire did what she could to help Frances but the older woman was grumpy about letting other people in. She always said she didn't want Alex to keep coming, but she persevered, partly out of guilt for a few pranks she had pulled on the woman when she was a girl and partly because every time she came, Frances had a box full of empty containers to give back to her, indicating she ate the food, Alex hoped. For all she knew, Frances might have just dumped it all in her disposal and ran the dishes through her dishwasher, but she wanted to think she was doing a little good.

"If you're going to bring all this food, even though I've told you again and again not to, why can't you leave out all the fancy froufrou ingredients? What's wrong with good, hearty basic food?"

Apparently rosemary was considered froufrou these days. Alex sighed. "Absolutely nothing, Mrs. Redmond. You're right, I love things that are simple. I promise, I only mixed a few herbs in a couple of the dishes. Nothing exotic, I swear."

"No sun-dried tomatoes like last time?"

"Nope. You told me you like plain old tomatoes and that's what I used."

"I suppose you put some of that Dijon mustard in this chicken salad, too."

Alex shook her head. "Plain yellow, just like you ordered."

"Good."

No *thank you*, no *how kind.* Alex wasn't sure why she bothered. There were others in town who would appreciate her efforts more but, then, she didn't do this to be showered with gratitude. She liked the warm feeling she received from helping others regardless of their reaction. Her mother and Claire had set a good example in that department.

Besides, she always felt a little sorry for Mrs. Redmond. Her life had been tough. She had lost a couple children and her husband had died young.

Some people—her sister Maura, for example—faced their sorrows with courage and grace and refused to allow hurt and loss to define them.

Others, like Mrs. Redmond, became angry and bitter, taking their internal pain out on everyone around them and keeping away anybody who wanted to reach out.

Alex considered her own outlook to fall somewhere in the middle. She could understand Frances Redmond's desire to huddle over her hurts and keep anyone else from inflicting more. Maybe that's why she could view her surliness with an exasperated empathy.

"I'll see you next time. Have a lovely week."

"It's supposed to rain every day," Frances grumbled.

"Then that soup I made will surely hit the spot, won't it?" She grinned all the way back toward her car.

Just before she reached it, a boy riding past the house on a blue mountain bike braked when he spotted her.

"Hi, Aunt Alex!"

Her heart lifted at the name. Claire's son had always called her Aunt Alex, even before his mother married her brother and made their relationship official. "Hey, Owen. How's my favorite dude?"

The ten-year-old gave her a grin that she imagined would break a fair number of hearts someday. "I'm good. What are you doing here?"

"Just passing by. Why aren't you in school?"

"We had early release today for some teacher work day thing and only had half a day. Riley is coming home early and we're goin' fishing. Mace and Mom are going shopping in a little while."

Her wild, once-hardened brother had definitely turned his life around and had become a fantastic step-father to Claire's two children, Owen and his sister, Macy, from her first marriage. She never would have expected him to be so good at it but he had transitioned smoothly into Claire's complicated life.

The two of them shared custody with Claire's ex and his wife. So far they all seemed to be making it work.

"Wow. How manly of you both," she said to Owen. "If you catch any trout, bring them by the restaurant and I'll fix them up for you."

She opened the door of her SUV and was greeted by a friendly "where have you been?" sort of bark.

Owen's head swiveled around. "You got a dog! I didn't know you had a dog!"

"Not mine," she said. "I found him wandering the streets last night. I'm looking for his owners now."

"What a great dog. You really just found him? Do you know his name?"

"I'm calling him Leo. It's a long story."

He seemed to accept that in his calm, unruffled way. "Cool. Hey, Mom," he suddenly yelled, "Alex is here."

She wasn't technically *there,* she was next door. And she didn't really have time to visit but she couldn't be rude now that she saw Claire walking around the side of the house.

She looked voluptuously pregnant and quite adorable in a loose denim work shirt that was probably Riley's, sleeves rolled up to her elbows, and a pair of rubber muck boots with green frogs imprinted on them.

"Hi! Did you ring the bell? Sorry, I must have missed it. I've been back in the garden. In a few months, I won't be able to bend over so I figured I should probably do what I can now."

"And after that, you'll be too busy to keep up with the garden. Or anything else, for that matter."

"I know. But isn't it wonderful?"

She beamed and touched her growing abdomen. Alex was hit with a fierce, aching sadness. She forced it away. "Fabulous. I still can't quite picture Ri with a newborn but I'm sure he'll be great at it. I know *you* will. You've already raised two of the greatest kids on the planet."

She rubbed Owen's artificially blond-tipped hair he

had horrified his mother with the last time he came back from staying with his father and stepmother.

"I was just finishing up. Have you got time for a cup of tea?"

"Better not. I've got to run to the restaurant. Technically, I wasn't stopping to see you this time. I took a few meals in to Frances."

Claire—who usually epitomized kindness and mercy—scowled. "I hope it was bland and tasteless."

"I did my best but sometimes my genius comes through anyway. Why are you mad at Frances?"

"Not mad, exactly, but she drives me crazy sometimes! Riley spent two hours at her house replacing a broken showerhead last week because she was too cheap to pay a plumber. And then the next day, she had the nerve to tell me she doesn't like the way it sprays and wanted exactly the same kind she had before. Ugh!"

"What did you do?"

"I went to four different home improvement places until I found the right one."

"Of course you did," Alex said, hiding a smile.

"She's a lonely old woman and we should have compassion, I guess, but she doesn't always make it easy."

Claire had plenty of practice with difficult women, considering her mother was the light beer version of Frances Redmond.

"So I heard a rumor about you," Claire said, changing the subject.

"That Brazen is going to be named the best new restaurant in Colorado and the Food Channel will notice and pick me to host a new show on regional cuisine and I'll put out a dozen cookbooks and retire to an island in the tropics, where I'll spend the rest of my days wearing muumuus and drinking mai tais?"

Claire laughed. "No, I must have missed that one. This one is just as juicy, though. I ran into Frankie Beltran at the grocery store this morning and she asked me about the hot guy you were with last night at the Liz. I had to confess my glaring ignorance, which is rather pathetic considering we had lunch together two days ago with the book club and you never said a word about any guy, hot or otherwise."

Yeah, only two days ago she hadn't known Sam Delgado as anything other than a name and the cause of one more delay in opening Brazen.

"Um, you know that contractor Brodie hired to finish the restaurant?"

Claire's eyes opened wide. "Seriously?"

She had absolutely no reason to feel weird about this. She had never intended her friendly invitation to turn into that hot kiss she couldn't shake from her mind. Or so she continued to tell herself.

"What's the big deal? He dropped by the restaurant the other day after everybody left. I thought it would be a nice gesture to show him around, welcome him to town, that sort of thing. We met at the Lizard for a game of pool and then we took a walk so I could point out the highlights of our little corner of paradise. I was strictly doing my civic duty."

"I'm sure it didn't hurt that he was, in Frankie's words, hotter than a firecracker lit on both ends."

He was all that and more. "He could have looked like a troll and I would still want to make sure he feels comfortable in Hope's Crossing. He's building my kitchen."

It sounded like a lame excuse, even to her, but Claire

didn't blink. One of the things Alex loved best about her was Claire's particular gift of letting people hang on to their own illusions without calling them out.

"Did you have a good time?" she only asked.

Good time? That was an understatement. She thought of his mouth, firm and determined, those hard, relentless muscles against her.

She sighed, then hoped the sound didn't come across as wistful to Claire as it did to her own ears.

"I almost beat him at pool. I won one game but we were playing two out of three."

"Wow! He beat you twice? Impressive. He must be fantastic, since you beat Riley most of the time and he's the best billiards player I know."

"Sam is pretty good."

"A gorgeous pool-playing contractor. We don't see those around Hope's Crossing every day. How did Brodie find him?"

"I don't know all the details but I gather Sam was working on a project at the hospital while Taryn was having some treatment, and the two of them struck up a conversation and have stayed in touch. He's done a couple other jobs for Brodie. From what I can tell, he does good work. And fast, too."

"So you had fun?"

Again, with the understatement. "Sure. He was with me when I found Leo here, isn't that right, bud?"

Leo was currently sniffing noses with Chester but paused long enough to give her a happy look, almost as if he recognized his name. He apparently didn't mind being used as a diversionary tactic.

Claire probably saw through her effort to change the subject but also didn't seem to mind. "Evie put the poster up you emailed us and she's been mentioning it to everyone who comes in. So far she hasn't found anybody missing a chocolate Lab."

"Keep looking. He's too gorgeous not to belong to somebody, somewhere."

"Are we talking about Leo here or Sam Delgado?"

Apparently diversions could only take a woman so far when it came to her best friend, who knew her better than anyone else on earth. But even Claire didn't know all her secrets.

"Ha, ha. He's actually a widower. Believe me, I asked. His wife died of cancer a couple years ago."

"Oh, the poor man."

"He was also an Army Ranger at one time, just like Dylan Caine. I guess he left the service after his wife's diagnosis."

"That's admirable. Not many men would give up their career to take care of their ailing wife. So do you like him?"

Entirely too much. And the more she talked about him—and thought about him—the more she liked him. Annoyance with herself and frustration with the situation made her tone sharper than she intended.

"Last I checked, we're not in junior high anymore. I'm past the stage of handing you notes about the cute boy in my social studies class."

Claire blinked but her gaze quickly sharpened and Alex could have kicked herself. She might be sweet and kind, but Claire was no idiot. If Alex acted touchy and hypersensitive about just the mention of Sam Delgado, Claire would quickly surmise there was more simmering between them than casual friendship.

She hurried to make amends. “Sorry. That was mean. I miss being in junior high with you.”

“Life certainly seems easier when a girl is twelve.”

In some respects, not all. Claire’s father had been murdered in a torrid love triangle when they were young, and even then her own father had had one foot out the door, though they had all been too blind to see it.

On impulse, she reached out and hugged Claire, pregnant belly, gardening gloves and all. She dearly loved all four of her actual sisters but Claire was her BFF. In their case, the *forever* really meant something.

“Sam is a nice guy but that’s all. He’s building my kitchen and I’m not going to do anything to screw that up.”

Claire pressed her cheek to hers. “Like break his heart, you mean?”

Or let him sneak close enough to break hers.

“Something like that.”

After a moment, she eased away. “I really do need to go. Sorry I can’t stay, but my shift is starting soon and I left a horrendous mess in my kitchen at home. Leo, come on. You and Chester can hang another time.”

She shepherded the dog into the backseat again, hugged Claire one last time, blew a kiss to Owen—busy now, untangling fishing line in the driveway—then drove away.

This was the important part of her life, she thought as she headed toward Currant Creek Valley. Her family, her friends, the people she cared about in town. She was perfectly happy with her life and didn’t need anything else—especially not a man with serious dark eyes and a mouth that tasted like heaven.

CHAPTER SIX

NEARLY A WEEK after that stunning kiss, Sam had reached the inescapable conclusion that Alexandra was avoiding him.

She seemed to have unerring instincts for visiting the restaurant to check their progress just as he stepped out for lunch or left to pick something up at the building supply store on the edge of town.

His crew all seemed to like her, even Silent Joe, and reported that she had told them all how much she loved the way her kitchen was coming together. To him, she had left only a quickly scribbled note the second time he had missed her, which read, *Looks great, Sam. You're a genius with a hammer.*

He might have resorted to stopping at her current restaurant up at the Silver Strike Resort just for an excuse to see her again, but every time he had considered making a reservation, he had decided against it.

After she had driven away so abruptly the other night without giving him an answer when he had asked point-blank to see her again, it had been easy enough to figure out that *was* her answer.

She obviously had her reasons for avoiding him. If that's the way she wanted things, what the hell else could he do? He wasn't some kind of creepy stalker guy. When a woman made it clear she wasn't interested, he moved on.

That didn't mean he had to be happy about it, especially after they shared a kiss that had rocked him to the core.

The gloomy, rainy morning matched his mood as he headed into her sister's coffee place and bookstore for a midmorning caffeine jolt for his crew.

He just finished ordering for the guys from their complicated list—who knew Silent Joe liked café au lait, extra foamy?—when some gut instinct kicked in. It was probably the same sixth sense that had carried him to the other side of so many dangerous situations when he had been deployed.

He turned around and there she was a few spaces behind him in line at the coffee counter, talking with an older woman who shared the same green eyes behind trendy glasses.

He knew he shouldn't be so happy to see her but he couldn't ignore the delight that burst through him like the sun between those clouds outside.

He just liked looking at her, plain and simple. All that long, wavy blond hair, those deep jade eyes, the sweet curve of her mouth. Alexandra McKnight was one hell of an appealing package.

As if she felt the heat of his thoughts, she finally broke off her conversation with the woman and shifted her attention to him. When she saw him, something bright and glittery flashed in those eyes before she shifted her gaze down.

"Wow. Somebody must be thirsty," Alexandra quipped.

He held up the carry tray with a half-dozen cups.

"Making a coffee run for the whole crew this morning. Somebody's got to do it."

All he wanted to do was stand there holding the coffee and stare at her. He realized in that moment of seeing her again after all this time just exactly how much he had thought of her in the past week, half the time without even being fully aware.

Thoughts of her had been simmering under his consciousness since he had last seen her drive away on a darkened Hope's Crossing street.

He had known the whole time he had worked at the restaurant that this was *her* kitchen. Did she prefer pull handles or knobs? Would she notice this or that extra little touch while she cooked in the kitchen? How could he make the space work best for her?

The other woman suddenly cleared her throat, and he realized Alexandra was staring right back at him, her glittery gaze fixed on his mouth. She had to be remembering that cataclysmic kiss.

And if it had affected her, too, why the hell was she avoiding him?

"Oh. Yes." She looked away and he saw a hint of color climb her elegant cheekbones. "Mom, this is Sam Delgado. He's finishing up the restaurant kitchen for Brodie. Sam, this is my mother, Mary Ella McKnight."

He smiled, juggling the to-go container to his left arm so he could shake her hand. She had auburn hair where her daughter was blonde but they shared the same finely etched bone structure, the same slender build.

"Nice to meet you, Mrs. McKnight."

"Hello, Sam. Alex was telling me how quickly the work is going at the restaurant. I do hope you're enjoying your stay in Hope's Crossing."

"I've only been here a week or so, but so far everyone has been very kind. Your daughter even gave me a guided tour the other night."

"Did she?" Mary Ella gave Alexandra a surprised look.

"You know me. Always doing my part to welcome visitors," Alexandra murmured.

Mary Ella's mouth tightened and he sensed some current between them he didn't quite understand. He probably should be on his way but he was loath to leave now that she couldn't avoid him, hot coffee notwithstanding.

"I saw the sign still up for Leonidas when I came in," he said. "No luck finding his owner, then?"

She shook her head. "For now, I've still got company."

"Leonidas? That's the name of the dog you've been keeping?" her mother asked.

He probably shouldn't enjoy sharing this little secret with her but he couldn't help it.

"That's what I've been calling him, anyway," Alexandra answered. "Remember those Belgian chocolates I gave you for Mother's Day last year?"

"How could I forget? I only let myself have one of them a week and savored them until Labor Day. This must be some dog."

"He is pretty great. I still haven't had any luck finding his home. Every day I call the two vet offices in town, the shelter, everywhere I can think of. I think they're getting a little annoyed with me. So far, no one has reported a missing chocolate Labrador. It's the weirdest thing. He had to come from *somewhere.* Someone certainly seems to have been taking good care of him, right? He was skinny but not starving."

Ethan had hounded Sam again for a dog when he talked to him on the phone the night before. His son seemed to think adding a canine member to their family was a given once they finally settled into their own place, after all these years of moving around.

He didn't have the heart to tell the kid they would be so busy settling in that a dog was somewhere far in the future.

At least he had made a little progress that morning finding somewhere to live. He was meeting with a real estate agent later, and Brodie Thorne had given him a lead on a couple places, including one house on the outskirts of town that needed some work but would be livable in the meantime. It was well within his budget.

He started to ask Alexandra if she knew anything about the neighborhood but she spoke before he could.

"My kitchen is looking fantastic."

Her approval was gratifying, he had to admit. "I'm glad you think so. Maybe you ought to stop by when I'm there so I can show you a couple things."

"Sure. I could do that," she said slowly. "I've stopped by a few times but…I guess I've missed you."

That color ratcheted up a notch or two, he noticed. He wasn't the only one who picked up on it. Her mother was giving her a very curious look. He wanted to ask why she was avoiding him but he couldn't very well do that with Mary Ella standing there.

"It would be good to have your input a little more directly. Could we arrange a time to…" He almost said *hook up* but didn't want her to think he meant that in the sexual sense. "Meet up?" he quickly amended. "I can meet you after your shift at the restaurant, if that works for you. I've got plenty to keep me busy."

"You've got the day off tomorrow, don't you?" her mother said, quite helpfully, he thought.

Alexandra frowned just briefly but long enough for him to pick up that she didn't appreciate her mother's input nearly as much as he did. "Yes. Yes, I do. I guess I could swing by at some point in the day."

"We should be there all day. Come over anytime that works for you."

"I'll do that." After a bit of an awkward moment, she gestured to the coffee. "You probably should go, unless your crew likes cold coffee."

"Right." He had completely forgotten his objective. "See you later, Alexandra. Mrs. McKnight, it was a pleasure to meet you."

Both women gave him smiles of varying warmth—Mary Ella's looked welcoming and friendly while Alexandra's struck him as guarded and wary.

Why? he wondered as he walked out of the bookstore and back to his truck, parked on a side street. They had a great time together, so why was she so determined to keep him at a distance now?

She obviously regretted their kiss. His ego might have been bruised by that if he didn't remember her heated response, the way her mouth had softened under his and how she had held on to him as if she couldn't bear to let him go.

He *did* remember those things, though, which made her reaction afterward all the more baffling.

The woman was a puzzle. A beautiful, funny, complicated puzzle.

One he very much wanted to figure out.

AFTER SAM WALKED OUT of Books & Brew, taking all that masculine strength with him, the fine tension that had clenched Alex's shoulders when she saw him standing there began to seep away.

She inhaled deeply, ridiculously aware that she had been holding her breath during the conversation, on edge and off balance.

Drat the man! He had no business bursting into her life right now and messing with her head and her hormones, not when she was so close to grabbing for everything she had ever wanted.

"I'm so glad you could meet me for coffee this morning," Mary Ella said. "I know you were working late last night."

She focused on her mother instead of this jittery mess of nerves in her stomach. "I love Maura's coffee."

"Your sister runs a fine shop, doesn't she?"

The pride in Mary Ella's voice made her smile. "She does indeed. Remarkably well, and all while raising the most beautiful baby in the world."

"Our Henry isn't that much of a baby anymore." Her mother's expression was soft, as it was when she talked about any of her children or grandchildren. "He's going to be a year old in June. Maura said he's been trying to take a few steps along the furniture."

"The time is just flying by. Any day now he's going to start growing a beard."

Mary Ella made a face. "Okay, he's still a baby for a while now. But the older I get, the faster time seems to spin."

They reached the front of the line and placed their orders, then found a couple padded chairs in one of the conversation nooks Maura had placed throughout her store for the convenience and enjoyment of her customers.

They chatted about Maura and Jack and Sage, just finishing her third year of undergraduate work at the University of Colorado in Boulder, then moved on to talk about Riley and Claire's upcoming happy event.

Throughout the conversation, Alex became aware that she wasn't the only one who seemed unsettled this morning. Mary Ella—usually calm as Silver Strike Reservoir on a summer morning—fidgeted in her chair as if she couldn't quite find a comfortable spot, and her fingers drummed with impatience on the padded armrest as they awaited their order.

When their drinks arrived, Mary Ella took a single sip of her tea and set the cup back on the saucer so abruptly some sloshed over the side and onto her lap.

Worry blossomed inside Alex like a noxious weed in Caroline's garden. This was *not* like her mother, usually the epitome of easy grace. Something was up.

"What's going on? You're acting like you've already had about a dozen cups of tea this morning."

Mary Ella set her tea—cup, saucer and all—onto the small table between them and tucked a strand of tastefully colored auburn hair behind her ear with fingers that trembled. "This is hard. Harder than I thought it would be."

That noxious weed of worry grew into a bristly, towering stalk. Something was seriously wrong. *Cancer* was the first thing that came to mind, maybe because of Caroline or because she had just seen Sam, who had tragically lost his young wife to the devil disease, though she didn't really have confirmation of that yet.

"What is it? Are you ill?" How would she bear it if

she lost her mother? Mary Ella was in her sixties, yes, but she was healthier than the rest of them and still walked four miles every morning and lifted weights at the gym three times a week.

"I'm trying to talk to each of you children separately. I've already called and spoken with Lila and Rose. I had a moment last night to talk to Maura and Angie and I'm going over to Riley's after I talk to you. It doesn't get easier, I can tell you that."

Panic fluttered inside her, dark and ugly, and she thought she just might be sick herself. "Is it cancer? If it is, I'll be there for you every minute. You know I will. I'll drive you to the chemo, I'll fix you anything that sounds good that you think you might be able to eat. I'll even shave my head when your hair falls out."

Mary Ella's eyes had gone wide during this little speech and if Alex wasn't mistaken, sudden tears swam in them. Her mother gave a shocked little laugh and reached for her hand.

Those fingers trembling in hers didn't set her mind at ease. "Oh, darling. I don't have cancer, but if I did, I would absolutely want you at my back. You have always been such a wonderful daughter. I couldn't ask for better children. All of you."

For a time in those rough teen years, she hadn't treated her mother very well and the memory still ate at her.

"Okay. Okay. You don't have cancer." Relief flooded through the panic. "What's this about, then?"

"I feel silly, especially now after that little side trip into terrible possibilities. I don't have cancer, I promise. Everything's fine. Better than fine, actually."

Mary Ella's throat worked as she swallowed hard.

"It's just… I don't know quite how to say this but…I'm getting married."

She stared for several long seconds as the words soaked into her brain, not quite sure how to react.

The news wasn't really unexpected. Mary Ella had been in a relationship for a year now, but accepting something as an inevitable outcome in the abstract was far different from being faced with the blunt reality of it.

"Does Harry know?" she finally quipped.

Mary Ella made a face. "Very funny. Yes. He's been asking me since Christmas. I just… It took me a long time to feel comfortable saying yes."

Their romance had shocked everyone in town, especially because Mary Ella had made no secret the past twenty years of her contempt for the man. She had always considered him greedy and soulless, someone who had betrayed his own son, traded his family away for a handful of gold.

Something had shifted between them the year before, however, around the time Harry's son, Jackson, had come back into Maura's life after he discovered they shared a daughter, Sage.

Tension tightened her mother's features and Alex knew Mary Ella was waiting for some other response from her than a joke. She didn't quite know what to say. Those strained and difficult teenage years aside, she loved her mother dearly and wasn't sure Harry Lange was good enough for her.

"Are you…okay with it?" Mary Ella finally asked.

She gave a rueful shake of her head, squeezing her mother's fingers. "I don't know, Mom," she said. "Don't you think you could hold out for someone a little more financially secure who might take better care of you in your old age so we don't have to?"

Mary Ella chuckled, some of the tautness of her muscles easing a little at Alex's light tone. "I don't care about his money. Harry knows that. I hope my own children do, too."

"You know I'm teasing, Mom. Though if you were any other woman, I might suspect you of marrying him just to get your hands on his Sarah Colville paintings."

"I'm considering that a very big bonus. I'm marrying the man I love and in the process gaining an entire houseful of paintings by my favorite artist."

Mary Ella no longer looked as if she were going to climb the walls in a minute, but anxiety still furrowed her forehead. Alex swallowed the rest of her conflicted emotions and reached across the space between them to hug her.

"I'm happy for you, Mom," she said, meaning every word. "I may not have been all that crazy about Harry when you started seeing him—you can't expect to unleash shock waves of epic proportions like that on the whole town without rattling a few people—but he's started growing on me."

Mary Ella's laugh was shaky with relief. "Thank you for saying that, my dear. Your sisters said much the same. Well, except for Lila and Rose, who haven't really had a chance to get to know him this last year, as the rest of you have. Even they said they trusted my judgment. I only hope Riley will be as understanding."

Her brother could be overprotective of the women in his family and often tried to boss them all around, but he and Harry also had a weirdly amicable relationship.

"I'm sure he'll be happy for you," she said. "If he's

not, Claire will make sure he comes around. So when's the big day?"

"We thought the holidays would be a special time for a wedding. Claire and Riley's was so beautiful a few years ago, all those silvery snowflakes. We don't want anything big, mainly for family and close friends, at Harry's house. It will be lovely in the winter, with a fire blazing and those windows that look out over the mountains."

"I'm doing the food, of course."

"Absolutely not," Mary Ella answered promptly. "You can plan the menu and hire the caterers if you insist on it, but I want you to be part of the family, front and center, not hiding away in the kitchen by yourself."

There went her escape plan. Ah, well. "Poor Maura. First she had to deal with Harry as a father-in-law and now he's going to be her stepfather, too."

"She's actually great with it. She and Jack both. We told them first. I hope you don't mind. Sage, of course, didn't seem at all surprised."

"None of us are, Mom. Everyone can see how happy you and Harry are together. He's been a different person this last year. Amazing, after all these years, to realize the man actually has a heart under all that bluster."

"A good, caring one. And healthier than it's been in years."

No matter her own misgivings about the relationship, she hoped for many joyful years for the two of them. Her mother didn't need more loss.

"Harry makes you happy. That's the important thing. You deserve somebody great in your life."

Mary Ella gave her a careful look. "So do you, my dear."

"Mom. Don't start again."

"I know. I know. It's just...you've been alone all these years. Don't you ever think maybe there's somebody great out there looking for you?"

Ugh. Slip an engagement ring on her finger and a woman seemed to think everyone else needed one.

"Mom, can't we just celebrate your happy news?"

"Hear me out. Last week I met this really nice young lawyer at the firm that handles Harry's affairs in Denver. He's been divorced about six months. No kids. He's great-looking. Brown hair, blue eyes. He dresses well and it's obvious he takes care of himself. More important, he's funny and charming and *kind.* We had dinner with him and the entire time, I kept thinking how the two of you would be perfect for each other."

"I'm not in the market for nice young lawyers, Mom."

Mary Ella looked undeterred. "Okay. That's fine. What about doctors, then? One of Harry's cardiac specialists is also unmarried. He looks just like that scruffy Irish fellow you and Claire think is so good-looking."

It took her a minute to figure out her mother meant Colin Farrell. Scruffy Irish fellow, indeed.

While she had to admit to being intrigued by the concept of a physician who looked like Colin Farrell, she couldn't help worrying that all of Harry's connections had apparently widened her dating pool, at least as far as her mother was concerned.

"I appreciate that. Really I do. But I'm not looking for a lawyer or a doctor. I'm really happy with my life. I just bought a house, after all, and the restaurant will be opening in a few weeks. Everything is perfect."

Mary Ella looked doubtful. "What about that nice

construction worker? He definitely looks like he could fill out a tool belt."

"Mom!"

"What? What did I say?"

She shook her head, trying to banish that image from her entirely too active imagination.

"I mean it. My life is arranged exactly the way I want it."

Mary Ella grew quiet. She sipped at her tea for a long moment then set her cup down on the saucer and faced Alex squarely, her green eyes a murky mix of sadness, concern and that lingering joy that couldn't quite be squelched.

"Not all men are like your father, Alexandra. You know that, right?"

They rarely approached the topic of James McKnight. She really didn't want to discuss it now.

"You think I don't want to make a commitment to a man because of Dad?"

"You were so close to your father." Mary Ella seemed to be picking over her words as carefully as Alex chose produce at the farmers' market. "I remember how you used to love cooking something special for him on weekend mornings. I would wake up and you would already be hard at work in the kitchen trying to come up with something unique. He would come in from his run, scoop you up in his arms and call you his little Julia Child."

She hated remembering those weekend mornings. "He had everything a man could want. But he still walked away from all of us."

"Oh, darling. Your father loved you and your brother and sisters. I have to think he loved me, as well. But there was always some core of him that could never be happy, no matter what I did or any of you children did. I'm not sure he had the capacity to be truly happy. We married so young and I think part of him could never stop wondering about the roads he didn't have the chance to travel and what might have been waiting for him there."

Mary Ella touched her hand. "That didn't mean he didn't love you, Alex. All of you. I know he did. The time he spent with you children was some of his happiest."

When she let herself see anything past her anger, she truly missed those happy times. Her father had been clever and fun, curious about everything around him.

Maybe, if she hadn't been dealing with the ache of abandonment, she might have been more discriminating in her choices later in life. She wouldn't have been so desperate for someone to love her that she completely ignored common sense and simple instincts.

"I'm going to tell you something I don't think I've ever voiced before," Mary Ella said. "If your father hadn't been killed in that accident at the dig, I honestly think he would have come to his senses and realized everything he was giving up. He would have come to see how very much his family meant to him."

"We'll never know, will we?"

"No. And that grieves my heart for you children more than I can say."

Alex shook her head. "Let's not talk about this. This is a happy day. You're getting married!" She injected all the enthusiasm she could in her voice, became as perky as Rachael freaking Ray sucking helium. "I'm so happy for you and Harry. As long as he treats you well, who cares that he has a reputation for being the crankiest man in town?"

Mary Ella laughed and allowed herself to be distracted, much to Alex's relief. They talked a few more moments about the wedding plans and the restaurant and then Mary Ella left, with the excuse that she was meeting Claire and Riley at the Center of Hope Café to share the news with them.

With all the tea she had already nervously consumed, Alex doubted Mary Ella would have room left for any of Dermot's food, but she wisely kept that opinion to herself.

After her mother left, she wandered around the bookstore for several minutes, purchased a couple foodie magazines and a cookbook for ideas.

She put them in her vehicle, which she had parked in the little lot behind Maura's store, then headed across and down Main Street to the little fenced yard at String Fever where she had left Leo to play with Chester while she met her mother.

The two dogs were nestled together in a patch of spring sunlight that had burst through the gloom while she was at the bookstore. The sight of them, Leo's head resting on Chester's plump haunches, made her smile and pushed away a little of her restlessness.

She left them to it and peeked her head into the store to grab the leash she had left in Claire's office. Evie stood behind the counter talking to one customer with another one waiting to grab her attention. She never disturbed her when she was busy so she only held up the leash and waved at her friend to let her know she was taking Leo with her.

By the time she walked back out, Leo was waiting

for her by the rear door of the store, his tail wagging a greeting. He really was a great dog. Somebody *had* to be missing him somewhere.

Outside the fenced garden, she paused, the leash dangling in her hand. Every instinct she might have for self-preservation was urging her to take the safe course for the rest of the day—to climb back into her SUV and head home and work on her fledgling vegetable-and-herb garden along the banks of the creek.

The day before, Caroline had supervised from the patio while Alex took some perennial starts from her friend's yards. Caroline, the expert gardener, had also offered some solid planting advice about what would work best for the soil she had.

Alex had big ideas for growing fresh herbs she could use in some of the dishes she wanted to serve at the restaurant and she couldn't wait to get started.

Still, she found herself turning up the steep Main Street toward Brazen. She would only stop for a moment, she told herself. Just to prove to both of them she wasn't running scared of him.

Clouds still hovered around the rugged mountaintops but the weather appeared to be clearing. In the wake of the early morning rain, everything looked clean and new, saturated with color, and the air smelled sweetly of spring growth.

She waved to Prudence Clover, riding down the hill on her cruising bike with the big straw basket in the front, and then to Darwin Leeds, who was out replacing a broken slat on his fence.

As she neared the restaurant, she told herself the little skitter in her chest was just happiness that she lived in such a beautiful place, surrounded by friends.

It certainly had nothing to do with anticipation about seeing Sam twice in one morning, only anticipation at seeing the familiar old fire station coming back to life.

The freshly painted wide red doors that had once opened for water tankers and ladder trucks gleamed a welcome in the morning light with their replacement windows. She couldn't wait to open them on summer days and put seating on the flagstone patio so people could sit and look out at the charming, bustling town below. It would be a beautiful place to enjoy the summer sunshine and the evening stars.

When she pushed open the side door, raucous classic rock music competed with the buzz of power tools. The smell of sawdust and wood glue filled the air.

She saw Sam first thing. His back was to her as he worked a board through some kind of big saw hooked up to a power compressor. He wore black ear protectors, which probably masked the sound of her arrival. From behind, his T-shirt accentuated those wide shoulders that tapered down to slim hips and the muscled biceps that flexed with each movement, complete with that very sexy tattoo on his right arm.

Nerves curled in her stomach, glittery and bright, and she tightened her grip on the dog's leash. This was stupid. He was just a good-looking man she happened to have kissed. Quite passionately.

Ignoring the clamoring impulse to just turn around and walk right back down the hill, she forced herself to wait a moment more until he turned off the power saw, then she cleared her throat.

He turned around, his brown eyes and long dark lashes magnified behind the clear safety goggles he wore.

"Alexandra! Hi. I didn't expect to see you again so

soon." He set the board aside and pulled off all his protective wear then headed toward her.

"And Leo. Hey, there."

She knew she shouldn't be charmed by this big, tough-looking construction worker bending down to give a stray dog the love, but a traitorous warmth trickled through her when he rubbed Leo's ears and throat.

"It stopped raining and he needed a walk anyway," she explained quickly. "I've been trying to exercise him whenever I can in public areas in the hopes that somebody driving by might recognize him."

"How's that working out for you?"

She held up the leash. "He's still with me instead of where he belongs."

"Maybe with you *is* where he belongs."

She made a face. "He has a home somewhere. I'm sure they're missing him. I don't mind watching him temporarily but once the restaurant opens, I won't have time to take care of him very well."

Saying that aloud made her sadder than it should. Already, the dog was seeping into her heart. She couldn't allow that. It would hurt too badly when he left.

"Have time to give me a quick tour so I can check out the progress?" she asked quickly, eager to change the subject.

He shoved work gloves in his back pocket. "Sure. Love to."

Did he sense the currents sparkling between them like dust motes in a beam of sunlight? she wondered as he showed her around the kitchen.

Eventually they circled back around to the spot where they had started. Alex planted her hands on her hips and gave a long look around at the total package. It was everything she had dreamed and more.

In her mind, she could see it in a few weeks' time, teeming with her crew instead of his, with the scent of delicious food cooking replacing the sharp construction smells.

"I'm very impressed. You do good work, Sam Delgado. I can't believe you've done all this in a week. You're nearly finished."

She should be jumping up and down with excitement about that, not fighting this vague depression that he would be out of her life soon.

"We're ahead of schedule. Another few days should do it, then we'll leave it to the painters and decorators. And speaking of work…I've been meaning to stop by the resort restaurant to have a meal so I can check yours out. Seems only fair, since you'll see mine every day while you work in here."

She would think of him. While she stood at that gleaming countertop, she would remember those big hands that had fashioned it. Eventually he would become just another memory in thirtysomething years of them.

That thought shouldn't have made her suddenly sad, either.

"I would have thought the divine hamburger I fixed you the other day was proof enough of my mad cooking skills."

He shrugged. "Still. I should have a second taste, just to be sure."

Was he talking about her cooking or that kiss? She wasn't quite sure…and wasn't sure she wanted to know.

Out of nowhere, she was struck by the desire to cook

him a really fabulous meal in her own kitchen at home. *Coquilles St. Jacques,* maybe, plump scallops in a dry white wine sauce with baby chanterelle mushrooms and Gruyère cheese.

The impulse unnerved her. She never cooked privately for anyone but close friends, and Sam Delgado was far from that. She swallowed the invitation before it could be anything more than an idea. Her cozy little house on Currant Creek was her haven. Just the idea of him in her comfortable space made her feel as if someone had dropped an ice cube down the back of her shirt.

The restaurant would do. She would make sure they served him a meal he would never forget.

"You do know I'm just the sous-chef there, right?" she said. Technically that was true, but the executive chef, Simon Petit, had two other restaurants, one in Denver and one in Aspen, so she had been doing the heavy lifting for years and had created about half of the items on the menu. With none of the credit, of course.

"Good enough for me. Do I need a reservation?"

She ought to tell him yes and that they were booked out for weeks, but this was the off-season and he probably could walk in any night of the week. "I'll take care of it. When do you want to come?"

"How about tonight around eight-thirty?"

That meant she would see him three times in one day. So much for trying to keep a safe distance. "Great," she said, lying through her teeth. "I'll make sure we have a good table ready for you."

"I'll look forward to it."

"Sorry to interrupt your work. I'd better let you get back to it."

"I'll see you tonight then."

His words were perfectly polite, innocent even, but she shivered anyway. Those nerves skittered around inside her like shallots in hot oil.

Firmly ignoring her reaction, she gripped the dog's leash, gave Sam a jaunty wave and headed back outside.

Once more in the murky sunlight, she marched briskly down the hill. Only when she was certain she was out of sight of Sam or any of his crew did she lean against a convenient tree trunk and press a hand to her stomach.

She had a serious crush on the man. It was ridiculous at her age and completely counterproductive. She was going to have to do something drastic to exorcise it before she made a complete fool of herself.

CHAPTER SEVEN

He was in heaven. Complete culinary heaven.

After finishing the best meal of his life, Sam sat back in his chair and wiped at his mouth with his napkin with a sense of total satiation.

Everything had been perfect, from the roasted fennel tomato soup at the beginning to the chocolate mousse layer cake he had just finished. He didn't consider himself any kind of foodie, though his late wife had done her best to educate his palate, but he did know when something tasted just right. This meal definitely fit the bill.

Though the waitstaff had been attentive and helpful, Sam's only regret was that he had missed the chance to see Alexandra. What was the point of coming out here to her restaurant if he didn't have the chance to tell her how delicious everything had been?

He was about to ask his server if he could finagle a few minutes of her time when the kitchen doors swung open and she walked out. All that silky blond hair was gathered under a tall chef's hat—a toque, he'd learned once when Kelli had been watching the Food Network from the hospital bed—and she wore a white jacket and black trousers. She looked crisply professional but every bit as beautiful as always.

Suddenly the whole evening seemed brighter. He didn't find that a particularly comfortable realization.

"So?" She gestured to his table.

"I'm not sure I want to ever move from this spot again. That was fantastic. I can't even describe how good it was."

She plopped down into the chair opposite, snagged his wineglass and took a sip without asking. "Go ahead. Try."

She really needed validation? He found that hard to believe, when she could produce such miraculous creations. "You do understand I'm not exactly a food critic, right? When I was a kid, a gourmet meal for us was a bucket of chicken. I'm only a dirt-poor kid turned soldier turned construction worker. Not sure if my opinion really holds all that much weight."

"It does."

"Okay. Well, I can't tell what was my favorite part of the meal. That soup where all those flavors mixed together perfectly, the beef tenderloin that literally melted in my mouth or the roasted potatoes with the herb crust. What was that?"

"Oh, this and that. Rosemary, oregano, thyme and a few other secret things."

He leaned back in his chair. "It was all divine. Every bit of the meal. But you knew that, didn't you?"

"It's always nice to hear it from somebody else." Her grin was bright and infectious and he wanted to kiss her again, right here, right now, in full view of all her coworkers and the remaining patrons.

"When does your shift end?" he asked on impulse. Yeah, she had shut him down the last time when he asked to see her again but he couldn't resist trying again.

"Now. We're basically done for the night."

If he were smart, he would thank her for a lovely dinner, head to his motel and try to sleep a little after a long day, preferably without frustrating dreams of her.

But sometimes the smart way seemed the coward's way and he felt like living on the edge tonight.

"Up for another game of pool?"

She wanted to say yes. He didn't know how he was so certain but for just an instant, something in her expression indicated she was seriously tempted, then wariness washed in like a dark cloud skating across the sky.

"I better not. I left Leo with Claire and Riley and told them I would swing by to pick him up after my shift."

She paused, as if weighing her words. "I was planning to take him for a little walk to help us both unwind. You're welcome to come along, assuming you can keep up."

Laughter bubbled up. If he could keep up? He was used to twenty-mile forced marches in the middle of the night in the desert, carrying seventy-five pounds of gear, and she was implying she could out-hike him.

He could fall for this woman in a big way if he wasn't careful.

Tonight he didn't feel like being very careful.

"I'll have to pry myself out of this booth first. After that delicious meal, that's easier said than done."

"Got a jacket handy, soldier? I was planning to hike up the Woodrose Mountain trail. It's got a nice view of town from up there but the mountains are chilly once the sun goes down. The trailhead is just at the top of Sweet Laurel Falls Road."

He loved the quaint place names in Hope's Crossing. Glacier Lily Drive, Willowleaf Lane, Sweet Laurel

Falls Road. Whoever went around with the naming pen had had a romantic streak. "I can find a jacket. Give me thirty minutes to run back to my motel for one and some hiking boots."

And a flashlight or two, he thought, *just to be safe.*

"That should give me just enough time to change and pick up Leo."

"Perfect. I'll meet you at the trailhead in half an hour."

She nodded. "I have a few things to wrap up here before I head down the canyon. It might be closer to forty-five."

"That works."

Though she had been the one to issue the invitation, he had the impression she wasn't entirely thrilled now at the idea of spending more time with him. Again, he had to wonder why. Awareness sparked and snapped between them every time they were within a dozen feet of each other. She had to sense it. Did it make her antsy, too?

She returned to the kitchen and he quickly settled his check then hurried outside the restaurant to the lobby of the Silver Strike Lodge, a massive timber structure built in the style of old national-park lodges that somehow managed to look rustic and elegant at the same time.

The lobby wasn't crowded but it was busier than he might have expected for the off-season. Then again, it was Friday. He could imagine the resort did a fair business with Colorado residents looking for a quick weekend vacation.

He had self-parked—he hated paying for valet parking when a few more steps could get him his own damn pickup truck—but as he passed a short line at the valet stand, one of the men standing there stepped out.

"Sam! You're just the man I wanted to see," Brodie Thorne exclaimed.

He stood with an older man with a shock of silver hair and a very well-cut suit.

"Hey, Brodie. What's up?"

When he was first starting out in the construction business, he might have been nervous when the guy cutting the checks told him he wanted to talk, but he knew he was doing a good job at Brazen and had no concerns on that score.

"Nothing, really. I just wanted you to meet Harry Lange. Harry, this is the man we were talking about at dinner. Sam Delgado."

The name rang a bell but he wasn't sure why. He tried to figure it out as he shook the older man's hand. "A pleasure."

"The pleasure is mine. It's rare I get the chance to meet a genuine hero."

He glanced at Brodie, who shrugged with an apologetic smile. He hadn't told Brodie much about his time in the Rangers but he fully expected the man had vetted him before bringing him to Hope's Crossing to finish the project. He would have heard things, just as he probably knew all about Sam's role in his father-in-law's downfall.

He shifted and pretended to misunderstand Harry's reference. "I'm not sure I'd call it heroic, but you're right. A good finish carpenter is tough to find these days."

The other man gave a rusty sort of laugh at that, earning him a surprised look from Brodie.

"Full of yourself, are you?" he said.

"About the things that matter in my life now," he answered.

"I like a man who doesn't live in the past. How are you enjoying our little corner of paradise, Mr. Delgado?"

He thought of Alex and this tangle of anticipation churning through him. "Everyone has been very welcoming."

"Good. That's what we like to hear. I understand you're thinking of moving your construction business up this way."

He glanced at Brodie, wondering just how much the two of them had talked about him over dinner and why his name had come up. This was the part he disliked about being an independent contractor, having to carry on polite conversations with people who might someday want to hire him. Especially when right now he wanted to be somewhere else.

"Not just thinking about it," he answered. "The wheels are already in motion. I'm committed. I'll be checking out houses tomorrow, as a matter of fact."

Not that it was any of the man's business. He wasn't sure if he liked Harry Lange. The man held himself with a confidence that bordered on arrogance. He was trying to figure out how to politely excuse himself from the conversation when Brodie spoke.

"Sam, Harry is the major shareholder and founder of the Silver Strike Resort Group," he said.

Was that supposed to impress him? He waited until he knew a man's character before he cared much about his accomplishments and how much was in his bank account. "Looks like that's working out well for you.

It's been nice talking with you but I need to go. I just made arrangements to meet up for a late-night hike with a beautiful blonde who said if I was late, she wouldn't wait around for me."

Harry laughed. "Let me guess. Alexandra McKnight."

He stared. "How did you know?"

"Beautiful, blonde, smart-mouthed. That's Alex. Besides that, I saw her talking to you at my restaurant. I like you, Mr. Delgado. I trust Brodie—and Alexandra, for that matter—to recognize quality, and I think you'll be a good addition to this town. I've got an opportunity that might interest you and I'd like to talk to you about it. I don't have much time to waste on this one. When you're done with the real estate agent, come and see me at my home office."

He rattled off an address, just assuming Sam would snatch it out of the air and remember it.

"I'm sorry. That's not convenient for me."

Both men looked at him, surprise on their features.

"How do you know until you hear what I have to say?"

"I meant meeting Saturday won't work for me. I'm picking up my son in the morning so he can spend a couple days with me. He's staying with my brother and his wife in Denver."

"Bring him along. I like kids. I've got a couple grandchildren myself and I'm about to gain a whole passel of step-grandchildren."

"Is that right?" Brodie asked, sounding surprised. "I hadn't heard you were making things official. You didn't say a word, all through dinner. When's the big day?"

"Don't know. I'll show up whenever Mary Ella tells me."

Mary Ella. He knew one woman named Mary Ella, had just met her that morning, in fact. It couldn't be a coincidence. Harry Lange was about to marry Alexandra's mother.

He wasn't sure if that changed his ambivalence about the man at all but he *had* liked her mother. If Harry had convinced Mary Ella to marry him, Sam had to be inclined to think more favorably about him.

"If you don't mind me bringing my son along, fine. I can be there tomorrow, late afternoon."

"Great. See you then. Now I suggest you get a move on, son. Alex is a woman of her word."

He had already figured out she would be. He nodded to both men and hurried to his pickup.

At the motel, he quickly changed out of slacks to cargo pants and suitable hiking boots. Back in his pickup, he was keying in the street address she had given him to his GPS when his cell phone rang.

Maybe she was backing out. Surprised by the fierceness of his disappointment, he reached for his phone and was happy on several levels when he saw his brother's home phone number, the one Ethan used to call him.

"Hi, Dad!" his son chirped when he answered.

He suddenly missed Ethan with a fierce ache. "I thought you would be sleeping. I tried to call earlier but Aunt Cheri said you were still at Luke's party. How was it?"

If not for the huge birthday celebration thrown by one of Ethan's classmates—the party he had been hearing about for weeks—Sam would have driven down to pick up Ethan that night to bring him back with him.

"It was really fun! Luke has a swimming pool and a slide and a trampoline. I was very careful to follow all the rules. Only one person at a time is permitted to jump on the trampoline, Luke's mom said so. It's a safety issue. I waited to jump until everyone else was done and having cake."

He wasn't sure how he felt about having a son afraid to do anything he wasn't supposed to. Pretty ironic payback for a guy who had broken as many rules as he could, once upon a time.

"I can't wait to see you tomorrow," he said.

"What time do you think you'll be here?" Ethan asked. "I want to set the alarm on my watch."

He laughed, even as he had another qualm. Since Kelli died, Ethan had been obsessed with setting alarms, keeping to schedules, probably out of some need to control the world around him that had turned so confusing and scary.

He wanted Ethan to be a regular kid, breaking rules, taking chances, missing the bus once in a while. Embracing life.

"I should be there around ten, then we'll come back here and have two whole days together. You're really going to like Hope's Crossing, I promise. Remember how nice it was when we came that day last month? They've got a park here with a cool climbing wall and a rocket you can play on inside. In the winter, we can go sledding and maybe you can learn to snowboard."

"I don't know about that. My friend William said his brother broke his leg snowboarding."

Further evidence of Ethan's fears. "It can happen sometimes, but it's a pretty fun sport if you know what you're doing."

"I guess."

"We can talk about it. We have a few more months to go before it snows again. Meantime, get some rest and I'll be there after breakfast tomorrow. I'll see you soon."

"Love you, Dad."

"I love you, Eth. More than anything."

They hung up and he stared out at the night for a long moment. His son was his priority. He had to be, especially during the transition phase while they both tried to adjust to their changing circumstances.

Ethan had lost so much. First his mother, then the relationship he had once had with his grandparents. Now he was losing something else important—his home for the past eight months, the cousins he loved and the aunt and uncle who had stepped up to help Sam.

Was it any wonder his son wanted to control as much as he could in his life? It was up to Sam to give him the most stable, supportive environment he could when they finally settled into life here in Hope's Crossing.

He was somber as he followed the GPS directions to the trailhead. As much as he wanted to see Alex again, he almost wished he had never gone to her restaurant earlier—and certainly that he hadn't pushed so hard for an opportunity to spend more time with her.

He liked her, probably too much. When he was with Alexandra, he could forget about the weight of responsibility dragging at him like that seventy-five-pound pack he'd been thinking about earlier—the constant worry that he wouldn't be able to give his son what he needed, that he wasn't enough.

He needed to be focusing on Ethan and creating the best life he could for the two of them, not remembering that moonlit kiss the other night.

He would enjoy his impromptu hike with Alex tonight and spend the time trying to ease things back to a friendly footing, he decided. He didn't see what other choice he had.

Still, when he drove into the trailhead parking area and his headlights picked up the sight of her waiting on a bench overlooking the town, a brown furry dog at her feet, he was aware of a fierce burst of something warm and bright he hadn't known in a long time. It felt suspiciously like happiness.

Leo barked a soft greeting when Sam parked and headed toward them. He reached down to pet the dog at the same moment he leaned in to give her a kiss on the cheek in greeting.

"You smell delicious," he said, then could have kicked himself for the spontaneous words. That sounded very much like a come-on, after he had just told himself to keep things friendly.

"I probably smell like a kitchen, since I've been cooking all day."

"You know us men and our stomachs."

She laughed. "Yes, but I also know you can't possibly be hungry. You just had a divine meal, which I happened to have fixed myself."

"Men don't always have to be hungry to want to eat," he pointed out.

"Are you talking about food or sex?"

So much for casual friendliness. He shrugged. "Either. Both. Does it matter?"

She shook her head but he saw she was fighting a smile. "Come on. Let's work off some of that…hunger… on the trail."

She took off, the dog trotting ahead of her on a leash.

He didn't even have time to hand her a flashlight. She didn't really need one—the moon was huge and full and lit up the terrain with a pale, unearthly glow.

The trail wasn't steep but the climb was steady. This part of the route was also only wide enough for one across so they didn't have much chance to talk.

He didn't mind. It was probably better that way since he couldn't seem to keep his big mouth shut. Despite all his good intentions, everything he had said to her since he pulled up to the trailhead had been provocative.

After maybe fifteen minutes of hiking, she paused at an area where the trail widened and the trees thinned, presenting a vivid view of the glimmering lights of the valley below. She pulled a water bottle out of the deep pocket of her jacket. Even as she drank, she didn't release her hold on the dog.

"You're not letting him off the leash?"

"Not yet. He's obviously a runner or he wouldn't have wandered down Main Street the other night. I don't want to take the chance of him losing his way, not with all the pitfalls up here. Bear, cougars, coyotes. Moose."

"Moose?"

She flashed him a look. "For your information, a bull moose could take out a Jeep if he had enough mad on."

"Yet you have no problem hiking up here in the dark."

"I'm tougher than I look, soldier. Besides, wouldn't you have been sorry to miss that view?" She gestured below them.

They stood, her shoulder brushing his arm, and admired the lights of the valley spread out below them.

"Beautiful," he answered. Lame as it seemed, he

wasn't only talking about the vista. In the moonlight, she seemed otherworldly, too, glowing with life.

"I don't know how anybody could ever want to leave this place."

She spoke almost reverently and he gave her a careful look. "You haven't ever wanted to go anywhere?"

"Been there, done that," she said, settling onto a slab of granite that looked as if it had been carved out of the mountainside.

"Oh?"

She was quiet for a long moment, the only sound the wind moaning in the tops of the pines and rustling the new leaves of aspen trees around them.

"After college, I lived for two years in Europe while I was in cooking school," she finally said.

Wow. He hadn't expected that. "What part of Europe?"

"France first and then Italy."

She spoke with a reluctance, her tone guarded, and he had to wonder what she *wasn't* saying. "You didn't enjoy it?"

"Parts of it, I really loved. The architecture, the art, the *food.* I mean, how can you not love all that fabulous food?"

"But you didn't stay."

"I planned to, but…I finally decided it wasn't the life for me."

"Why not?"

She hesitated. "I missed my family too much."

Even through his envy at all she had, he sensed that wasn't the whole story.

"Don't take them for granted. Your family, I mean," he said when she didn't seem willing to add anything else. "If you get along with them, consider yourself lucky."

"I do. Believe me I do. You mentioned a brother. What about your parents?"

"Don't have any. It's just the two of us."

"You had to have had them once. It's kind of a biological imperative."

"Technically, yeah. Our dad, if you want to call him that, took off back to Colombia when Nicky was only a few months old. We never heard from him again."

"You don't know what happened to him?"

He shrugged. "I barely remember him, if you want the truth. We didn't miss him much after he left. I tried to find him years ago when I was stationed in that part of the world. I'm not sure why. Stupid curiosity, maybe. Or maybe just to tell him off for abandoning his kids."

"You couldn't find him?"

"Not a trace. The trail went cold."

Judging by the little he knew of the man, he had probably come to some violent end while trying to screw somebody out of money or drugs, but he decided not to mention that.

"What about your mother?"

She wasn't going to stop until she heard the whole grim truth, he sensed. He rarely talked about his parents but something about the night and the woman seemed to wrest the words out.

"She wasn't really much of a mother. She was in the life, you know? Drugs, alcohol. The whole thing. Nicky and I were in and out of foster care from the time I was ten until I turned eighteen. Not always together, though I tried."

"What happened when you were eighteen?"

He remembered that time, both the determination and the fear. “I found a compassionate judge who gave me custody of him.”

“How old was your brother?”

“Fifteen. The biggest smart-ass you could ever meet when he was a kid, but now he’s a hotshot attorney with a great wife and a couple kids. He just got a job in Belgium working for an international company there.”

He wasn’t sure how, but he and Nick had somehow made it work. He had done odd jobs for two years, until his brother graduated high school at seventeen, when Sam had enlisted. With his army wages, he had managed to live on nothing, saving every penny to help Nicky through school.

“You sound proud of him.”

“I am. It’s amazing that he came out of what we did and became somebody.”

“So did you.”

He shifted, uncomfortable with her words. Before he could find some way to deflect the conversation—and before he quite figured out what she intended—she leaned in and kissed him, her mouth warm and soft against his.

He sensed the kiss was completely spontaneous, that she hadn’t given it much thought ahead of time and probably wouldn’t have done it if she hadn’t acted on impulse, but he wasn’t about to argue.

She was here, touching him, kissing him, and that was the only thing he cared about.

After that first delicate brush of her mouth against his, as soft and sweet as butterfly wings, she started to ease away, as if she believed he would be content with that little taste after he had savored so much more than that the other day.

Knowing only that he couldn't let her go yet, he grasped her hands in his and tugged her closer. Her fingers fluttered in his like that butterfly but after a moment's hesitation, she opened them and twined them together with his, all while her scent—vanilla and spices and delicious female—made his head spin.

So much for good intentions. He forgot all the reasons this wasn't wise. With the sparkle of stars overhead, the sprawl of lights from the town below and the cold mountain air that smelled sweetly of spring wrapping around them, the moment was perfect. He didn't want it to end.

He kissed her, tasted her, until they were both breathing hard, until his body ached, until he wanted nothing so much as to find a soft patch of grass somewhere and explore every warm, curvy inch of her....

She was the first to pull away and he realized she was practically on his lap. He wanted her to stay exactly there.

"You are one fine kisser, Sam Delgado."

He smiled against her mouth. "I'm good at a lot of things."

Her body trembled, ever so slightly, but before he could stop her, she slid out of his lap and gave a light jump to the ground, reaching for the leash she had dropped in the midst of their kiss. The dog hadn't gone far; he was curled up on the ground looking far more comfortable than either of them right now.

"I like you very much, Sam," she said, "and I would be lying if I didn't admit I find you incredibly sexy, but

I'm not going to sleep with you. I suppose it's only fair to tell you that up front."

He managed a rough laugh, dangerously close to falling hard for Alexandra McKnight. "Just because a woman happens to enjoy the way I kiss her doesn't automatically mean I expect her to fall into bed with me."

In the pale moonlight, her features looked almost fey. "Then you are truly a man among men. Come on, Leo. We should probably be heading back."

He stood for just a moment on the mountainside with the cool breeze rippling his hair, then shook his head to clear away the lingering arousal and followed after her, wondering just how the hell his best intentions had gone so wildly off the rails.

ALEX GRIPPED THE HANDLE of Leo's leash so hard she was quite sure when she finally made it down to the trailhead, she would have an imprint on the skin of her palm that would last for days.

She was completely self-deluded to think she could keep things casual and friendly with Sam.

The only reason she had invited him along on this little walk with Leo was to convince herself she had the strength of will to resist this attraction that simmered between them. Ha. That certainly turned out well, didn't it? A half hour into it, she was once more in his arms.

She couldn't seem to help herself. Her brain warned her to keep a safe distance but the rest of her just wanted to grab hold and not let go.

Leo led her down the dark trail, easily dodging the small rocks and weedy growth along the way. He moved fast, probably eager for bed, and she followed right behind him, hoping she didn't trip and go sprawling.

Wouldn't that be a lovely conclusion to the evening, if she ended up in the emergency room?

She was aware of Sam not far behind her. The beam of his flashlight cut ahead of all three of them, but he was silent, concentrating on the trail.

By the time the trailhead came into view, endorphins pumped through her and she could feel each beat of her heart.

"Why are you running so hard?" Sam asked when they reached their vehicles.

She caught her breath. "That wasn't a run, soldier. That was just a little stroll down a mountainside. It's not my fault you can't keep up."

"I wasn't talking about the pace."

Yeah. She figured that out. She hated feeling like a coward but she had a very powerful feeling it wouldn't take long for her to fall head over heels for this strong, sexy man who'd raised his younger brother and nursed his dying wife and who made her feel as if she would catch fire in a dry wind. For some crazy reason, she suddenly remembered the phrase Frankie Beltran had said to Claire, telling her Sam was hotter than a two-sided firecracker.

She was the firecracker, at least where he was concerned. He only needed to look at her out of those big, long-lashed dark eyes and she wanted to explode across the sky in a big flash of heat and color and sparkles.

"I like you, Sam. A lot. But I told you I'm not going to sleep with you and I mean it. I don't do relationships very well. Casual, flirty and fun I can handle but I'm not interested in more than that."

"Nothing wrong with casual, flirty and fun. For now."

She pounced on the last two words. "See, right there. That's the problem. I only want the *now.* And actually, I don't even want that in this particular *now.* Nothing personal, but I just don't have the energy for you."

He studied her in the moonlight and she felt exposed to the bone, as if he could sift through layers of skin and muscle and sinew to the very heart of her.

Oh, the wonders of self-delusion. She thought she could handle a man like Sam the same way she treated the fun-loving ski bums and river guides she usually dated. It was no coincidence they were usually a few years younger than she was and more than willing to let her set the terms and make up the rules.

Sam was different. With him, she felt extremely out of control, as if she were floating down level-five rapids with no life preserver, no raft, no helmet, no protection but her own wits. Flimsy help, there.

"This is an important time for me, preparing to open the restaurant after months—*years,* really—of planning. I just can't afford the distraction."

"Distraction."

He spoke the word softly and it hovered between them like a pesky deerfly.

"Yes. What else would you call this?"

He was silent for a long moment. "You're definitely distracting. I can't seem to get you out of my head, try as I might. I thought seeing you again would help in that department but I think we've only made things worse."

He sighed. "As much as I'm tempted to give you all the casual, flirty fun you can handle," he went on, his voice low, "I think you're probably right. This isn't a good idea."

She was so busy trying to ignore the burst of heat

from his words, it took a moment for the second part of what he said to seep through.

"It's not? I mean, no, it's not. What a relief that you agree with me."

"The timing isn't great for either one of us."

"Horrible," she agreed.

"Neither of us is looking for a relationship right now."

"Absolutely right."

"So no more midnight walks. Are we agreed on that?"

"Probably smart."

They both looked at each other for a long moment and then Sam smiled, one edge of his mouth lifting just a little higher than the other. "It's too bad, really. I like you right back, Alexandra."

"No reason we can't still be friendly with each other."

"Except every time I'm with you, I'll want to kiss you again."

"You'll get over it."

He laughed and unexpectedly reached out and pulled her into his arms, kissing the top of her head with an affection that stealthily sneaked into her heart more effectively than a passionate embrace.

"I'll do my best." Too soon, he released her and she opened her car door and climbed inside.

"Good night, Sam."

"Night. Thanks for the hike and the company."

"You're welcome."

She closed the door quickly, firmly, and shoved the transmission into Reverse. She didn't quite squeal her tires, but it was close as she backed out of the parking space then quickly headed toward her house in Currant

Creek Valley before she could surrender to the fierce urge surging through her to turn off the engine, fly out of the SUV and jump back into his arms.

CHAPTER EIGHT

FOUR HOURS AND SIX HOUSES after starting out with the Realtor, Sam picked the house he wanted five minutes after walking through the front door.

"This is the one. It's perfect."

His perky real estate agent—the aptly named Jill Sellers—quickly concealed her dubious expression. "Are you sure? It needs *so* much work! I only showed you this one because you insisted."

He should have trusted Brodie Thorne's instincts. This was the very house Brodie had suggested he consider, a two-story early-century bungalow in serious need of some love and care.

The rooms were small and dark and the trim looked as if it had been painted over at least a dozen times. The last kitchen makeover was probably circa 1970, at least judging by the green appliances and lovely orange cabinetry, and the main bathroom would have to be completely gutted.

All in all, it was exactly what he wanted. The challenge of the work it needed was a huge part of the appeal.

"What do you think, Ethan?"

His son sat on the bottom step of the porch, chin in hand. Rodin's *The Thinker* with missing front teeth and dark curls. “I believe it’s my favorite so far. I really like this house. It feels happy in here.”

He grinned. “There you have it. That’s good enough for me, kid.” He turned back to Jill. “Looks like we’re going with the happy house.”

She frowned as much as her Botox would allow. “You really should have a home inspection first. I doubt the electricity is up to code and the plumbing might have to be entirely replaced.”

“The structure is solid and the foundation decent. I had a good look when we came in. I figure I can fix just about anything in between.”

“What about all the other houses we looked at?” she said, a little desperately. “Some of those had real potential.”

“I agree, but they’re not for me. I’m sorry to waste your time and energy. We should have started here.” Which he had suggested, several times, but he figured he should probably refrain from pointing that out.

“We Delgado men know what we want when we see it, don’t we, kid?”

Ethan grinned. “Yep. Can I have the bedroom upstairs with that window seat and the huge closet?”

That was the one with the water damage that would need some serious drywall repair. In the win column, the two downstairs bedrooms were just fine and the upstairs bathroom only needed new paint.

“We might have a bit of work to do first,” he warned his son.

“But after that, can I?”

“Sure thing.”

“Are you sure about this?” The real estate agent looked aghast, probably because the asking price was much lower than any of the other houses they had seen, which meant her commission would take a corresponding hit.

He regretted that but he wasn't about to buy a house he didn't want just so she could have a bigger payday.

"Dead sure."

"It's barely livable!"

"It's got a working bathroom and kitchen. What more do a couple guys need? Let's go down 5 percent on the asking price, see if the seller will bite. With that price, especially for this area, I could raze it to the foundation and start over and still probably come out ahead."

The neighborhood was perfect, as far as he was concerned, a mix of old and newer houses on lots separated by looming pine trees. A silvery creek threaded through some of the houses in the neighborhood—not his, thank heavens, with an inquisitive son to worry about—and the mountains soared as a backdrop.

He could picture watching sunsets over those mountains from the porch on summer evenings, raking leaves with Ethan on crisp autumn afternoons with the smell of wood smoke in the air, the whole neighborhood lit up with twinkly lights at Christmastime.

Apparently Jill could see his mind was set. She shifted from pointing out the pitfalls to some of the positives.

"Well, it *is* quite historic, built during the mining boom in the latter part of the nineteenth century. It's one of the original houses in this neighborhood. Really, most of the other houses grew up around it. The yard is nicely landscaped, with all those beautiful mature trees and even some cherry and apple trees in the back. It's been neglected the last few years because of the owner's health issues but should only need a little elbow grease to bring it back."

He didn't mind hard work, though he knew little about gardening. He would just have Ethan read some books on the subject. The kid could be a walking encyclopedia when you gave him a research topic.

"The seller is actually the grandson of the original owner," the real estate agent went on. "He was pastor here in Hope's Crossing for many years. He and his wife raised all their children here. Hank had a heart attack a few years ago and hasn't been able to keep up the house as he'd like. From what I understand, they're moving to Arizona to be closer to grandchildren."

He had sensed the house had known families, children, love.

"Let's not keep them waiting then. Make the offer, see if they bite."

Her carefully coiffed hair didn't move when she shook her head, he noticed. "I hope you're not rushing into things, but let me go make a call."

She walked into the kitchen, leaving him and Ethan alone. After she left, he felt a moment's misgivings. Buying a house was a huge decision. Buying a house in a completely new community felt monumental.

No, he wouldn't second-guess. Moving to Hope's Crossing was the right decision, for him and for his son.

"What did you think about that creek we saw on the way in? What are the chances we can hook some trout in it?"

Ethan appeared to give the matter serious thought. "There are too many variables for me to be able to answer that. We don't even know if there *are* trout in it, for one thing."

He laughed. “It was a figure of speech, son. That’s all. What do you say we go take a look at it, see if we can find any.”

“Sure.”

They headed into the April sunshine and Ethan slipped a hand in his, his fingers small and vulnerable.

“Does it snow a lot here?” Ethan asked as they headed across the street to an area where the creek ran close to the road before curving through the trees.

“More than in Denver, that’s for sure. You think you’ll be okay with that? You’re going to have to learn to ski or snowboard. I think it’s the law.”

Ethan frowned. “I don’t think that’s possible. It wouldn’t be constitutional, would it?”

He laughed and rubbed Mr. Literal’s head. “Maybe not the law. Maybe it’s just a strongly worded suggestion. Don’t worry, I think you’ll like it.”

Before Ethan could answer, a very familiar dog came bounding across a nearby yard toward them with single-minded intent. Ethan gasped and edged behind him. For all his talk about wanting a pet, he wasn’t a fan of big, strange dogs.

“You don’t have to worry about this dog. He’s friendly.”

“How do you know?”

“We’ve met before.”

“Is he a stray?”

“The answer to that particular question is a little complicated. Leo, what are you doing up here?” he asked. “Did you run away again? Don’t you know you had a good thing going?”

The dog looked at him for a moment out of those beautiful hazel eyes then barked happily and turned back around the way he had come, heading up the street in the slanting afternoon sunlight.

Sam muttered an oath but cut it off when he caught Ethan watching him carefully. He wasn't at all in the mood to chase down a dog, but he also knew he couldn't let Leonidas wander aimlessly.

"Come on."

"Where are we going?"

"To catch that rascal of a dog," he answered.

"Really?" Ethan's eyes were huge. "Are we going to keep it?"

When they were a little more settled, maybe they could consider getting a dog, but that seemed months away.

"Right now the dog belongs to someone else. Come on, let's see if we can grab him before he gets too far."

They hurried down the street, Ethan's hand still in his, past a couple houses that showed clear signs of children living there, with bikes parked beside the garage, and a trampoline in one backyard. Finally the dog paused at a particularly charming small log home, almost hidden from the street by trees.

"Oh, I like this house, too," Ethan declared. "Maybe we could buy this one instead."

"Looks like somebody already lives here. See, no for-sale sign."

The dog slipped around the side of the house as if he belonged there and cut through a gap in the fence. Sam felt a little weird about going into someone's backyard but he was afraid if he took time to knock on the door to ask permission, the dog would escape through some other gap and Alexandra would never be able to find him.

"Where have you been?" He heard a low, exasperated voice as he turned the corner of the house and suddenly there she was.

Alexandra was on her knees next to a flower garden that bordered a wide flagstone overlooking the river and the mountains. She had one hand firmly around the dog's collar, the other still holding a gardening spade.

She wore pink flowered gardening gloves and a floppy straw hat and he was seized by a powerful urge to toss it off and throw it into the garden before he pulled her against him and kissed her once more.

Fortunately, he managed to tamp it down.

She hadn't spied either of them yet as she continued to talk to the dog. "I don't want to use a chain on you or lock you in the garage when I'm outside but I will if you run off again. How are we ever going to find your owners if you wander off like that when I'm busy? And how on earth did you open the gate?"

The dog grinned at her as if to say, *Look who I found,* and Sam moved closer. "You've got a gap in your fence that looks just big enough for a troublesome dog to sneak through. Though I suppose he could also escape across the creek."

She had whirled at his first words, her eyes stunned. Dismayed, even. "Sam! What are you… How did you find out where I lived?"

"Is it a secret?"

"No, I just…I don't remember telling you."

"You didn't. Leo did."

At the temporary name, the dog barked happily and plopped on his belly. Still looking stunned, Alex rose and joined him. She didn't appear to notice Ethan, who had become distracted by a bird feeder next to the house where a couple of colorful little finches darted in and out.

"Seriously, what are you doing here?"

"House hunting. I just made an offer on that bungalow a few doors down and across the street."

If he thought she looked stunned to see him before, it was nothing to the complete shock in her eyes now. "You…what?"

"If all goes well, it looks like we're going to be neighbors."

"Neighbors? Here? Don't be ridiculous."

"Ridiculous?" He hadn't expected that particular reaction. She was looking at him as if he had just announced he was opening a strip club next door to the elementary school.

"You…you have a business in Denver. You're only here for a few weeks, to finish Brazen."

"*Had* a business. I'm moving my whole operation. I'm keeping my crew so I can still do some jobs in the city, but as of now the address on my letterhead will say Hope's Crossing."

She continued to gape at him and he couldn't help wondering why this news seemed almost catastrophic to her.

"We were ready for a change, weren't we?"

For the first time, she seemed to register Ethan's presence. He saw her gaze move rapidly from the boy to him and then back to the boy again, lingering on Ethan's blue eyes and curls and the wide mouth he knew they shared.

"We."

He hadn't meant to tell her like this. A completely unaccustomed—and unearned—guilt made him squirm.

He had every right to protect his son, he reminded himself. "This is my son. Ethan, this is my friend Alex McKnight."

"Alex is typically a boy's name. I have a friend named Alex at school and he's a boy."

"Yes, but sometimes it's short for Alexandra," Sam answered.

"Oh. Okay. I'm very pleased to meet you, Alexandra. I think I like your dog."

She hadn't stopped looking at his son since becoming aware of him.

"Thanks." Her voice sounded thready and she had to clear it before she spoke again. "I like him, too, except when he wanders off. But he's not really my dog. I'm just watching him until we can find his owner."

She smiled at the boy and Sam suddenly remembered she had several nieces and nephews. Of course she would be comfortable with children.

"Would you mind if I played with him? I would very much like to throw a stick and see if he'll bring it back."

"He'll be in heaven. He's a retriever. That's kind of what they do. We've been playing fetch all afternoon. You should be able to find some tennis balls over by the back door."

"Even better! A spherical object will be easier to throw."

"That was my theory, too."

His son and the woman he was fiercely attracted to smiled at each other in perfect accord and Ethan headed off, the dog at his heels, to find a tennis ball.

Alexandra turned back to him and her smile dropped away like that spherical object falling out of the sky. "A son. You *are* a man of mystery."

He shrugged. "I like to keep a woman guessing."

"I can see maybe keeping your favorite color a secret but this seems like pretty important information to withhold. You didn't say a word."

"I'm a little cautious about mentioning Ethan to people when I first meet them," he admitted. "It probably comes from being in the military but I tend to be overprotective about sharing my personal life, especially about my family."

"An understatement."

He felt guilty, for reasons he couldn't have explained. He hadn't done anything wrong but the way she was looking between him and Ethan made him feel otherwise.

"I guess I should have mentioned him but I didn't quite know how. I'll admit I'm a little rusty about this. I haven't dated since my wife died, in part because Ethan tends to get…attached very easily."

A trait he and his son apparently shared. He had a feeling he was becoming very attached indeed to this woman with the blond curls and big green eyes.

"Nothing wrong with a little caution. Since we both decided we're not really dating, it shouldn't be an issue with us."

"There is that." He didn't want to think about that so he quickly changed the subject. "I like your house. I'll admit, it's not quite what I would have imagined for you."

"Why not?"

They both watched the boy and the dog play in the yard but he noticed she kept a safe distance from him, almost as if she didn't trust herself to come too close.

"I don't know. I guess I would have imagined you

in some kind of modern apartment somewhere. This is homey."

"I like it. I bought it for the kitchen."

"You must enjoy living by the creek."

"I'm not here that often, but yeah."

"What you need is a big comfortable chair right there on the back patio so you can unwind out here with the sound of the water. While your dog plays in the grass, of course."

She snorted and wiped the back of her hand against a smudge on her cheek, which only served to leave more dirt trailing there. "I don't have a dog, only a temporary houseguest. And I'm opening a restaurant in a few weeks, in case you forgot, so I don't plan to do much unwinding for a while."

"All the more reason why you need a sanctuary."

"THE KITCHEN is my sanctuary."

Alex could barely string together a coherent thought but she managed to answer honestly enough.

She called him a man of mystery. Ha. He was a ghost, a shadow, an enigma. They had spent several hours together, at least, and had engaged in two very passionate, very intimate embraces.

Not once, in all that time, had he happened to mention two important facts about himself—that he had a son and that he and said son were contemplating a permanent move to Hope's Crossing.

And not just any neighborhood. *Her* neighborhood—her freaking *sanctuary*—with his *son,* for heaven's sake.

Obviously, he hadn't considered her someone important enough that he was willing to share those vital details of himself. That shouldn't hurt. She knew it shouldn't but she still couldn't seem to help the little spasm under her breastbone.

Why *should* he tell her? They had spent a few pleasurable hours together and kissed exactly twice. He was building her kitchen. That was the sum total of their relationship.

None of this would be an issue if she hadn't been shortsighted enough to invite him to play pool that first night. If she had just looked at him as a really gorgeous guy who was doing good work on her restaurant kitchen and left it at that, she wouldn't be standing here in her backyard feeling stunned and stupid and, yes, hurt.

What a disaster.

She was still mulling how she could handle this major wrinkle when Jill Sellers peered over her back fence.

"There you are! I've been looking everywhere. I knew you couldn't have left because your truck was still parked out front but I couldn't, for the life of me, figure out where you'd gone until I heard voices over here."

Jill blinked big blue eyes at her. "Oh, hello, Alex. I didn't notice you there."

Nothing new there. Alex was used to being invisible to Jill and her tight circle of friends. Most people moved past their high school cliques once they picked up their diploma from the principal at graduation but Jill and a few of her friends still seemed to delight in thinking they ran the town.

"I forgot you lived in this neighborhood," Jill went on.

Despite hard lobbying to the contrary, Alex had used a fairly new real estate agent, which apparently still irked Jill.

"Yes. I was just about to tell Sam some of the downsides of the area," Alex said. "You know. The deer that come down in the winter and eat all the shrubs, the high water table we can have in bad runoff years because of the creek, the hikers wandering along the Currant Creek Valley trail."

"Hold on. Don't tell him that!" Jill beamed her thousand-megawatt smile, all jocular charm, but it couldn't quite outshine the edge in her voice. "You know those are minor little details, Al. I was just looking for him to tell him I have some great news and some *really* great news."

"Great," Sam said, his voice dry, but Jill didn't appear to notice.

"It is. The seller is *so* excited about your offer, what with this soft market and all the *work* that needs to be done to the place. Nobody else has looked at the property in *weeks* and Bob and his wife are anxious to move it so they can make an offer on a condo in Arizona. He's given preliminary approval to your offer!"

"That *is* great news."

"Even better, when I told Buzz, his agent, that you were looking for a place to live sooner rather than later, he seemed to think the sellers would be willing to sweeten the deal and offer a short-term lease while you all work out the details. You could move in tomorrow if you wanted!"

And there went the neighborhood.

Alex gripped the trowel she hadn't realized she still held, wishing she could dig a big keep-out sign on her front yard. She didn't want him here, living just a tennis ball's throw away. She would consider anywhere in Hope's Crossing too close but right here in Currant Creek Valley was unthinkable.

"I don't need to move quite that quickly," Sam was saying. "Ethan still has another month of school in Denver and will be staying with my brother and his wife until then."

That explained what he did with the boy while he was here finishing kitchens and taking midnight walks and kissing her until she couldn't think straight.

"Well, if you change your mind, we just have to say the word to Buzz and he'll set the wheels in motion. It's a cash offer and you don't have to wait for bank approval, only the inspection and the title search, so that will speed things up considerably."

At that moment, Ethan laughed at something the dog had done. Sam turned his attention to his son, a softness to his features she hadn't seen there before.

"Good. The sooner the better. We have our work cut out for us, making the kitchen and the downstairs bathroom usable. If we can move quickly, Ethan and I can work on it during the weekends when he comes up."

"We have so many details to hash out." Jill gave a faux apologetic look to Alex. "Maybe we should work through some of these issues back at the office where we don't have quite so many…distractions."

She gestured to the boy and the dog but Sam's gaze didn't leave Alex. "We wouldn't want any *distractions,* would we?" he murmured.

She had used that very word the night before, she remembered.

His very obvious implication that *she* could disturb his concentration wasn't lost on Jill. Her mouth tightened for just an instant before that fake smile stretched wider. "Shall we go back to my office then?"

Sam glanced at the complicated-looking watch he wore and swore suddenly. "I'm sorry. This is going to have to wait. I'm afraid I lost track of time and I'm supposed to be somewhere in about twenty minutes."

"Now?" Jill blinked at him.

"Yeah. Come on, Eth. We've got to go."

"What about the offer?" she pressed.

"You can handle it. I already told you my terms. What else do you need to know?"

Alex hadn't seen Jill this frustrated since their senior prom, when her date—who had ended up as her first husband—had ignored her and spent the night sneaking beers with his friends behind the old community center building.

"I guess I have your cell number. I can call you if I encounter any problems."

"You do that. Thanks a million." He gave her a wave then turned to Alex. "I'll see you later, neighbor."

Before she could think of a way to block him, he leaned in and kissed her on the cheek, surrounding her with his heat and that distinctive scent of his soap—bergamot and cedar leaf and something citrusy that tugged an instant response out of her.

Drat the man! It was completely unfair of him to shake up her world like this now, when she had so many other plates spinning.

She smiled weakly. "See you."

He walked away holding his son's hand, and Alex wanted to cry. Or at least throw a few dirt clods at him for being so damn irresistible.

"He's really a lovely man," Jill said. "And that boy is completely adorable."

"Isn't he?" Alex smiled tightly.

"I think he'll be a wonderful addition to the town, don't you? Who knows? I might even hire him to do some work at my house."

"I didn't realize you were remodeling. Didn't you just move into a new house a few years ago? Right before your second husband left town, wasn't it?"

Alex regretted the dig as soon as she said it. Apparently she was still as bitchy as she had once been in high school in retaliation against Jill and her vicious cronies.

"Sorry," she muttered.

Jill didn't seem offended, for once. "Honey, I was glad that loser left. Without the extremely generous alimony my attorney insisted on, I wouldn't be able to stay in that beautiful new house. I think I might have just enough of that bastard's money set aside to add some new built-ins to my home office."

If Alex knew Jill, she intended to get more out of Sam than some new cabinetry. She considered warning him that Jill could be, er, predatory, but decided he was a big boy. He could probably take care of himself. Maybe he liked slick, polished real estate agents better than frazzled, smart-mouthed chefs.

It wasn't her business what he did, who he saw, where he lived. He had made that crystal clear by his echoing, cavernous silence.

CHAPTER NINE

"LESS THAN A WEEK before the restaurant opens. You've got to be going crazy making sure everything is ready. Are you certain there's nothing I can do to help you?"

She smiled at Claire for her ever-ready willingness to help. She loved her friend dearly, even when she tried a little too hard.

"You're doing it. I needed the distraction of some company and I needed taste testers. This is the perfect combination. Thanks so much for coming over on short notice."

"Sign me up for taste testing and distracting anytime," Maura piped in, smiling at Henry, who currently sat on Alex's lap chortling away at Leo, who watched him out of careful eyes as the baby banged a wooden spoon on a plastic bowl Alex had sacrificed for the cause.

Maura seemed a different person than she had been a year ago, when she had been tangled up in grief and pain, closed off to all of them.

Married nearly a year and mother to the very adorable Henry, she glowed with happiness, and Alex couldn't be happier for her. Her sister deserved to find joy again after the hell of losing a child.

"Are your nerves completely shot?" Mary Ella asked.

"This is something you've wanted for so long and it's almost here."

Panic fluttered in her stomach with barbed wings. "You could say that. If I blow it, who knows when another chance like this might come along, right?"

"But you're not going to blow it," Claire insisted. "Everything will go perfectly. You'll see."

She wasn't so sure about that. Every time she turned around, she remembered something else she needed to do before the Friday night.

The past three weeks had been a whirlwind of preparation, trying to make sure every detail was perfect. She had worked her last day at the resort restaurant more than a week ago and spent every waking moment since devoting all her energies to Brazen.

"You're all coming, right?"

"Wouldn't miss it," Claire said firmly. "We already have reservations and are planning to drive over with Evie and Brodie. We better get a fantastic table, since we're sitting with the owner."

Those barbed wings flapped harder. She would *not* screw this up. She could do this. One of the first things she learned in culinary school had been that a good chef had confidence in herself and the unique gifts she had to offer.

She knew her food was good, but all the minutia was killing her.

It didn't help that her two sous-chefs were engaged in a pissing contest that was beginning to affect morale among the rest of the crew. She had a meeting with both of them later to go over final details and she planned to rattle their cages a little, remind them she was in charge and refused to keep either of them on staff if they couldn't figure out how to bury their differences and get along.

Should be a pleasant evening, all in all.

"You know I'll be there," Mary Ella declared. "Both Harry and I are eagerly anticipating it."

"I'm coming," Maura said. "Jack will even be there. He's flying in from Singapore and should be home Friday afternoon. Should be just enough time to shower and shave."

"He's coming home just for my restaurant opening, I assume."

Maura laughed. "I'm sure that was right at the top of his list while he was scheduling his trip dates."

Maura's husband always had several international projects spinning. Alex had been inclined to dislike the guy for abandoning her pregnant sister more than twenty years ago but Jack had managed to achieve what none of the rest of them did, help Maura see that her life could go on again.

"Who's watching this adorable guy?" She nuzzled Henry's warm, sweet-smelling neck. His giggle just about drowned out the little pang in her heart at what might once have been.

"Macy. She insists she's fourteen and plenty old enough."

How could Claire's daughter be fourteen already? She had vivid memories of holding her just like this, giving her raspberries on her neck and changing her diaper, and now she was becoming a young lady.

The world moved on and she just stayed the same.

Not true, she corrected herself. Look at all she had done in those fourteen years. She was happy. Not every woman needed one of these little munchkins to feel complete. She loved being an aunt and was damn good at it. That was enough for her.

"So what do you think?" She gestured to the plates she had prepared for the women. That was the reason she was holding Henry, so his mother, grandmother and Auntie Claire could devote their full attention to the pumpkin risotto.

"I like it," Claire declared. "It's got an almost smoky flavor."

She waited for Maura and Mary Ella and didn't miss the quick look they exchanged.

"What's wrong with it?"

"It's not my favorite thing you've ever cooked," Maura said honestly.

"Mom?"

"I have to agree. It needs something. I can't quite figure out what."

That panic fluttered faster, stronger. Brazen would be a disaster. No one in town would ever be able to look her in the eye again.

She forced herself to breathe. Confidence. So she made one dish that didn't resonate. So what? They had all raved about the apple-pear salad, the roasted artichokes and the pan-seared turkey cutlets. She hadn't even been planning to add the pumpkin risotto to the menu.

"Okay. That's fine," she said. "I'll table that one and work on it a little more. Thanks for the input."

"It's not bad," Mary Ella assured her. "Just…not as fantastic as everything else."

"I'm a big girl. I can take criticism," she said, and hoped it was true. She had better be able to, anyway, since after Friday night, she couldn't hide away behind someone else's failures or successes.

Needing a bit of comfort after that little ego burn, she played her trump card. "This isn't for the restaurant, just for you guys, but I made some of those three-layer chocolate-and-caramel brownies you like."

"Wow. Is it my birthday?" Claire asked.

"As good as."

She handed Henry over to Mary Ella for some grandma love, then plated the still-warm brownies, adding a drizzle of caramel and one of chocolate from the squeeze bottles she kept in the refrigerator.

For the next several moments, her warm, comfortable kitchen was full of her favorite sound: people enjoying her food. The brownies took a great deal of effort by the time she made the fudge sauce and layered the blond and dark chocolate batters, but the effort was almost universally appreciated.

"You know, of all the things you make, I think this very well might be my favorite," Mary Ella said. "I gain five pounds just breathing in the smell of them, but it's worth it."

"I can make them for your wedding reception if you want," Alex suggested.

"You can give the recipe to someone else to make but I told you before, I don't want you doing the food for the wedding. And I don't think we're having a reception. Just a small gathering for family and friends."

"Is that what Harry wants?" Maura asked. "If I know him—and I venture to say I do a little after being married to his son this last year and raising his clone of a granddaughter for twenty years before that—I would guess he wants to throw a big party and brag about his beautiful bride to the whole town."

"We're both too old for that kind of business, don't you girls think?"

"Are you kidding?" Maura grinned at their mother. "You're the sexiest sixtysomething bride I know. Besides, we were all robbed last year of the biggest social event of the season when Genevieve called off her wedding. Somebody has to fill that void. You owe it to Hope's Crossing."

"I've still got her wedding dress hanging at the shop," Claire said. "I have no idea what to do with it. Genevieve told me she never wants to see it again."

"There you go, Mom. You could wear that." Alex grinned.

Even when she scoffed, Mary Ella managed to make the sound classy. "My bust is a little bigger than Genevieve's. And can you just see me in that lovely designer white gown, veil and all, at my age? I would look completely ridiculous!"

"You would look beautiful," Claire said stoutly. "At least that way, all the work I did—twice—of custom-beading the bodice wouldn't completely go to waste."

"Who knows?" Mary Ella argued. "Gen's young. She might want to wear it again in a few years."

"Seems to me, wedded bliss is the last thing on her mind," Alex offered. "Did I tell you I saw her one night last month, shooting pool with some pretty rough customers at The Speckled Lizard?"

Had it only been a month ago when she and Sam had spent that first evening together? When they had gone for a walk through the quiet streets of Hope's Crossing and laughed together and shared that first kiss?

She had only seen him a couple times in the past few weeks, once at the restaurant when she had delivered a celebratory lunch for him and his crew on the day they finished the kitchen and turned the work over to the interior design crew, and once when she had bumped into him briefly at the grocery store in town.

Both had been short, stilted encounters—on her part, mostly, she suspected—and had left her unaccountably depressed.

She knew he had moved into the house down the street. For the past week or so, she had seen lights burning at all hours. She couldn't seem to escape the man. Every time she drove past, she thought of him, wondered how he and Ethan were getting along, remembered the sizzle and churn of her blood when he kissed her.

Though she had been tempted several times to drop by and welcome him to the neighborhood as she would any other new move-in, she kept telling herself she would do it later, after the restaurant opened.

She was a coward. She knew it, but the truth was, she hadn't yet recovered from the bombshell he had dropped that Saturday afternoon.

All along, she had been thinking he would be out of her life as soon as the restaurant was finished, only to discover the man was moving in down the street…with the son he hadn't bothered to mention.

Had she ever been so completely wrong about a man before?

Well, okay, once. Horribly, disastrously. She turned her attention away from the past and back to the conversation when she realized Claire was asking her a question.

"You saw Gen here in town?" Claire frowned. "That doesn't make sense. I thought she was working in Paris."

"Last I heard, she had some big hotshot public-relations job with a fashion design company there," Maura added.

With that tight clothing and her heavy makeup, Genevieve had looked pretty far removed from someone in the Parisian fashion design world, but that was none of Alex's business.

"It was definitely her. If I had any doubt, it would have disappeared when I saw the way she turned up her nose when she saw me, like a family of skunks had just wandered past."

"Have you heard any news about what she's doing lately from her mother?" Claire asked Mary Ella.

"Laura tends to avoid me these days." Mary Ella didn't look particularly upset by that development. No surprise there. The ill will between the McKnights and the Beaumonts was deeply rooted in the events of the past two years.

Genevieve's brother Charlie had been driving impaired in the accident that had killed Maura's daughter Layla. While Maura seemed to have made her peace with the boy, Alex wasn't as forgiving a person as her sister.

Then the previous year, the scandal erupted about Maura's other daughter, Sage, having a brief affair with Gen's fiancé, who happened to be the son of a very influential Denver family, and Gen had broken off the engagement and sent back all her wedding presents.

Alex had her own opinion about the social-climbing Beaumonts as a whole, but she still couldn't get over Gen standing up for her future like that.

The result of that unexpected pregnancy—the beautiful little boy on Mary Ella's lap—started to fret and rub at his eyes.

"You're tired, aren't you, little man?" Maura said.

He stuck out his bottom lip and held his hands out to his mother, who swooped him out of her mother's arms.

"I should probably take off," Maura said. "I'm hoping I can get him down for a nap before I have a conference call with a couple distributors later today."

"Thanks for dropping everything to come over."

"You know I'm here whenever you need somebody to eat your delicious concoctions. It's a sacrifice, but you know me. I'm all about my family."

"You're a giver, Maur."

Her sister laughed as she bundled Henry into a cute little denim jacket and hefted him into her arms, where he promptly laid his head on her shoulder, perfectly content in the arms of his mother.

Again, that old pain tugged at Alex's heart but she ignored it with the ease of long practice.

She returned to the kitchen, where Claire sat alone, leafing through a culinary arts magazine she had left on the table.

"Where's Mom?" she asked.

Claire gestured to the French doors. "She walked out to your patio to take a phone call. I was assuming it was Harry, since they were all lovey-dovey."

"Eww."

"I think it's wonderful," Claire said. "Your mom's been alone a long time. She deserves to find someone who treats her so well, after all these years."

"I guess."

Claire had plenty of experience dealing with Riley's

reaction, who also felt squeamish about his mother's relationship with Harry, and she was wise enough to deftly change the subject. "This was so fun today. Thanks for the invite. I hate that we never have time to hang out lately."

Some of that was Alex's fault, she knew, because of her hectic schedule and the late hours she had to work in the restaurant business.

Some was simply the inevitable fact that Claire was busy with two—soon to be three—children, the bead store she owned and her husband.

"Once the restaurant opens and things settle a little, I'm sure we'll be able to find a little more time."

"But then I'll have a new baby," Claire pointed out. "You certainly remember how crazy that was."

"Not really. I wasn't here, remember?"

"Right. You were off having your grand adventure in Europe."

She forced a smile as she transferred the leftovers to the many containers that filled her cupboards for that very purpose. Grand adventure. Right. After a dozen years, she still didn't have any intention of telling her loved ones otherwise.

"I'm actually glad we have a minute alone," Claire said, her voice a little hesitant. "I've been wanting to ask you something."

"Sure," she said absently as she separated the dozen or so brownies and packaged them individually in cling film. Caroline Bybee loved them. She could freeze them individually and stick a few in her freezer next time she stopped by for a special treat.

"Riley and I would like you to be the baby's godmother."

The words seeped through her consciousness and she set down the spatula. Godmother. Good heavens.

"I… Really?" She stared. "Come on. Be serious. You honestly think I'm the best one to be a guide and example to your baby?"

"Who better?"

She could think of a couple dozen others. "What about Angie? Or Maura, for that matter? They've done a fine job with your other kids, haven't they?"

"You're my best friend, Alex. You weren't around when I had either of my other kids. You're finally home now and it would mean so much to both Ri and me if you would consider it."

Another obligation that threatened to overwhelm her. All these babies. Sometimes her arms ached with it.

But, just like Maura had joked, she was all about her family. "Of course," she answered after a moment's hesitation. "It can't be much harder than being the favorite aunt and I've had plenty of practice there."

Claire laughed and hugged her. "Yes. Yes, you have. Thank you, my dear. You've taken a big weight off my mind."

"You're welcome," she replied, just as the doorbell chimed through her house.

"Maura must have forgotten something." Claire looked around. "One of Henry's toys or a bottle or something."

"She knows she doesn't need to ring the doorbell, for heaven's sake," Alex exclaimed, hurrying to answer.

When she opened it, she found not her sister but a very cute, curly-haired boy with big blue eyes and his father's long lashes.

"Hi, Alex. How are you this afternoon?"

She smiled at his formal, polite greeting. "Hello, Ethan! I'm fine. And how are you?"

"Great. Hi," he greeted Claire. "My name is Ethan Delgado. I just turned seven years old. My dad and I live down the street."

Claire shook the small hand he held out, swallowing her own smile. "Hi, Ethan. Nice to meet you. I'm Claire McKnight."

Despite making the first overture, he looked uncomfortable at speaking with a stranger and quickly turned back to Alex. "I'm sorry to interrupt but I was riding my new bike down the street and I thought I heard Leo bark. I was checking to see if you found his owners. I guess you didn't."

"Not yet. Still looking, though." She had tried everything. After nearly a month, she didn't hold out much hope that she would succeed.

She would soon have to figure something out with the dog. She still didn't have time to take care of a dog but now she was very much afraid she had passed the point where she could give him to someone else, without her heart breaking apart.

"I could exercise him for you, if you want," Ethan said eagerly. "Do you think he would like to take a walk with me? You could pay me if you wanted to."

At the magic *W* word he recognized only too well, Leo sat up straighter and his tongue started to loll eagerly.

"I think that's probably a good guess," she answered drily. "Tell me, what's the going rate for dog-walking these days?"

"I was thinking a dollar would be fair."

"More than fair," she assured him. "What a great

deal for me! I'm sure Leo would enjoy taking a walk very much. How thoughtful of you to offer! Come on inside while I find his leash. Would you like a brownie while you wait?"

Ethan's eyes lit up. "Oh, is that what I smell? I bet they're delicious. They smell good, anyway."

"Trust me, they're good," Claire answered.

He seemed to warm up a little to her. When Mary Ella walked in after finishing her phone call, Alex introduced her mother to the boy and left Ethan in the capable hands of both women while she placed a brownie on a napkin and then retrieved the leash off the hook by the back door.

"Here you go," she said, giving him the brownie and then attaching the leash to Leo's collar before she handed that over, as well. "The big question is, can you hold on to the leash and eat a brownie at the same time?"

His brow furrowed as he considered his answer. "I think so. I can hold the leash with one hand and the brownie with the other, see? If it's too difficult to manage both, I'll eat the brownie first and *then* go on the walk with Leo."

"You, my friend, are indeed a man who thinks things through."

He gave her that sweet, swift smile of his, obviously delighted at being called a man.

"You remember to stay away from the creek, right?"

"Yes," he said. "My dad only reminds me of that every time I go outside. We'll stay on the sidewalk and we'll only go to the end of Currant Creek Valley Road and back, I promise. Is that okay with you?"

They should be fine for the four-block round trip, she

figured. Leo was very well behaved on a leash—another indication that someone somewhere had once loved him.

"Sounds perfect. You boys have a wonderful time."

He had a mouthful of brownie and just waved to her, leash and all, as he walked out the door and down the steps with the dog leading the way.

The three women watched him go down the sidewalk and she was happy to see that Leo didn't tug or jerk.

"Oh, my word. Is he not the most adorable thing you've ever seen?" Claire exclaimed, smiling as she watched them go.

Well, personally Alex thought the kid's father was pretty darn adorable, too, but she decided not to comment. Her mother and Claire would both make too much of her opinion.

"Did you know Sam is working on the new recreation center?" Mary Ella looked delighted to reveal that particular tidbit of information.

"No. I hadn't heard," she said, trying to inject just the right note of casual interest in her voice.

She should be happy for Sam. He wanted to settle in Hope's Crossing, to build a business here. Working for Harry Lange's pet project up Silver Strike Canyon was a great start and would probably lead to future jobs.

That's what he wanted but she had still been clinging to the hope that maybe he would decide he and her town didn't fit, after all, which was pretty small-minded of her when she stopped to think about it.

"Harry has really taken a liking to him and his work," her mother went on. "He says Sam is an old-time craftsman who cares more about quality than quotas. His military record doesn't hurt anything, of course.

He's a genuine hero, though I get the impression you won't hear him say anything about that."

He was closemouthed about his past and downplayed that aspect of his life. She could admire that about him. She supposed he kept plenty of secrets about his past.

"It's nice when regular people move in," Claire said. "People who want to make Hope's Crossing their permanent home instead of just buying a place for a vacation spot or a tax write-off."

"Isn't it?" she murmured.

"I think so. We need new people, new blood," Mary Ella said. "That's the reason Harry and Jack are trying to build more affordable housing in that development they're working on together west of town."

Yes. New blood was important. She just didn't want it to belong to Sam.

"Look, I hate to run after you went to so much trouble for us," Mary Ella said, "but I told Angie I would help her pick out some curtains to go with the walls she just painted. She texted me when I was on the phone with Harry."

"Absolutely. You'd better go."

"What time is it?" Claire looked at the clock. "Oh, I can't believe I stayed so long. The kids are with their father but I said I would pick them up about twenty minutes ago. I'm sorry!"

"Nothing to be sorry about. The kids come first. It's completely understandable. I appreciate you both taking the time to come."

After ushering them out to their cars with a package of leftovers each, she returned inside. Without the happy chatter, the house seemed to echo with silence, especially while Leo was busy taking a walk. She hadn't realized how accustomed she had become to his company in just a few short weeks.

She only had a few moments of silence before she heard a bark outside and an instant later the doorbell. She grabbed her wallet and opened the door while digging out some change.

"How was your walk?" she started to say, but bobbled the last word when she discovered Ethan and Leo weren't alone on the doorstep. The boy's father stood behind them, big, dark, gorgeous.

This time the nerves in her stomach had wings tipped with feathers and it was all she could do not to shiver.

"Oh. Hi."

"Hi, there." He gave her a long look, that mouth that tasted so very lovely lifted in a half smile. "Apparently we've gone into the dog-walking business."

"And a very valuable service it is, too. Were you a good boy, Leo? Were you?"

The dog slobbered all over her while she rubbed his scruff. When she looked up, she found Sam watching her with a sharp, hungry look in his eyes but he blinked it away so fast she wondered if she had imagined it.

"We walked to the corner and back and stayed away from the creek, just as I promised you," Ethan said proudly.

"Excellent! Then I think you've earned *two* dollars."

She handed them over and he couldn't have looked more thrilled.

"Thanks," he exclaimed. "Thanks a lot."

"Don't thank me. You earned them."

"I was telling my dad you make the very best brownies I have ever tasted and that he should try one." He paused, a crafty look in his eyes. "Maybe I could have another one, too, just to make sure. If you have any left, I mean."

Sam cleared his throat, a faintly embarrassed look in his eyes. "That's not why I came over," he said. "You don't have to give me brownies."

"You're in luck. I happen to have exactly two extra brownies and was looking for someone to take them off my hands."

"We can do that, can't we, Dad?"

"I've learned to never turn down brownies. Who knows when the chance for more might come along?"

She couldn't resist raising an eyebrow. "Isn't that true? For brownies and…so many other things."

His eyes glazed, just a bit, and she hid her smile even as she tried to rein in the natural instinct to flirt with the man. She just couldn't seem to help herself around him but she vowed to try harder.

She was supposed to be mad at him for not telling her he was moving to Hope's Crossing or that he had a son. And she was, honestly. Anger and hurt and a whole host of other emotions seemed to clot together in a big ball inside her whenever she thought about Sam, but she also couldn't help thinking the afternoon suddenly seemed much brighter.

He was a loving father who had been trying to protect his son. How could she be angry about that?

She ought to send them both on their way with the brownies, but she had all those leftovers and it didn't seem very neighborly not to share.

"Are you guys hungry?"

"Yes," Ethan declared. "We haven't had anything to eat since lunchtime. Well, technically I had a brownie, but that's it."

"Then you are both in luck," she said. "Come on back to the kitchen. My family was just here having a taste of things to come when the restaurant opens and I happen to have plenty of leftovers."

"You don't have to feed us. That's not why I stopped by, either."

"The way I see it, the more guinea pigs, the better."

"I'm not sure I like the sound of that, Eth. We're guinea pigs."

"If I can't have a dog, can I at least have a guinea pig?"

Sam smiled at his son, rubbing a hand over his son's curls. "We're going to have to see on that one, kid. Maybe we should check out what guinea pigs eat first."

She managed to tear her gaze away from the tenderness between father and son. "In my kitchen, they eat fabulous food. Just wait and see. And if the guinea pigs are very good and try a little of everything, they get to have some of my fantastic brownies as a reward."

"They really were good," Ethan told his father.

"You must know some very happy guinea pigs," Sam said.

"You don't know the half of it."

She couldn't seem to look away from his smile. "Why did you? Stop by, I mean?"

He blinked a little, as if he'd forgotten. "Oh. To say hello, for one thing. That's what neighbors do, isn't it? I hadn't seen you in a while and I…well, wanted to see how you are."

Had he missed her, too? Probably not. He probably only wanted…brownies.

"I'm fine," she answered. "Nervous about this weekend, but otherwise fine."

"Good. That's good. I, uh, also wanted to ask you about the blue recycling can. I can't seem to figure out when they come pick that one up."

"Every other Monday, so tomorrow would be the day. You probably just missed the first pickup of the month when you moved in."

"That makes sense. Okay. Thanks."

They gazed at each other and she remembered the delicious heat of his mouth and the implacable hardness of his body against hers and the slow, heady churn of her blood.

"Are we going to eat?" Ethan asked.

She looked down at his son as color rushed to her cheeks. "Right. Yes. Come on back to my kitchen."

CHAPTER TEN

SAM FOLLOWED ALEXANDRA and her dog into the warm, delicious-smelling kitchen, wondering just how he had managed to stay away so long.

He had missed her. A dozen times he had wanted to stop by and see her when he had driven past and seen lights on at her house, but he had reminded himself every time of that shock and dismay on her features when she had discovered he was moving permanently to Hope's Crossing.

She didn't want him here. She had made that much clear, so he had just figured he was better off not bothering her.

The dog hurried in ahead of them all and began licking his water dish, looking completely at home.

"Before you say anything, no, I haven't found his owners yet. I'm beginning to think maybe he was dumped off here, although that doesn't explain the collar."

"Maybe he wandered into town from some far-off location and his owners don't even know to look for him here."

"It's been known to happen," she answered. "Hope's Crossing has always been a haven for strays."

That described him perfectly. A stray, somebody who

didn't have connections anywhere else. He wanted to make this a home for him and for Ethan.

"On the menu today was turkey cutlets, a really delicious apple-pear salad, pumpkin risotto and roasted artichokes. According to the reports, the risotto is not the best thing I've ever made but I actually thought it was quite tasty."

"My dad was going to grill a couple of hot dogs later for us but he's been too busy installing a new toilet," Ethan announced. "I was helping him but eventually I got bored and went for a ride on my new bike."

He made a face at his son for the overshare. "Plumbing. Always such a fascinating topic of discussion."

She smiled even as she pulled plates out of the cupboard and began arranging food on them for him and Ethan.

"This looks delicious."

"Thanks."

"Guinea pigs eat really fancy food," Ethan observed with a worried look. "I wonder if they like hot dogs and chicken nuggets, too."

Alexandra laughed. "Guinea pigs actually have pretty special food. They would be sick if they ate any of this. I was teasing before. When I said you were my guinea pigs, that was only a figure of speech. It meant I was going to let you taste the food I fixed so we can tell whether you like it and if I should serve it in my restaurant."

"Oh. Okay."

Ethan took a nibble of the rice dish and then apparently liked it enough to try another and another. He didn't touch the artichokes—a personal aversion—but ate all the turkey she set on his plate.

They ate at her little kitchen table in a bay that overlooked the wide patio and the river, and he wondered again why she didn't have any furniture out there so she could sit and enjoy the sound of the rippling water. It seemed to him a little like someone who lived by the ocean but kept the windows and doors closed against the soothing sight and sound of the waves.

She sat with them but didn't eat anything. "I already had some with my guests," she explained when Ethan asked her why she wasn't eating her own food. "I'm pretty stuffed right now."

To Sam's surprise, she and Ethan seemed to hit it off brilliantly. The two of them talked about all sorts of topics, from LEGO creations to Harry Potter trivia to the scientific basis for how yeast acted to make bread rise.

It was the most pleasant hour Sam had enjoyed in weeks. Probably since the night he went hiking with her on Woodrose Mountain.

He hadn't realized how hungry he had been when he walked inside but he had seconds of everything. When he finished, he pushed the plate away. "Fantastic. As always. Your restaurant is going to be a huge hit, Alexandra. Seriously."

He wanted to bask in the warmth of her wide, bright smile.

"Thank you," she said, her voice soft. "I don't want you to think I'm constantly in need of approval but I'm not going to lie to you, right about now I really appreciate the vote of confidence."

She was a contradiction of boldness and insecurity. One of the many things that fascinated him about Alexandra McKnight.

All his reasons for staying away from her seemed

really ridiculous right now, especially as he sat here in her kitchen and realized how very much he had missed her.

What would it take to convince her to make a little room in her hectic life to see where things might develop between the two of them?

"I'm finished with my dinner. It was very good. I do still like hot dogs, especially the way my dad cooks them on the grill, but this was quite tasty, too. I ate everything except the artichokes. I wouldn't have eaten those even if they had been dipped in ice cream. I just don't like artichokes."

"Good to know. I'll keep that in mind next time," she promised.

Sam wanted to believe she meant something by the words but he recognized polite conversation when he heard it. They likely wouldn't have a *next time,* unless he figured out some way to persuade her otherwise.

"Is it all right if I play with Leo for a while?" Ethan asked.

"I don't mind, as long as it's okay with your dad."

He probably ought to excuse them both and take Ethan home. On the other hand, it seemed rude to sit here in her kitchen, eat her food and then rush out like a soldier who only had ten minutes for chow before report.

"Not too rough inside the house," he told his son. "You wouldn't want to break anything of Ms. McKnight's."

His son and her dog headed into the great room, leaving the two of them alone in the kitchen.

She was the first to break the silence left behind

them. “So I hear you’re working on the new recreation center.”

“News travels.”

She smiled, tucking behind her ear a wavy blond curl that had slipped out of her loose ponytail, and he had an insane urge to tug the rest of it free, to unleash all that silkiness and dip his fingers in it, as he had done twice before.

“You’re moving to the wrong place if you want to keep any secrets around here,” she told him. “You may not know this but my mother is marrying Harry Lange.”

“So I hear.”

“She probably knew you were going to work on the recreation-center project before you were even asked. Harry has a well-earned reputation of not taking no for an answer. If he wants something, he won’t stop until he finds a way to get it. That’s not an exaggeration, by the way. It’s simple reality.”

“Good to know.”

“What does Harry have you doing at the rec center?”

“Same thing I did at the restaurant, just on a little bigger scale. Finish carpentry. That’s kind of my area of expertise. Apparently I’m picking up the slack for the same guy who was supposed to be wrapping up the work at Brazen.”

“Oh, right. The contractor with the family issues.”

“I hate taking the guy’s jobs since I know all about trying to work through family stuff, but somebody’s got to do it. People can’t wait around indefinitely.”

Through the doorway he could see Ethan on the floor, wrestling with her dog and looking as if he were having the time of his life. He was really going to have to think about adding a dog to their little family unit once things settled down. A chocolate Lab, maybe…

"So what's the completion date for the recreation center?"

"It's a rush job. The whole thing isn't going to be finished by the end of the summer but we're trying to get some of the main reception areas done by early June. Something about a special memorial event on that day. You probably know more about that than I do."

"Aah. The annual Giving Hope Day." Her mouth tightened, a shadow of sadness drifting over her features.

"Giving Hope. That sounds ambitious."

"It's actually in remembrance of my niece, Layla. My sister Maura's daughter. She was killed a couple years ago in a car accident in the canyon—not very far from where you're building the recreation center, actually."

"Is that the same car accident where Brodie's daughter, Taryn, was injured?"

"Yeah. The very one. A group of teenagers sort of went on a rampage, I guess you could say, causing trouble and just being stupid. Vandalism, breaking and entering, some petty theft. They were drinking. A few of them got high. The driver had a couple drinks in his system and rolled his pickup truck on the way down the canyon, trying to flee a police chase."

Some of his surprise must have registered on his features because she nodded.

"I know. Shocking, right here in happy little Hope's Crossing. If you moved here because you think of small-town life as this idyllic paradise where everything is perfect, you're going to suffer a rude wake-up call."

"I served three tours of duty in Iraq and Afghanistan. I do believe that's the first time anybody has ever implied I'm naive."

"I'm sorry if I gave that impression. I just hope you understand we're not insulated here from the problems the rest of the world has to face. Hope's Crossing isn't perfect. We have our share of troubles. Teen pregnancies, suicides, drugs. Just like anyplace else."

"Understood."

"Maybe more so because we're a tourist destination and that brings its own challenges. I guess the difference is that those of us who have chosen to make this our year-round home work really hard to build community. People care about each other here. Have you heard about our Angel of Hope?"

"A little. Just that somebody goes around secretly doing nice things for people," he answered. "Sounds like a fine concept to me. And nobody knows who it is?"

"Rumors are always flying but no, we haven't figured it out. At this point, I think the Angel has taken on a life of its own. Kind of a pay-it-forward kind of thing. People do nice things for others and let the Angel take the credit for it. Whoever started the whole thing is a genius. Because of the Angel, Hope's Crossing has come together like never before."

Her features glowed when she talked about her town and the people she loved. She looked so lovely, he just wanted to sit here and gaze at her.

"And the Giving Hope Day?" he managed to ask, taking a sip of water.

"This is our third annual event. My friend Claire organized the first one as a way to honor Layla on what would have been her sixteenth birthday. It's kind of grown beyond the original idea and now it's a huge day of service where everybody comes out to do projects around town. Painting fences for senior citizens, yard cleanup for single mothers, reorganizing the shelves at the food bank. Anything we can do to make life better for someone else."

She narrowed her gaze. "Come to think of it, you're just the kind of man we need. A guy who has your mad skills with a hammer will definitely come in handy. I'll have to remember to tell Claire she should put you to work."

"Absolutely," he answered without hesitation.

This was exactly what he wanted, for himself and for Ethan. A town with its own Angel of Hope and a day set aside to help each other. She might talk about all the problems Hope's Crossing had, but from the perspective of an outsider, what he saw now was a place where he and his son could settle in and shove down roots to build a new life.

"Sign me up. I'm willing to do anything."

She laughed. "You better not let Claire hear you say that or you'll be working from before sunrise until midnight, straight through the gala auction and dance."

"You didn't tell me dancing was involved. That is *not* one of my mad skills."

"Don't worry. Plenty of people sit out the dancing part. I'm usually in the kitchen, for instance."

"What a shame."

He only meant he was sorry she had to miss the fun but somehow his words came out low, almost sensual.

For several long moments she blinked at him, her eyes wide and those soft lips slightly parted. He remembered the taste of them, sweet and lush, better than any triple-chocolate brownie.

He wanted to kiss her again, so badly he ached with it, but he knew he couldn't. His son's laughter rang out only a few yards away. He and the dog could race back into the kitchen any moment now.

Beyond that, she had made it clear she didn't want him—though right now the heat waves shimmering between them would tend to contradict that.

Apparently he wasn't very good at maintaining a friendship with a woman when he wanted more. He would just have to try harder to put his attraction to her on a shelf somewhere, tucked way out of sight and out of mind. Neither of them needed this awkwardness.

She was the first to break the tension. She folded her hands together on the table and cleared her throat. "I prefer the kitchen, actually. I'm not very good at dancing, either. I only end up pissed off when a man won't let me lead."

"Maybe you just haven't found a man you find worth following, once in a while."

Her laugh seemed to surprise her. "You could be right about that, soldier."

Before he could answer, Ethan chose that moment to return to the kitchen.

"Can I give Leo a treat?"

Her smile to his son was bright and open. "Sure thing. See that big jar on the counter by the microwave? That's where his goodies are."

Leo apparently knew the drill. He planted his haunches on the tile floor and waited while Ethan shoved a hand in the jar and emerged with a treat.

"These are different. I've never seen a dog treat like this." He held it up.

"Looks homemade," Sam observed mildly.

Alexandra gave him a rueful look. "Yes, I made them, okay. I made homemade treats for a dog who doesn't belong to me. I bake them up all the time for my friends' dogs. Don't read anything into it. It doesn't mean I'm keeping him. I don't have time for a dog."

"I didn't say otherwise," he protested, but he was charmed nonetheless. She already loved Leo. He didn't need to see the evidence of a jar full of homemade dog treats to be certain the dog had somehow wormed his way into that well-protected heart.

"We'd better go. Ethan, can you tell Ms. McKnight thank you for letting you walk her dog and for sharing her delicious food?"

"Thank you very much," his son said promptly. "May I walk Leo for you again next weekend when I come back to stay with my dad?"

She slanted a look at Sam as if asking whether he minded. He shrugged a little. How could he discourage his son from showing initiative?

"Sure," she answered. "If I haven't found his owners by then, anyway."

Ethan rubbed the dog's head. "Why *can't* you just keep him? He's a really good dog. They must not have taken very good care of him if they let him run around wild."

"But think how sad they must feel if they've been looking for him all this time? They're probably lonely without him."

"If you *do* find his owners, won't you be the lonely one?" Ethan pressed. "You don't even have a kid of your own."

Sam winced at his son's bluntness, especially when

he saw her inhale sharply. Something dark and pained flashed in her gaze before she forced a smile.

"No kids here," she agreed pleasantly enough. "But I do have a really big family with tons of nieces and nephews, and one more on the way in a few months. I spend a lot of time with my family and friends, and I'm very busy working most of the time. It's hard to be lonely when you're so busy."

Did staying busy help stave off the loneliness for her the same way it had for him since Kelli had died?

"I think my dad is lonely when I'm not here," Ethan offered. "He lives all by himself while I'm with my aunt and uncle and my cousins. I don't see why I can't just move here with him now."

Ugh. He got so tired of rehashing the same argument. Ethan just couldn't let it rest. "A few more weeks. School will be out before you know it and you'll be coming here for good. Then you'll be missing your life back in Denver."

"We always want what we don't have, Ethan," Alexandra said. "Let that be a lesson for you. And here's another one. Brownies always make everything better."

She held out a plate where she had piled several more of those luscious people treats. As Sam took them from her, their hands brushed and that little sizzle of current arced between them. He didn't miss the way she quickly slid her hand away and curled it against her leg.

They walked through the great room. When they reached the front door, Ethan rushed outside first and stood on her sidewalk, looking up at the stars beginning to appear in the twilight. They had spent far longer inside her house than he had intended, but it sure as hell beat fixing the plumbing.

"I meant to tell you, I'm coming Friday night to your restaurant opening," he said. "Brodie invited me to join him and Evie."

Something wild and a little panicky flickered briefly in her gaze and he was sorry he brought it up.

"Great," she said in an overly cheerful voice. "The more the merrier, right? Oh, and you'll have a chance to meet Claire and Maura and their husbands. We were just talking about it when they were here. They're all sitting with Brodie. Are you taking anyone?"

The question came out of nowhere and it took him a moment to process it. A date? Did she really think he wanted to date anybody else while this inconvenient heat bubbled and seethed between them?

"I hadn't planned on it, no."

"You really should. You wouldn't want to be the only one at the table without a date. Awkward."

Evie and Brodie struck him as very warm and casual. He doubted anyone would make him feel like a loser for showing up alone at a social event like a restaurant opening.

"My wife has been gone for two years. It won't be the first time I've spent an evening without a date. I'll survive a little social anxiety."

"Have you met my friend Charlotte yet? She runs the candy store in town. I think you would really like her."

He glanced at Ethan, who was too busy trying to pick out constellations to pay them any attention. "Are you really trying to set me up with one of your friends?"

She tossed that mischievous strand of hair behind her ear again. "If you want to look at it that way."

His rough laugh sounded strained, even to him. "How else am I supposed to look at it?"

"I just thought the two of you might get along, that's all. Charlotte is really wonderful. Warm and kind and a little bit shy. She doesn't date a lot. She's made some amazing changes in her life lately and I'd like to see her go out a little more."

"With me."

After everything between them, she really wanted him to date one of her friends. If he needed further proof that she wanted to ignore this attraction, she had just handed it to him, served up as prettily as she arranged food on a plate.

He knew he shouldn't find that so damn depressing.

"Forget I said anything. It was just a suggestion." She sounded defensive, flustered, and he didn't know whether he wanted to shake her or kiss her.

Okay, yes, he did. Kissing would always be the clear winner.

"I have no problem going by myself but if it makes you feel any better, I understand Brodie's mother will be part of the party. She can be my unofficial date."

"Katherine?" She laughed, looking enthralled by the idea, and he decided he would never understand her. "You might have competition there. Both of them try to play it cool but she and Charlotte's dad, Dermot, have this funny little unspoken thing going between them."

He could certainly relate to that. "Good to know. I'll try to keep her from breaking my heart."

"Well, if you change your mind, I can still give you Charlotte's number."

He just barely refrained from rolling his eyes. "Good night, Alexandra."

"Good night, Samuel. See you, Ethan."

His son waved cheerfully at her, then slid his hand in Sam's and the two of them walked down the side-walk toward home.

CHAPTER ELEVEN

FOR THE FIRST TIME she could remember, her snug little house didn't surround her with a calming peace when she arrived home Thursday night.

Usually any tension of her day started to seep away just from pulling into the driveway and seeing the warm welcome of those burnished logs.

If she had known how much she would love owning her own place, she would have purchased one years ago. Somehow it had always seemed so much trouble, with the yard work and home repairs and property taxes. She had managed to convince herself she enjoyed the freedom and flexibility of apartment living and didn't need anything else.

Since buying this house, she had come to appreciate so many little things. The smell of fresh-mowed grass, the thwack against the door of the newspaper she rarely had time to read but still faithfully subscribed to, the satisfaction she found in fixing something inside the house herself instead of calling someone else to do it for her.

This time, as she turned off her engine and opened the door, that sense of welcoming peace remained hauntingly out of reach. The logs still glowed honey-gold in the porch light, and the night air smelled of the sweet lilac hedge just beginning to bloom and the tart pines rising into the night, but her mind was too tangled up to properly appreciate it.

In less than twenty-four hours, Brazen would open its doors for business. She was alternately consumed with excitement that this moment had finally arrived—everything she had dreamed of for so long within reach—and paralyzed by fear that she would fall on her face in front of her family and friends and everyone she held most dear.

Every single muscle in her body ached with exhaustion and she was physically as tired as she could ever remember. She had been working every waking moment all week long to make sure every detail was perfect. As tired as she was, she wasn't sure how she would ever be able to settle down enough to sleep.

When she opened the door to her house, Leonidas raced to greet her and ran around her as if she had been gone for months. Guilt pinched at her. Poor neglected stray.

She hadn't left him here alone all day. That morning, he had set out with her and spent part of the day in the little yard beside the restaurant. When she returned home at dinnertime to pick up some paperwork, she had brought him back to the house and left him here, but that had been five hours earlier and the poor thing had been alone ever since.

"This is why I can't have a dog," she informed him as she dropped her armload—bags, keys, phone—onto a console table in her entryway so she could love him up. "It's a time thing. I'm sure you understand. It's not you, it's me."

Leo cocked his head to one side and gazed at her out of those wise hazel eyes.

She sighed, still feeling guilty at neglecting a creature who depended on her. What was she going to do with him? She had decided by default to put off making a decision until after the restaurant opened but with another turn of the earth, that day would be here. She was going to have to give him away. One of her new servers had mentioned his kids wanted a dog. Or maybe she could find someone old and alone who could dote on him.

She wasn't going to figure this out tonight. Right now she needed something to work these kinks out of her body. The sweetly scented spring air called to her. Combine that with a dog who needed attention and exercise and she knew instantly what she should do.

"Let's go for a walk," she said. "What do you say, hmm? Want to burn off some of that energy?"

Leo gave one of his low, happy barks and padded to the front door to wait for her. Smart thing.

"We won't go far, only a little way up the Currant Creek trail, how does that sound? It's eleven o'clock and I really do need to try to sleep if I can. People are counting on me to be awesome tomorrow."

Leo tried to nudge open the door she had left ajar. She closed it firmly with a laugh. "Hold on. Give me a second. It's not going to help my stress level if you take off without me tonight, trust me on that."

She quickly grabbed a warm jacket out of the closet and her flashlight, as well as the can of bear spray she had taken to carrying since a few black bears had been seen recently on trails around town.

A few moments later, she hooked the leash on Leo and the two of them walked toward the bridge that would take her over Currant Creek to the trail that ran on the opposite side from the houses.

The night was beautiful, warmer than usual for May. If the weather held, the Brazen outdoor seating that had just arrived would be the perfect place to spend a pleasant May evening, especially with that lovely view down Main Street. She did have kerosene warmers ready but she would really prefer not to use them if she didn't have to.

As they made their way up the trail accompanied by the burbling creek, just a silver ribbon in the moonlight, the tension in her shoulders began to ease, along with the steady throb of a headache.

Leo loved the excursion, sniffing at every rock and clump of growth.

No other creatures disturbed their walk except an owl hooting in the trees, and some kind of water inhabitant—a muskrat or beaver, maybe?—that splashed upstream.

They didn't go far, only about a mile to the fence that marked the edge of the Forest Service land. Sometimes a walk amid the steady mountain beauty that surrounded her soothed her even more than yoga. By the time she turned around and headed back toward her house, her muscles were loose and relaxed.

She was so relaxed, she wasn't paying much attention to her surroundings. If she had been, she might have noticed she wasn't the only one awake in her neighborhood.

"You're out late."

The low words came completely out of nowhere and she shrieked and jumped about a half foot in the air.

What was the point in having a big dog if he didn't

warn her of that kind of stuff? She jerked her head around in the direction of the voice and saw a dark shape on Sam's front porch.

"Not cool! You scared the life out of me!"

He gave a rueful-sounding laugh. "Sorry," he said. "I forgot you couldn't see me up here in the dark."

The smart thing would be to just say good-night and keep on walking but she couldn't seem to make herself do that. She was only being neighborly, she told herself. It seemed rude to just walk on by and she certainly couldn't stand out here on the sidewalk and yell back and forth with him, not at this late hour. She would wake up Mr. Phillips, especially, on Sam's other side, who liked to sleep with his bedroom window cracked even in the coldest weather.

She moved up his walk, assuring herself she would only stay a moment.

"Leo has been cooped up all day," she explained. "We both needed to stretch our legs a little before bed."

"Next time, grab me. I'll go with you."

As if she would have found *that* at all restful. "I was fine."

"Maybe so, but it's pretty foolish to go walking by yourself after dark. Anything could have happened to you. One slip and you could have fallen into the creek. And who knows what scary wild animals might be lurking out there?"

She was more concerned about the scary male lurking right here. "I was fine," she repeated. "I had Leo with me and I'm sure he could be pretty fierce if the need arose. Besides that, I always carry bear spray."

"Which wouldn't have been particularly useful if

you had fallen into the creek, unless a bear fell in at the same time."

Okay, there was some truth to that, but she refused to live her life in fear. About exploring the Currant Creek backcountry, anyway.

"Nothing happened. Here I am, safe and sound."

She always felt very protected in the mountains around Hope's Crossing, though she knew that feeling was likely illusory. A woman on her own could never be completely complacent of her safety. Her brother could probably tell her stories that would raise the hair on the back of her neck.

"That's good. But seriously, call me next time. Or at least send me a text letting me know where you're going so we have a starting point for a search if you don't come back."

With all the stress in her life, this was one more thing she didn't want to worry about right now so she quickly changed the subject. "I like your swing."

He gave her a long look, obviously aware of her transparent conversational ploy. Apparently, he decided to let it stand.

"I've always wanted one," he answered. "A porch swing just seems to represent home to me. Somehow in base housing the opportunity never arose to put one in, and then we moved into a condo near the hospital for Kelli's treatments and didn't have a good spot. This is the first time I've ever had a front porch. I saw this swing while I was shopping for new bathroom light fixtures today and I couldn't resist."

She knew she shouldn't find that so blasted endearing but she couldn't seem to help it. The man continually surprised her. She was also more than a little touched, given their history, that he would open up and share something so personal with her.

"Want to give it a trial run with me?" he asked.

"Now, that sounds like a line."

His low laugh sizzled down her spine. "No. This is a line. I've always dreamed of sitting on a porch swing on a lovely May evening with an even lovelier woman."

"Nice. A little cheesy, but surprisingly effective."

She saw the gleam of his teeth in the night as he smiled. "Is it?"

Her dog flopped onto the top step of the porch. Again, that warning voice told her to just say good-night and go home, where she was safe.

This didn't seem a night for making wise choices. Before she could talk herself out of it, she took the final steps to the swing and sat down.

The chains rattled softly as he set the swing in motion and they moved gently there in the darkness, Leo's panting and the night creatures peeping and humming and the rustling of the leaves against the porch for company.

"In case you're wondering," he said after a moment, "I'm not going to ask the obvious. If you're nervous about tomorrow night, I mean."

She made a face, though she knew he couldn't see it. "Thank you. I appreciate your forbearance."

He laughed softly and the swing moved forward, backward, forward. He was right; this was the perfect spot for a swing, looking out at the mountains.

"In answer to your unasked question, yes. I believe I've moved past nervous to scared as hell, venturing into what-was-I-thinking territory. In fact, at this point I'm beginning to think jumping into Currant Creek teeming with bears—and me with no bear spray—would be less intimidating."

"You'll be great," he answered. "I've tasted your food, remember. You've got the stuff, Alexandra."

Warmth burst through like a bright sunbeam. "I appreciate the vote of confidence. It helps take me just south of panic."

"I'm still planning to be there at the opening. I'm looking forward to it."

"No Ethan tomorrow?"

"No. Nick and Cheri are bringing him up Saturday morning and I'll drive him back Sunday night. Only two more weeks of school and then he can come permanently."

"He seems to be excited for the move."

"He complains about the separations during the week but I think he's going to miss his cousins when Nicky and his family move to Europe."

"What about you? Are you going to miss your brother and his family?"

"They've been incredibly supportive since Kelli died. I don't know what I would have done without them these last few years. So, yeah. I'll miss them but I guess it was time for all of us to make a change."

"Why Hope's Crossing? I'm not sure you've ever given me a straight answer on that. Colorado is a big state. A guy with your particular skill set probably could have landed anywhere."

He was silent. "You're going to think this sounds ridiculous."

"Try me."

"When Brodie first talked to me about taking over and finishing the work at Brazen, Ethan and I came out from Denver to see what needed to be done on the site. I remember, it was a Saturday afternoon in March, sunny and cool. After walking through the restaurant, we stopped for lunch at the pizza place in town."

"They make a good pie. Certainly not worth uprooting your whole life for, though."

"The food was good, yeah. But while we were eating, at least three different people stopped to say hello and ask if I needed directions anywhere."

She smiled at the stunned note in his voice. "Yeah, we can all go a little crazy trying to help out lost tourists. It can be annoying."

"I didn't think it was annoying. I thought it was wonderful. I still do. I've never experienced that sense of community. I want Ethan to have what Nick and I didn't, you know? Roots. Traditions. A place to belong."

He was a loving father who would do anything for his child. "What about you?" she asked, mainly to avoid thinking about how sexy she found that. "What do you see in the stars for your future?"

"Same thing, I guess," he said after a moment. "It will be nice to have my feet planted in one spot for a while."

He was quiet while the swing continued its hypnotic movement. "I basically went from the chaos of our childhood straight into taking care of Nick and then into the military, and spent the next decade and a half going where I was sent. When Kelli was diagnosed, we were living in Germany. We both decided being near her family during her treatment was our best option. Not one of our smartest decisions, by the way."

"They weren't supportive?"

He sighed. "You don't need to hear this ugly story tonight. Tomorrow's a big day for you."

"Distract me."

"I could come up with far more interesting ways to distract you than talking about the mess I'm leaving in Denver."

His words vibrated through the night and her insides quivered. She firmly ignored her instantaneous response.

"How about we stick with you telling me what happened with your wife's family? Why are you leaving a mess?"

"Her father owns a big construction company. Tanner and Sons. A major player in the area. Despite the name, neither of his sons has much interest in construction. One is a teacher and one is an artist and neither stuck around Colorado. I think J.T., Kelli's father, had some vague idea of eventually handing over the reins to me. He had been after me for a long time to quit the army and go into business with him."

That would have meant the world to Sam, she thought. Coming from the hardscrabble beginnings he had shared with her, she could only imagine how he must have wanted acceptance from his wife's family.

"Once I started working for him, I quickly realized our, uh, ethical baselines didn't quite mesh."

"What does that mean?"

"It's not unusual in huge construction contracts to underbid the competition and then cut corners so you can still make a profit. J.T. took that to extremes. I guess I was too distracted while Kelli was dying to really pay much attention to anything else. A few months after her death, I sort of woke up one day and realized I couldn't do some of the things he was asking of me."

Sam had a strong core of honor. It was one of the things she most admired about him. How had he developed such a thing through the turmoil of his childhood, with a father who had abandoned him and a drug addict for a mother?

"So you quit."

His rough laugh held little amusement. "I took things a little further than that. I actually ended up turning him in for gross building code violations for an elementary school he was building. Six months ago, I testified against him and the building inspector he was paying off to look the other way. He was convicted of fraud and bribery, among a host of other things, and is headed to prison pending his appeal."

"I think I read about that case," she exclaimed. "It must have been ugly."

"You could say that. I guess it's also safe to say J.T. and Margeaux won't be inviting me over to any family barbecues in the near future."

She didn't miss the pain in his voice. How hard it must have been for a man who had grown up in chaos and probably craved a family to make choices he knew would cost him dearly.

Despite knowing it probably wasn't the wisest thing she'd ever done, she reached a hand out and placed it over his fist curled on his thigh, compelled to offer comfort.

"Losing them must have been hard for you."

He seemed to freeze at her touch and she could hear the quick inhalation of his breath. He held himself stiffly for just a moment and then seemed to relax on a sigh. He even turned his hand over and entwined his fingers with hers.

The sweetness of the moment nearly took her breath away, sitting here in the darkness with him while the breeze ruffled the new leaves of the big elm beside his house and the dog snuffled softly at their feet.

“It was harder on Ethan,” he said. “He loves his grandparents and doesn’t quite understand another loss.”

“Kids are resilient. They learn to bounce back.”

Ethan would always have a hole somewhere in his heart for his mother and the grandparents, just as she did for her father. People learned to patch up those holes and throw on a little drywall mud and tape until it was almost as good as new.

“I hope so. Being a parent is just about the toughest thing I’ve ever done, especially without Kelli.”

She thought of a tiny baby she had loved inside her for a few short months, that magical time when the world had seemed full of joy and possibilities…until all the pain and hurt came later. Sometimes all the patch jobs in the world couldn’t cover some holes.

“I’m sorry,” she murmured. For so many things. For his wife’s death and her parents’ betrayal, for a boy who had grown up without a home he could call his own but had been determined to give first his little brother and then his son something more, for her own mistakes and the chances she had lost because of foolish choices.

The swing continued its endless rhythm, like life, and a soft, tender intimacy swirled around them.

“What am I going to do with you?” he asked, his voice low.

It seemed the most inevitable thing in the world—

natural and sweet and perfect—when he shifted that big, rangy body to face her, cupped her cheek and lowered his mouth to hers.

She sighed, so very drawn to his strength, to his heat, to this hunger that blasted away every thought in her head but *more.* He kissed her softly, his mouth firm but easy as he delivered slow, tender, barely there kisses that left her achy and trembling.

He pulled her against him, until she was half lying across him on the swing, her legs tucked up beside them. She wrapped her arms around his neck and let him sweep away all her fears about the next day, every doubt, every qualm, every fretful thought.

He held her close while the swing swayed, while her dog snored, while the night seethed with quiet life around him, and she never wanted the moment to end.

In his arms, she felt this strange sense of safety, peace, comfort.

This wasn't merely physical desire. Yes, she wanted him in a hundred different ways, but this was something more, something so wild and bright and terrifying she was almost afraid to examine it.

She had to, though. She couldn't run away from it, couldn't hide under her bed and pull the covers over her head and pretend this wasn't happening.

She was falling in love with him.

CHAPTER TWELVE

THE IDEA BURST across her mind like the sun exploding over the snow-shrouded mountains on a winter morning.

Wild panic fluttered in her chest and everything inside her seemed to go cold.

No. Not now. She had so much going on at this point in her life. She didn't have *time* for another heartache.

Like it or not, she was very much afraid she was too late.

She was falling in love with Sam Delgado—his sweet smile and that strong sense of goodness and honor and his longing for home.

Throw in that adorable, motherless little boy who completely tugged at her heart and it was a miracle she had resisted the Delgado males this long.

Oh, what a disaster.

Though it sliced at her more acutely than her best knife, she slid away from him on the far corner of the swing. He was breathing hard, his eyes slightly dilated in the dim light.

"I thought we decided it was a bad idea to make out again."

His laugh was rough-edged and sexy. "*You* might have decided that, but I'm a guy. For us, it's never a bad idea to make out."

She wanted so much to nestle back into his chest—or better yet, go inside his half-finished house and work out her restlessness the very best way she could imagine—but she had already made a mess of things. Making love, no matter how much her body craved him right now, would turn a disastrous situation into a catastrophe of epic proportions.

"Isn't it a good thing one of us has better sense," she finally said. "I've got a long day tomorrow. I need to go."

"You don't have to. Stay, Alexandra."

She could come up with a dozen reasons why she needed to slide off this porch swing, grab her dog's leash and keep walking.

Sam needed someone soft and warm, giving, not a prickly, neurotic chef who sucked at relationships.

Beyond that, her restaurant was opening in less than eighteen hours. How on earth could she possibly indulge in this wild heat with him tonight and expect to have any powers of concentration left for Brazen, especially when she had a feeling once they started, she wouldn't want to stop?

Finally, and most significantly, she was already falling in love. Contrary to popular belief, she didn't sleep around. She had slept with exactly three men in her life and each had carved away a little chunk of her heart. She thought she had cared about each of them at the time but those feelings were nothing compared to this soft, seductive tenderness.

She could run a restaurant staff of two dozen, she knew exactly how much produce to order for a busy restaurant, she could juggle eight or nine deliveries at a time, but she had absolutely no idea how to keep fighting what she wanted so very desperately.

"I can't," she whispered, giving it one more try. She managed to make it to her feet but couldn't seem to move down the steps and away from him. "I told you I'm not going to sleep with you. I'm not sure how many times I have to tell you I'm not interested."

"I don't know. Maybe I would believe you if you didn't kiss me like I'm your favorite dessert and you've been on a hunger strike for weeks."

Oh, he was so very right. Every time they kissed, she forgot all the reasons she shouldn't indulge in all those wonderful, glittery feelings.

"I can't be what you're looking for, Sam."

"And what's that?"

He sounded genuinely curious but she didn't miss the edge to his voice.

"You're looking for a home. A warm hearth. You all but admitted it yourself. That's why you moved to Hope's Crossing. You need somebody sweet and giving who can offer the home you've never had. If she wasn't five months pregnant and deeply in love with my brother, I would have said Claire was the perfect woman for you."

"How do you know what I want or what I need?" His voice was tight, each word clipped, and she realized this might be the first time she had heard him angry.

"This porch swing, this house. Moving to Hope's Crossing in the first place, just because a few people said hello to you in a pizza parlor, for heaven's sake. It's all proof."

"That I'm looking for a woman like your friend Claire."

"Maybe not Claire exactly but someone like her. Calm and serene. Sweet. That will never be me. I was born sarcastic. I'm moody and unpredictable. I can be downright bitchy. Just ask my two sous-chefs, who are both ready to quit right now."

"Maybe I like that about you. You always keep me guessing. Don't take this the wrong way but Claire would probably bore me to tears in about ten minutes. Maybe five."

She bristled. "What's that supposed to mean? Claire is my best friend. She's a wonderful person!"

He shook his head and then had the effrontery to laugh at her, and she had to fight the urge to slug him.

"Yeah, moody and unpredictable just about covers it. There's absolutely nothing wrong with Claire. I never said that. She seems lovely. But she's not you. What if I like all those things you spewed out as faults? I like that I can never figure out how that mind of yours works."

She could feel the ache of tears behind her eyelids and they completely appalled her. She never cried, damn it. It was only exhaustion, because she had been working so hard at Brazen. It certainly had nothing to do with Sam, sitting there so big and tough and wonderful on the swing he had put up to provide his son with a better life than he had known.

"I need to go. Tomorrow's only the biggest night of my life and I don't have the time or the energy for this right now."

He looked as if he wanted to argue but he finally only stood up. The chains rattled a protest at the shift. "I'll walk you the rest of the way to your place."

"You don't have to do that. I've got Leo."

"Tonight, you'll have me, too."

She supposed it took less energy to let him walk her the three hundred feet to her house than it would to stand here and continue arguing with him.

"Fine."

She walked down the stairs, gripping her dog's leash. Her *temporary* dog's leash. Look at her. She couldn't even open her heart and her life to a *dog,* much less a man and a boy who needed so much more than she could give them.

SAM DIDN'T KNOW when he had ever been so tangled up over a woman.

Things with Kelli had been so easy. He couldn't remember ever being this stirred up, even in the beginning of their relationship.

He had been temporarily stationed near San Francisco, where she had been going to graduate school for social work. He had walked into a bar with a couple of buddies, seen her there with some of her girlfriends and asked her to dance.

Six months later, they were engaged, married a year after that, and Ethan had come along almost two years to the day after that.

He couldn't say their marriage had been perfect. Kelli had been on the spoiled side and had been frustrated living on an enlisted soldier's salary. She could be petulant when she was mad at him and generally spent way too much time on the phone with her mother and her girlfriends in Denver.

Still, he had spent two years grieving for the life they could have made together.

Alex, on the other hand, was the antithesis of easy. For all her prickliness, there were glimpses of something else, something soft and sweet she seemed to think she needed to hide away from the world.

Why? What was she hiding?

None of his business, he reminded himself. As she had so bluntly told him, she wasn't interested. He needed to back off, no matter how frustrating he found her.

"Have you met any of the neighbors yet?" she asked when they passed the house just to the north of his.

"A few. The lady who lives across the street from you dropped by with some cookies."

"I'll bet she did."

"Meaning?"

"Meaning Anita Adams has been divorced for about five months now, something of a record for her. She's probably looking for husband number four. Gorgeous single guys aren't exactly thick on the ground in Hope's Crossing, as you might have noticed."

"I guess I haven't really been paying attention," he said drily.

Though tension still tugged and stretched between them, she smiled. "That was probably mean of me. Forget I said anything. See? I told you I can be bitchy. I actually really like Anita. She is a lot of fun under the right circumstances. You should ask her out."

He somehow managed not to growl under his breath, though it was close. She was trying to throw him at someone else again, just minutes after that heated kiss, and it bugged the hell out of him.

"Thanks for the dating advice, but I'll probably pass on that one, too." He changed the subject. "I understand the house to the south of me is a vacation home for a couple from California."

"Bob and Cindy Whittal. They only come out a couple times a year, usually at Christmas and for a week or so in the summer. They're really nice. He's a plastic surgeon to the stars or something like that. They make a point of always coming to the restaurant up at the resort and saying hi. I guess I'll have to let them know about my new situation now."

"I haven't met my neighbor on the other side. I haven't even seen him, but I know someone's there because I've seen lights on and someone moving past the curtains. Seems a bit of a recluse."

"Mr. Phillips. You and Ethan should really take a moment to stop in and say hi. He has health problems and doesn't get out much but he's very kind."

"I'll do that."

They reached the walk leading to her house, and Leo strained on the leash, eager to be home.

They walked up the steps and she unlocked her door. For a minute, he felt uncomfortably like a sixteen-year-old kid on his first date, not sure if he should swoop in and steal a kiss.

"I'll see you tomorrow evening," he said.

She had left a porch light burning when she and Leo went for a walk. In its glow, he watched her mouth twist into a grimace. "We'll have to see if you're still talking to me on Saturday after you try to force down the gag-inducing dinner I'm sure will be in store for everyone."

"Would you stop, already? You know perfectly well it's going to be fantastic, just like everything you cook. You've worked damn hard to get here and you need to just relax and enjoy this moment."

She looked at him for a long moment, then, to his

delight, she started to laugh. "You're right. Absolutely right. That was the perfect thing to say."

Before he quite knew what she intended, she stood on tiptoe and kissed him just above his jawline but stepped quickly away before he could sweep her into his arms and give her a proper good-night kiss.

She opened her door and would have stepped inside and probably closed the door on him but he shoved a hand out to keep it open, framing her with his arm.

"You probably ought to know that my nickname in the Rangers was Unstoppable. When I go after something, I'm all in. I don't back down."

She was silent and he saw her throat work as she swallowed.

"Then I guess it's a good thing there's nothing here you need," she said softly.

"Wrong," he murmured.

She looked at him and for the first time he saw something in her expression that made him pause. She looked…wretched.

"This isn't some mission, Sam. This is your life. And Ethan's, too. Remember that."

Without another word, she tugged her dog inside and closed the door, leaving him standing on her porch wondering how in the space of about five minutes, she could leave him just about trembling with hunger one minute, frustrated enough to pull his hair out the next, and aching to comfort her after that.

CHAPTER THIRTEEN

BRAZEN WAS A HUGE HIT.

He had always figured as long as a meal was filling and tasty, he didn't need to quibble about spices or cooking methods or whether the flavors melded together in just the right proportions.

He freely admitted his ignorance on culinary matters but even *he* could tell Alexandra's restaurant was destined to be a smashing success, just as he had predicted.

For one thing, the place was packed to the gills on opening night, with a waiting list that spilled out the door.

She had enough friends and family around that he imagined a huge first-night crowd wasn't necessarily enough to guarantee success. The appreciative murmurs and exclamation of delight he heard all around him, on the other hand, were much better indicators.

He sensed a buzz of excitement about the place as palpable as that pleasant evening breeze rippling the trees around their large table on the outdoor patio.

He sat beside Katherine Thorne, adjacent to Brodie and his beautiful wife, Evie, and listened to the conversation flow around him like water around his waders in the middle of a fly-fishing stream the few times he'd gone.

"You're getting married at Harry's house, aren't

you?" Katherine was asking Mary Ella, who sat across from her, beside Harry Lange.

"We haven't made any final decision yet," Alexandra's mother said as she took a bite of her entrée, a delicious-looking plate of salmon with some kind of fruity salsa on the top.

"What about a date?" Claire asked.

"We thought Christmastime, but we haven't made a final decision about that, either. We need to time it right so we don't interfere with all of you children getting married and having babies."

"I think you're safe for a while," Maura put in. "Alex and Lila are the only unattached McKnights left and they're both committed to the fancy-free single life."

"For now," Mary Ella answered.

He shouldn't be so shamelessly eavesdropping upon a conversation that didn't concern him but he was fascinated by everything about Alexandra.

Pretty pathetic, actually, how he couldn't get her out of his mind.

He wondered how she was holding up. He couldn't imagine a restaurant opening was all that pleasant for the chef, despite his advice to her the night before to relax and take joy in what she had accomplished.

She was probably too busy chopping and stirring and whatever else she did to truly savor what she had accomplished here, knowing she had given all these people a truly memorable meal.

He hoped he had the chance to tell her but so far she hadn't appeared in the dining room.

A few moments later, when their server appeared to check on their table, she discreetly pulled a note out of the pocket of her short black apron and set it beside his plate.

It had his name written on it in the big, bold hand he recognized as Alexandra's. *My kitchen is perfect,* it read. *It's better than I could have dreamed. Thank you.*

He laughed softly but beneath his amusement simmered something else, something warm and tender. In the middle of what she herself had called the most important night of her life, she had taken the time to think about him.

He wasn't quite sure what to do with that.

He grabbed a pen from the inside pocket of his jacket and scribbled back, *Just breathe. You're rocking the house.*

He folded it and wrote *To the Chef* on the outside and handed it back to the server when she returned to take their dessert orders.

He didn't think anybody noticed the little interaction but after the server left, Claire McKnight leaned over and spoke to him in a low, amused voice. "Why am I suddenly reminded of our eighth-grade social studies class?"

He smiled. "You tell me."

Despite what he had said the other night in the heat of the moment about finding Claire boring, he actually really liked the other woman. She struck him as a very kind and giving person.

"You have to remember, we didn't have cell phones in those days," she said now. "None of this texting business that takes all the fun out of things. Alex and I had to pass our notes to each other the old-fashioned ways."

"Poor things."

"I know. Primitive, right?" She smiled. "You'll have

to ask her about the most embarrassing moment of her junior high school life, when I accidentally dropped the note she had just written me about the boy she had a crush on, Tony Coletti, and it was picked up by our social studies teacher, Mr. Kaiser, who then proceeded to find it highly entertaining to read it aloud to the whole class."

He tried to picture both of them as girls. It took a little more imagination than he could come up with, especially after such a delicious meal. "You've been friends with her for a long time."

"You could say that. The first day of first grade, Corey Johnson stole my brand-new Barbie lunch box before school and put it way on the top of the big jungle gym that only the older kids played on. I was afraid of heights at the time, too chicken to go after it. Guess who came to my rescue?"

"Um, Wonder Woman."

"In the form of Alexandra McKnight. Alex climbed right up there without fear, grabbed my lunch box and then jumped all the way down and started hitting Corey with it for being so mean. One of the teachers had to step in to stop her. She and I have been best friends ever since. Oh, and she ended up going to the junior prom with him. He's a mean drunk now, something we should have guessed by the way he liked to torment little girls."

He smiled at the story, entranced at these little glimpses into Alexandra's past. "This is a huge day for her."

"She's worked amazingly hard to get here. I hope…"

Her voice trailed off, a worried light in her eyes.

"You hope?" he prompted.

"I hope Brazen is everything she dreams it can be."

"What do you mean?"

"I don't know. It's just...have you ever wanted something with all your heart, worked for it, sweated for it, even sacrificed other important things along the way in pursuit of it...only to discover your dream wasn't exactly how you pictured it?"

He thought about how much he wanted to create a home here for Ethan. So far it was turning out to be everything he wanted and more.

"Not really," he said honestly. "What about you?"

She glanced at a couple sitting at a nearby table, then turned back with a smile.

"Funny you should ask. Yes, actually. While Alex was mooning over Tony Coletti, all I could ever see was that particular man sitting over there. My ex-husband."

Startled, he looked closer at the couple. The man was well dressed, if a little too trendy for Sam's basic-guy tastes, and had artificially streaked blond hair. He sat holding hands with a very pretty brunette who looked to be about fifteen years younger.

He never would have pictured Claire McKnight as being divorced—but then, he remembered Alexandra telling him she had only recently married Alexandra's brother. That explained how she had older kids then.

"I thought if I only married Jeff Bradford, my life would be perfect. For several years of our married life, I thought it was all I could ever want. One boy, one girl, a husband who was a doctor, a lovely home."

"I'm guessing by virtue of the fact that he's your ex-husband, you discovered otherwise," he said.

She glanced at the man beside her, who was engaged in animated conversation with Jackson Lange, and her eyes were soft with emotions that made a weird lump rise in his throat. “Dreams change. Lives change. We have to do our best to adapt. What we think we want or need isn’t always the best thing for us.”

“Are you saying you don’t think Alexandra should have opened the restaurant?”

“Oh, no. Not at all! She has been working for this since she came back from culinary training in Europe more than a decade ago. She had many chances to have her own restaurant but none of them seemed right for her until now. I just hope…” Her voice trailed off. “I hope it makes her happy.”

He had to wonder if others could see the loneliness that seemed to twine around her like an ugly scarf she couldn’t untie.

“I get the feeling Alex thinks the name of the restaurant is particularly self-descriptive,” Claire said after a moment. “Brazen. She likes to think she’s tough, bold.”

“You think otherwise.”

Claire was quiet for a moment while silverware and glasses clinked and the conversation murmured around them. “She just might be the most vulnerable person I know, with the biggest heart. Even that bold, brave girl in first grade had a soft spot for someone she perceived as weaker than she was.”

If he wasn’t careful, he was going to end up falling very, very hard for that particular bold, brave girl. The same girl who couldn’t seem to go five minutes without telling him all the reasons they couldn’t be together.

To avoid spending too much time thinking about that depressing reality, he said, “I understand you’re the person I need to talk to about volunteering to help out with the Giving Hope Day in a few weeks.”

The change of subject worked just as he hoped. Claire's soft, pretty features lit up. "Yes!" she exclaimed. "Oh, can I put a man with your skills to work!"

She launched into an explanation of some of the projects on tap that year while the efficient servers cleared away dessert. He listened to her with half an ear while he tried to puzzle out the mystery of Alexandra and his growing feelings for her.

She was the only woman who had evoked even a glimmer of interest in him since Kelli died. If his interest were only a glimmer, he could deal, but this was becoming a tidal wave of hunger and, yes, tenderness.

He was beginning to care deeply for her. Meanwhile, she sent him sweet little notes to make him smile and she kissed him with her whole heart, all while insisting they couldn't have a relationship.

What was a guy supposed to do with that?

He had a few ideas—and a few plans—but he was very much afraid he was spinning his wheels. Stubbornness was another of her traits.

He sipped at his wine, wondering why it suddenly had an edge of bitterness to it.

THE DIGITAL READOUT on her dashboard clock read one-fifteen when she finally drove down Currant Creek Valley Road toward home.

Her neighbors slept, their lights out and their window shades closed against the beauty of the May night. They were missing this perfect night, she thought.

How long had she been a night owl? Forever, maybe. Even when she was a kid, she remembered waking up in the room she shared with Maura and sneaking downstairs to watch a scary movie on TV at a rare time when she didn't have to share the remote and the viewing choices with five siblings.

Her mom used to say she couldn't sleep because she was too afraid she was going to miss something.

That had been another thing she had shared with her father. No matter how low she turned the television set, even when she was sitting right in front of it with the sound almost off, he would still sometimes hear and come downstairs in his plaid pajamas.

He never yelled at her to go to bed, even on school nights. Sometimes he would pop a batch of popcorn or she would come up with some kind of elaborate snack and they would nosh while they watched the end.

Riley or Maura would sometimes join them but Maura always preferred having a book in her hand to watching television and Ri often fell asleep midmovie, something he still tended to do.

Maybe that's why she loved this quiet time, when most of the world slept. It reminded her of a happy period in her childhood when she felt important and cherished and safe.

She pulled up in front of her house and sat for a moment with the windows still rolled down and the engine off. A *genuine* night owl hooted as she climbed out of her car. The sound slid around and through her, leaving her strangely restless.

This was supposed to be the most triumphant moment of her life. Opening night of her own restaurant, after all these years, an evening she had shared with nearly all of those she loved most in the world, all but the twins, Lila and Rose.

Opening night had gone better than she could have dreamed, even with the inevitable kitchen dramas. For starters, she had ordered too few napkins from the linen service. They had ended up—horrors!—having to use paper for the last four tabletops.

And then her two sous-chefs had almost come to blows over a mushroom soup that had charred on the bottom.

To top it all off, one of the servers had chosen that very afternoon, of all possible days, to break up with a troublesome boyfriend and had consequently spent the evening alternating between tears and a giddy relief.

Despite everything, she knew the evening had gone well. The rave reviews alone weren't enough to convince her. Her family and friends loved her and probably would have raved if she had served them up mac and cheese from a box.

But she had worked in enough fine restaurants to pick up the vibe when diners were very happy with what they were eating.

Judging by the reaction, she sensed Brazen was on its way.

Where was the huge burst of joy she had expected? Expected and *earned,* damn it. She had just conquered a summit she had been struggling toward for most of her adult life. She should be euphoric, effervescent. Instead, she felt...oddly deflated.

She let herself into the house, expecting for an instant to be greeted by a slavering, enthusiastic dog, until she remembered she had dropped Leo off to stay with Claire and Riley for the weekend because of her hectic schedule.

Her house seemed to echo with a vast emptiness. She told herself that was the reason she felt so unsettled. She had become used to the dog these past few weeks and didn't quite know now what to do without him.

She had worked hard for the restaurant, just as she had worked hard to make this place her home.

She was happy and content—though she had a feeling people who were truly happy and content didn't have to try so hard to convince themselves of it.

Though she hadn't had time for dinner, she couldn't bear the thought of food right now. A glass of wine, maybe, to celebrate. She found a bottle in the back of the refrigerator and pulled out a wineglass from the cabinet.

She poured a small amount and then on impulse headed for the door leading to her small backyard and patio. She could sit on the back step in the moonlight and listen to the rippling water of Currant Creek and toast herself for a job well done.

She decided the moon offered enough illumination so she opened the door without turning on the outside lights.

Her mind on the long day at the restaurant and all the preparation she needed to do for the dinner crowd tomorrow—tonight, now—she made it down three steps before she suddenly realized something was very different from the way she had left things.

The wineglass almost slipped from her finger but she managed to hang on to it.

What in the world?

In the moonlight, a dark low-slung shape took pride of place, angled toward the creek. A chair, wrapped in a bow.

For just an instant, she thought this might be a gift

from her very own Angel of Hope but then reality intruded. The Angel visited the wounded, the downtrodden, those who were struggling with pain and loss.

Everything in her life was going exactly the way she wanted. Why on earth would the Angel waste time on her?

Not the Angel. Sam.

What you need is a big comfortable chair right there on the back patio so you can unwind out here with the sound of the water. While your dog plays in the grass, of course.

Those had been his words, the day he and Ethan had first come to her house. She remembered them as clearly as if he were standing here now.

Sam had done this. She was suddenly sure of it. She rushed back up the steps and flipped on the porch lights so she could see better.

It was stunning. Built in the Adirondack style, of red cedar stained to show the wood grain, the chair had wide armrests and a curving back. A matching leg rest angled down and looked just the thing for relaxing on a summer afternoon.

Beside it was a small round table of the same cedar, the perfect size for holding a pitcher of lemonade and a paperback novel.

She traced a hand over the wood, smooth as chocolate ganache. Beautiful. Simply beautiful.

He had made this. She knew it. Warmth burst through her like fireworks over Hope's Crossing in July and she quickly peeled away the ribbon in the half light of the moon.

That owl—probably the same one who had been

keeping her company on her late-night walks—hooted from the treetops of the cottonwoods along the creek. For once, the sound didn't leave her melancholy. She was too busy being delighted at the gift.

He'd left a note, she saw, taped to the back of the chair. It was too dark to make out the words, even with plenty of moonlight, so she held it up to the glow from the light fixture beside the back door.

With all your hard work today, I figured your bones would probably need a place to rest. Now, this *is a sanctuary.*

She clutched the note to her chest. Oh, she was in trouble. Sam Delgado was becoming very good at sneaking his way under all her defenses. She was beginning to forget all the reasons she needed to keep trying.

All evening, she hadn't been able to resist peeking through the kitchen doors every once in a while and somehow her gaze had always seemed to fall on Sam. The only thought that had played through her mind whenever she had seen him was how *right* he looked, laughing and joking with her family and friends, just as if he had been part of the group forever.

She eased into the chair cushion he had thoughtfully provided. The chair was ergonomically perfect, providing exactly the right support. Her weary bones definitely needed this.

She smiled and then laughed out loud as she sat on her back patio while the creek rippled over rocks, its song an endless comfort.

Yes. Finally, here on her back patio, came the joy and happiness that had been missing all evening. How had Sam instinctively guessed what would make the night perfect?

And how on earth was she supposed to be able to resist a man who was capable of such sweet thoughtfulness?

CHAPTER FOURTEEN

EVERYTHING SEEMED TO BE falling into place. Well, nearly everything. Tuesday night, four days after Alex opened her restaurant, Sam turned onto his street just as the sun sank down behind the mountains. He was starving and exhausted but also filled with a great sense of achievement.

The recreation-center work was ahead of schedule, on schedule to be finished on time for the Giving Hope Day. His four-man crew from Denver had been working double shifts to finish the job, in addition to six temporary workers he had hired on to help.

Like Alex's restaurant, the work had been nearly done at the rec center before he had been hired on. He felt a little like a cleanup batter in baseball. His job had been to come in and wrap up all the little details—finishing the trim in a few rooms, hanging some doors, putting in cabinets for the administrative offices.

The town leaders, through a generous grant from Harry Lange, had spared no expense on the facility. From the exterior landscaping to the enormous exercise facility to the meeting rooms spread throughout, the building seemed to be a labor of love.

The vast indoor pool, especially, with those full-length windows overlooking Silver Strike Canyon, should be a huge hit during the long high-mountain winters when it was finished.

Ethan would love it and Sam had found unique satisfaction working on something he and his son and the rest of their adopted town could enjoy for years to come.

He smiled thinking of his son. He had ended up staying at his brother's house in Denver all weekend, helping Nicky with a few last-minute repairs on his house in preparation for renting it out while they were in Europe.

Ethan had helped him, proud as punch to wear his miniature tool belt. This morning when he left to drive back to Hope's Crossing, he put the pickup in gear and started to hit the gas to back out of the driveway and heard a noise coming from the backseat of his king cab.

Upon investigation, he found Ethan hiding under a jacket he had tossed on the backseat.

"I miss you, Dad. Why can't I come with you now? We're not doing anything in school but dumb stuff like Field Day and cleaning out our desks."

He had hugged his son. "Two more weeks, kid. We can both make it, can't we?"

As much as he missed his son, he needed a few more weeks to ready everything. He had spent his lunch hours looking into possible summer day-care situations that might work for his extended hours. Ideally, he would like to hire a housekeeper-slash-nanny—but until he had time to whip the house into shape, he wasn't sure he could find anybody willing to work in a construction zone.

He had finally managed to get Ethan back into his brother's house for breakfast and school before making the long drive here to the recreation center.

Now he had a full evening of work to make sure his

son had a place to sleep where the ceiling wouldn't fall in on him during the night.

Both of them deserved to have a little stability, especially after the chaos of the past few months.

He was so busy thinking about the tasks ahead of him for the coming evening that he completely missed the visitor waiting for him on his front porch until he started to climb the steps.

Some ex-soldier he was. Out in the field, that could have been a deadly mistake.

He actually had two visitors, he realized. A long-limbed dog with fur the color of fine Belgian chocolate sat waiting for him on the top step, tongue lolling out and tail sweeping across the wooden slats of the porch floor.

If Leo was here, Alexandra had to be, too. His heartbeat kicked up, much to his dismay. He had missed her these past few days, as ridiculous as that seemed. He looked farther on to the shadows and found her curled up on his porch swing, sound asleep.

Apparently she was working overtime, as well. She looked comfortable, with her face pressed into the pillow and one hand tucked under her cheek. She was more relaxed than he had ever seen her, soft and warm and lovely.

He remembered what her friend Claire had said.

She likes to think she's tough, bold.... She just might be the most vulnerable person I know, with the biggest heart.

She probably wouldn't appreciate him seeing her like this but he couldn't bring himself to wake her, not when she had that smudge of exhaustion under her eyes.

If the swing had been a little bigger, he would have

climbed on there with her. Instead, he leaned a hip against the porch railing and reached a hand down to pet her dog, aware of a rare and precious contentment seeping through him.

She didn't sleep for long, much to his disappointment. Maybe she sensed his presence or maybe she simply had too much energy coiled up in that compact frame to sleep soundly in these conditions.

After a few moments, her eyelids began to flutter. She came to full consciousness in an instant. One minute she was breathing deeply, the next she jerked upright and scrubbed at her face.

"I fell asleep."

She said the words in an accusatory tone, as if he were to blame, and he had to smile.

"Looks like."

"How did that happen?"

"I'm guessing you finally stopped moving for five seconds and closed your eyes."

"Probably." She raked a hand through her tangled hair. "I didn't mean to. I've just been so busy. The swing was so comfortable. I was only going to rest for a second, while I waited for you…."

She crossed her arms across her chest suddenly and that delicious sleepy-eyed warmth turned into a glower. "Where have you been?"

He raised an eyebrow. "I'm sorry. Did I miss curfew?"

"I've been trying to find you for three days and you just…disappeared."

He knew he shouldn't have this little spurt of happiness that she had been looking for him, not when she had made it clear she thought they were a disastrous combination.

"I spent the weekend in Denver with my brother and his family. Ethan and I were helping do some things around their house to help make things ready for them to rent it out while they're in Europe. I drove back this morning and headed straight for the job site."

"Oh. That explains it."

"And I've been working every spare minute at the recreation center."

"Are you finished?"

"Close. We've got a few more things to do."

Hard work was good for the soul, right? He continued to pet her dog, something else good for the soul.

"You needed me for something?"

She gazed at him for a long moment and he saw something hot flash in her eyes before she quickly concealed it. "Er, yes. This is for you."

From the other side of the porch swing, she slid out a cooler he hadn't noticed.

"What's all this?"

Pink bloomed on her cheeks. "That chair. That was… an amazing gift."

He wanted to kiss those cheekbones. Start there and work his way to her mouth and then wherever else he could touch. "It seemed a shame to waste such a perfect spot, there along the creek. You needed a proper chair."

"It's perfect," she said, her voice soft. "Really wonderful. I've sat out there every night since you left it for me."

"That's what I was hoping."

He didn't tell her the chair was part of his master strategy, demonstrating to this prickly, independent woman that she didn't have to do everything by herself. Sometimes leaning on somebody else once in a while could be immensely rewarding.

"Thank you. It was…extraordinarily thoughtful of you."

"I had fun building it," he assured her. "Ethan helped, as I'm sure he'll be sure to tell you when he sees you again. He hammered in several of the nails."

"Then I will cherish it even more."

The chair had only taken a couple of evenings the week before. Yeah, it was time he could have been spending working on making the house ready but he was suddenly very glad he had decided to devote a little energy to this. He liked seeing her flustered and a little off balance.

Her foot nudged the cooler. She was wearing flip-flops and her toenails were painted a rosy pink. He could always start there and kiss his way up….

"This pales in comparison as a thank-you," she said, "but it's the best I could do."

"Okay, you've piqued my curiosity. What is it?"

"Stick with what you do best, right? In my case, that's food."

He opened the lid and discovered three stacks of neatly wrapped containers, each with handwriting on the top. One read Chicken Parmesan, he saw at first glance, another Portobello Ravioli, Pork Tenderloin on yet another. There were more but that was all he could see.

"I guess you could say this is my version of TV dinners. Everything should be labeled and most of it can be heated in the microwave. Of course, it won't be as good as when I originally cooked it, but it's the next-best thing."

"There must be a dozen meals in here."

She shrugged. "I didn't really count. But most of the serving sizes are probably big enough for you and Ethan both."

He hated cooking and considered it his hardest task as a single father, coming up with something nutritious and half-decent that Ethan would actually eat. Having that worry taken away would be a huge plus.

"I'm astonished," he said honestly. "Completely astonished. This will be a great break from fast food."

She shrugged. "Like I said, I know my strengths and most of them involve a kitchen somewhere."

"I will love this. So will Ethan. Thank you."

Color seeped along her cheekbones. "It hardly seems commensurate. I'm a little embarrassed, if you want the truth. I'll be enjoying the chair you made me for years to come while you'll probably polish off the last meal in a few weeks."

"You didn't have to do anything like this, Alexandra. I gave you that chair because I wanted to. I didn't expect anything in return."

That seemed to fluster her. "Yes, well, I appreciate it. More than I can say. Um, we should probably put these in the freezer as soon as possible. I can't believe I fell asleep and left them sitting out this long. I should have just gone back to my house and put them back in the freezer while I watched for you from the window."

"You looked as if you needed the nap."

"It's been a crazy few days. The restaurant is closed on Tuesdays but I spent most of today cooking for you and some other friends."

He hoped she still considered him a friend, despite everything else that simmered between them. "Come on inside. Let's see if I can find room in the freezer."

He unlocked the door and led the way inside, aware as he did that the house was cluttered with construction mess, especially the living room. The family room in the back was moderately livable but he had been using this room to store all the supplies and paint cans. Saw-horses, trouble lights and ladders cluttered the floor.

She apparently didn't notice. "Wow, look at all the progress you've made!"

"All I can see is how much I still have to do."

"No, it's beautiful. Those crown moldings are gorgeous! I never would have guessed they were hiding beneath all those layers of paint."

"Amazing what a little elbow grease can do. Let me put these things away and then I'll take you on the grand tour."

In the kitchen, she exclaimed again over the new cabinetry he had installed and the pendant lights over the island that replaced the old fluorescent fixture.

"Wow! I can't believe how far the house has come in only a few weeks. Do you ever sleep?"

"When I can."

The few hours he did catch had been more than a little restless lately, occupied with a certain lovely chef, but he decided telling her that particular detail would only make him sound pathetic.

"Well, it's amazing."

He lifted a shoulder. "You like cooking things, I like this. Taking something rough and unfinished, turning it into a warm, comfortable space. Finish carpentry is the very best part of construction work, in my opinion.

The bare-bones work has its place, but I get to see immediate results."

"I am really impressed, Sam. I guess I shouldn't be. I've spent plenty of time in the kitchen you built. and the chair you—and Ethan—made me has become the most comfortable spot in my house or outside it."

"Come on. Let me give you the tour."

He showed her Ethan's room, close to completion, the new tile work in the main bathroom, the shower he was completely rebuilding in the master bathroom.

"Wonderful," she said when they circled back to the kitchen. "You're doing a fantastic job. I'm sure you and Ethan will be very comfortable here."

"I sensed that from the first moment I looked at the house. It felt *right.* I can't explain it. I only know this is where we need to be."

"Just like you knew Hope's Crossing was a good place to call home after one afternoon at the pizza parlor."

"I know you think I'm ridiculous."

"No. I get it." Her voice was soft. "Sometimes you have to go with your gut. You're a good father. Ethan is lucky to have you."

Her words were warm but her expression was resigned, almost sad, for reasons he didn't understand.

"I'd better let you get back to your evening. All the instructions should be on the food. I know from experience they're all freezer friendly and should warm up well. And when you run out, let me know and I can drop off more."

"Keep a ready supply of meals-on-wheels, do you?"

"Something like that. Good night."

She reached for the door but he made a countermove and blocked her way. “Can I ask you something?”

She stood only a few feet from him, and her clean, sweet scent of vanilla and Alexandra reached right in and grabbed his gut.

“What?” she asked, her voice and her stance wary.

“What am I doing wrong?”

She shifted and he saw nerves flicker in her green eyes. “I don’t know what you mean.”

“Yeah. Yeah, you do. We’ve got this heat between us. I know you feel it. But you seem determined to treat me like just another of your many casual friends. Like you would Brodie Thorne or Mr. Phillips next door.”

“I hope you and I are friends. I’m a generally friendly person.”

“We’re more than that or you wouldn’t shiver when I touch you.”

“You’re imagining things.”

“Am I?”

For purely illustrative purposes—not because of any overwhelming need to touch her burning inside him or anything—he slid a hand out and cupped her face. When she trembled, quite predictably, that familiar hunger exploded.

She almost immediately went still but he sensed it was taking a tremendous effort. “How do you even have room for a cell phone while you’re carrying around all that ego?”

A ragged laugh escaped and he did the only thing he could think of. He drew his thumb over her cheek and then leaned down to kiss her.

She remained frozen for all of perhaps three seconds and then her arms slid around his waist and she kissed him fiercely, passionately, as she always did, as if she couldn't help herself.

Why did he do this, again and again? He couldn't keep torturing himself. They seemed to follow the same pattern. He would kiss her, she would respond, then something would make her freak out and she would run away, leaving him aroused and frustrated.

He knew why he did it, why he couldn't seem to stay away. He had known for a while now but hadn't wanted to face it.

He was in love with her.

The truth of it settled over him like puffs from the cottonwoods along the creek, gentle and sweet and completely natural. He loved Alexandra McKnight, this strong, independent, beautiful woman who fought him at every turn.

What the hell was he going to do about that?

Right now, he was going to go on kissing her. He had no choice, not when she was wrapped around him, her tongue in his mouth and her hands drifting under the edge of his T-shirt to the skin beneath.

He was instantly hard, instantly ready. Unstoppable.

Except by her.

"This is more than physical. You know that, right?"

The instant the words escaped, he knew they were a fatal miscalculation. Why, oh, why couldn't he keep his big mouth shut?

Every single one of her muscles went rigid and he could almost see her coming back to reality. An instant later, she wrenched away from him.

And here you have the freak-out section of the program, folks.

"No, it's not. It's *only* physical. We happen to have highly compatible pheromones, that's all."

She reached for the door again, always running away, but he held a hand out and stopped her, suddenly sad and angry and frustrated.

"Is it me, specifically, you're running from, or anything with a Y chromosome?"

She lifted her chin. "Does it matter?"

"Damn right, it matters. You've obviously been hurt. I have no idea who did it to you but it wasn't me! It's not fair that you've decided to tar me with every other man's sins."

"No. It's not."

She didn't explain herself or defend herself, which only pissed him off more. In fact, she looked wretched again, her green eyes huge amid suddenly pale features.

"What do you want from me? What can I do to show you I'm not all the other jackasses who have hurt you? Because I have to tell you, I'm tired of you taking off at a flat-out sprint anytime I get too close. To be perfectly honest with you, Alexandra, I'm at a place in my life when I have to wonder if the chase is worth it, especially since you obviously have no intention of letting me catch up."

"Maybe you should stop trying then!" Some of the color returned to her features. "I've been nice about it. I've tried being bitchy. If you want me to paint it in big red letters on the street in front of your house, I can do that, too. I'm not sure what else I can do to convince you I'm not interested in a relationship."

He gave her a long, steady look. "I guess that's where I'm having problems believing you. Call me crazy, but

I think you *do* want more. I think you're terrified to let yourself care, for some reason I can't comprehend."

"Is it impossible to believe I'm perfectly happy being on my own? Plenty of people are."

"Absolutely. I'm just not sure you're one of them. Can you tell me straight that you're not lonely?"

She snorted. "Yes, Sam. You're crazy. Between the restaurant and my girlfriends, I'm surrounded by people nearly every moment of my life."

"We both know that doesn't mean anything."

"I'm tired of people telling me I'm not happy!" she snapped. "Doesn't anybody think I know my own mind?"

He was quiet and sad all over again. She wouldn't open up to him. He had given her the perfect chance to tell him about the parts of her life she kept secret from him and she had shut him out. Again.

"I care about you, Alexandra. I think I could fall for you very easily, with a little encouragement."

The words were a bit of a lie, since he was already there, but he decided that was information he should keep to himself for now.

"The thing is, I've never been much of a masochist," he went on. "I'm not going to keep beating my head against a wall when I'm getting nothing out of it but a headache."

"Then stop. Please, Sam. I thought we could still have a friendship, even with this whole inconvenient pheromone thing between us, but apparently I was wrong. When you touch me, kiss me, I forget all good sense. So now I'm asking you. Please. Leave me alone. Thank you for the chair and…everything, but I don't…

I can't…" Her voice caught and his heart broke right along with it.

"I don't want this!"

She jerked the door open and raced out the door before he could move, grabbing her dog and her cooler as she rushed down the stairs.

CHAPTER FIFTEEN

"RILEY'S WORKING a late shift tonight and the kids are with Jeff and Holly. Want to come over and rent a chick flick?"

Before answering, Alex finished the headpin she was looping to make a charm out of a particularly pretty turquoise bead. "I can't tonight. Sorry. I've got a date."

Claire raised an eyebrow, the glasses she wore when she beaded making her look smart and sweet at the same time. "Seriously? Again? Isn't that like your third date this week? Who's the guy?"

She gripped the small needle-nose pliers more firmly. She was here to bead, not talk about her love life, she wanted to snap. But when her best friend owned the shop, she supposed she had to expect an interrogation.

"A couple different guys. Three, actually," she answered without looking at Claire.

"Three dates in a week? Impressive. Even for you."

"What's that supposed to mean?" She bristled.

"You don't need to jump down my throat. I was just asking. It seems a little…frenetic, especially when you only opened the restaurant two weeks ago."

Okay, she had to agree with that. She probably should have said no when the last guy asked her out, but she hadn't been able to bring herself to do it.

She supposed she had some vague idea that maybe

if she threw herself back into a social whirl, returned to her status quo of serial dating, she could start to get her head on straight again. She did best with one or two weeks of dating, where all parties concerned just wanted fun and company, right? Maybe that way she would stop aching for a certain man who wanted more than she could ever give.

She had gone to lunch with one man to check out the competition in Telluride, a matinee of a summer blockbuster action movie with another, and she was meeting a third for drinks and conversation this evening, her one day off this week.

"When do you have time to meet all these men?" Claire asked.

"Oh, here and there. You know."

"No. I have no idea. It's still technically the off-season, so I'd like to know how you happen to find every available guy who happens to wander through town."

"I struck up a conversation with someone while I was mountain biking. Another I helped find the potato chip aisle at the market, and a third was a guy I met several months ago at a trade show who happened to be in town for the weekend."

"So do you like any of these guys?"

"I like all of them or I wouldn't have agreed to see them, would I?" Her tone was a little more belligerent than she intended and Claire must have picked up on it.

"You tell me."

She wanted to give some fast and flippant answer but she couldn't. The truth was, she wasn't really being fair, she supposed, especially when the guys wanted at least the possibility of another date and she couldn't even give them that.

"I like to have fun," she said. "What's wrong with that?"

Claire gave her a long, searching look, which Alex studiously tried to ignore while she attached a jump ring to the earring finding. "Nothing at all, if I thought you were really having fun."

She couldn't come up with an answer to that, simply because she didn't have one. She wasn't having fun. She was miserable. All the frenzied dating was only making her aware how much more she could have.

Damn Sam Delgado, anyway.

"Well, you'll be happy to know I've decided to take a dating break after tonight." Okay, she had only just reached that momentous resolve as of right this very moment, but she didn't have to tell Claire that. "Who has the time or the energy?"

Again, those big, magnified eyes scrutinized her. After all these years of being best friends, nobody knew her like Claire, not even her mom or her sisters.

She still had a few secrets left but she had a very strong suspicion Claire had to guess some of the things she wasn't about to say.

"I really thought you were hitting it off with Sam. He seems like a great guy."

Yep. Claire knew her entirely too well. "He is. Terrific. Hey, is that a new line of crystal beads I haven't seen yet?"

"Yes. And why are you trying to change the subject?"

She made a face that she was pretty sure didn't fool anyone. "I want to finish these earrings today for Caroline before I have to go meet a supplier at the restaurant. I have very limited time with my best friend here. Why would I want to waste some of that precious time talking about my boring dating life?"

One of the things she loved best about Claire was that she respected Alex's wish to keep some things to herself without being hurt that she sometimes needed space and privacy.

Claire had guessed something was seriously wrong when Alex came home from Europe. For long months, she had looked at her with concern but after several bouts of her gentle prodding, she had accepted that some things Alex needed to keep private, for her own reasons.

To her relief, Claire seemed to know this was one of those times.

"How is Caroline?" she asked after a pause, though that familiar concern was a shadow in her eyes. "I heard she's not doing well."

This wasn't exactly a restful topic for Alex, either, but she didn't avoid it. "She's going to be fine," she said firmly. "I stopped yesterday morning and visited with her. I think she's just a little down, that's all. I thought a few new pairs of earrings might help."

"Help you or her?"

Claire really did know her too well. "Okay, both. It's a helpless feeling, you know? Cancer sucks."

Claire reached across the table and squeezed Alex's hand around the pliers. "Yes, it does. You're a good friend, Alexandra McKnight."

Was she? She had to disagree. Claire put up with her moods and her silences but not many people would.

She managed not to show that part of herself to Caroline. Right now, she needed to be her best self for the elderly woman. Caroline didn't have that many others in her life, only one son who lived on the other side of the world with his Japanese wife and rarely made it back.

"I wish I could do more. I've been taking her food as often as I can but right now she's not eating much. I'm taking some of her favorites today and I thought the earrings would be appreciated, as well. You know how fussy she is about how she looks."

"What can Riley and I do for her? I've got her on the cleanup list for the Giving Hope Day this coming Saturday, but please let me know if you think of anything else she might need."

"I will. I'd like to be on her yard crew."

This year she had already asked for some other assignment than food. While she was on the committee that organized the lunch provided to the volunteers and the dinner that was part of the gala, both events were being catered this year by one of Brodie's other restaurants.

She didn't mind. Between the restaurant and the other meals she cooked for her elderly friends, she needed a bit of a rest from the kitchen.

"I'll put you down. I've still got you on Evie's decorating committee for the ballroom, right?"

"Oh. Right. I forgot that part. What other projects are you doing this year?"

As she had hoped, Claire launched into a recitation of the various activities planned. The big one this year was the construction of a badly needed concession stand at the Little League ballpark.

Through carefully inserted questions, she was able to keep Claire talking about the Giving Hope Day—instead of Alex's tangled love life—until she finished seven pairs of earrings for Caroline, one for each day of the week made of beads the same bright colors as the flowers in her tangled garden.

She didn't mind. Even talking about Claire's pregnancy and impending birth and the old pain that inevitably dredged up would have been preferable to talking about why she was dating all these other men who weren't Sam.

"YOU NEED TO…stop bringing me so much food, my dear. I'll never…be able to eat it all."

She had to strain to both hear and understand Caroline's words. Every day, her voice seemed to become more garbled and quavery. It broke her heart—and so did Caroline's implication that the food would go to waste because she didn't expect to be around long enough to finish it.

"Don't be ridiculous. Of course you will. When you're feeling better and ready to work in that garden again, you're going to have a ferocious appetite. I want to make sure you've got plenty of good stuff in your freezer to help you keep up your energy."

Caroline didn't answer, only tangled her fingers in the fringe of the cashmere pashmina Katherine Thorne had recently brought her back from one of her frequent travels, this one to New Delhi.

"You just sit there and I'm going to heat you up some of this delicious soup. It's mushroom and rice, your favorite."

"You don't have to…do that. It sounds good but… I'm afraid I'm not very hungry."

"I'll warm it up anyway and you can try a spoonful or two."

Maybe once Caroline had a taste, she would rediscover her appetite and want more. At this rate, she was going to waste away before the cancer took her.

Alex made a mental note to talk to the hospice nurse who had been coming in for the past few weeks about some recipes she thought might tempt Caroline.

While the soup heated, she spent a moment cursing the vagaries of life out in Caroline's beautiful garden, now wild and overgrown. One moment a person could be hale and hardy, out-gardening the rest of the town on her worst day, the next she became a shadow of herself while her life slipped away ounce by ounce.

She cut some flowers she thought might make Caroline smile—spiky lavender that smelled divine; a burst of elegant yellow irises; plump, showy pink peonies and some humble, early-blooming daisies.

She wasn't much of a floral arranger but she found a pretty jar in one of Caroline's cupboards and did a passable job, then dished the warm soup in her fanciest bowl and set it on a tray along with some gourmet crackers she had brought along in hopes of tempting that capricious appetite.

Caroline was dozing in her comfortable recliner by the front window but she blinked away when Alex came back.

"Oh, thank you, my dear. And…thank you for the earrings. They're all so beautiful, I couldn't decide. I ended up doing…eeny meeny miny moe."

"Good choice."

Caroline wore the pair she had made out of translucent pink heart-shaped crystals. They reminded Alex of the delicate, draping bleeding hearts that were among the first flowers to bloom in that splendid garden.

She sat with her and coaxed her to swallow a spoonful and then another. All told, Caroline probably ate about a half cup of soup and two of the crackers, which was more than Alex had hoped.

"Thank you. That was so delicious."

"You're welcome, darling. There is plenty more in the refrigerator. You can share some with Helen when she comes again," she said, referring to the hospice nurse.

"I'll do that."

She left the flowers in the living room where Caroline could enjoy them but carried the tray back to the kitchen, where she loaded the dishes into the dishwasher and then spent a moment washing down the cabinets and countertops, dusty from nonuse.

"I guess that's all," Alex said. "Is there anything else I can get you before I go?"

"I wish…you didn't have to go, my dear. I love… your company."

She studied her friend for a moment, frail and ill and living alone here in the house, and thought of her date with a man she had met once and would likely never see again. She could barely remember his name. Brent something. Or was it Trent?

What was she doing, wasting precious moments of a life that would be gone entirely too soon?

"Will you excuse me for a moment?" she said, and walked back into the kitchen, reaching for her cell phone.

She was glad she had backed out of the date, she thought a few moments later as she hung up. If a guy could get so pissy about a little disappointment, he wasn't worth even a minute of her time.

"There," she said to Caroline when she returned to the living room. "Looks like my evening just freed up."

"What about your date?"

"I would much rather spend my night with you," she said honestly. "You know, Claire was looking for something to do tonight, too. Why don't I call her and we can have a girls' night, just the three of us? I can have her pick up a movie and pop some of my gourmet popcorn."

"Not...a chick flick," Caroline insisted. "Action-adventure. Something that has...hot guys...with muscles."

Alex laughed and kissed Caroline on the top of her gray hair. "You got it. Hot guys with muscles coming up," she said, feeling better about life than she had in a week.

THE EVENING WAS A BLAST, even if Caroline fell asleep during the second half of the movie, just when the action was ramping up to full throttle.

She and Claire enjoyed it anyway and then helped Caroline with her medications and into bed. Claire was endlessly patient, a much better person than Alex could ever be.

She didn't complain when Caroline sent her out to the kitchen on the third errand, this one to find the reading glasses she had left out there.

After she went out, Caroline reached a hand out and grasped Alex's, her bones as thin and fragile as *pâté feuilletée*. "I'm sorry...you canceled your date to spend time with...boring me."

"Are you kidding? This was the most fun I've had in weeks. Anyway, the guy turned out to be a jerk. And he was nowhere *near* as hot as Matt Damon."

Caroline smiled a little, her fingers trembling ever so slightly. "Have I ever told you…about my Thomas?"

"Not really," she said carefully. Like her, Caroline had some secrets she held close to her heart. "My mom told me once he died in the Korean War."

"Yes." Caroline had a faraway look in her eyes. "We were married only a year and I was pregnant with our Ross when he was drafted. He was killed six months later. He never saw his son."

Her chest felt tight and achy as she pictured a young war widow, alone and grieving. "Oh. Oh, darling. I'm so sorry."

"I had a chance for…love…again a few years later. His best friend came back…from the war and stayed around town for a few months, working in the…silver mine, before they played out. Joseph Baxter. Joe. He looked…just like that Damon fellow. Maybe that's why I like his…movies so much."

Alex smiled through the tears she was trying not to shed. Out of the corner of her gaze, she saw Claire had returned but waited in the doorway, one hand on her round stomach and the other pressed to her heart.

"He loved Ross and…wanted to marry me but…I was too afraid. I had already lost someone dear to me, you see, and I didn't want to go through that again. The pain…when Tommy died, was…unbearable. And so I pushed away Joe. Again and again. Until he gave up and left Hope's Crossing. Last I heard, he moved to Nevada to work in the mines and…married a girl he met there."

Caroline was quiet for a long moment, her face averted on the pillow. Alex would have thought perhaps she had fallen asleep again if those frail fingers didn't continue to tremble in hers.

Finally she turned back and her gaze met Alex's with more clarity and purpose than she had seen there in weeks. "I've been alone…all these years…sleeping by myself in this cold bed. Who can say what I missed out on, because I was too…afraid?"

Even in her illness, Caroline didn't do anything by accident. She was telling this story, tonight, out of some motivation Alex didn't understand.

"He worked in a mine," she murmured, compelled to defend that long-ago version of her friend. "What if a tunnel collapsed on him or something? You would have had to go through the pain of losing someone all over again."

Claire made a low sound in her throat but Alex didn't turn around and Caroline apparently didn't hear her.

"I…should have…risked it." She grasped Alex's hand in both of hers as if she were cupping life-giving water. "Life isn't…meant to be spent…hiding in the corner with your arms huddled over your head, protecting… yourself from anything that might hurt you. Life should be…embraced."

"You've done that. Everyone in town loves you."

Caroline dismissed that with a shrug of her slight shoulders. "When a woman is ready to turn another… chapter in her life, she begins to see things with… unforgiving clarity." Despite the struggle to speak, she gave them both a mischievous smile. "I've spent fifty years…without a man in my bed. Think…of all the orgasms I missed."

Claire sputtered a laugh. Even with her emotions in turmoil, Alex managed to laugh, as well.

"There is that," Alex murmured.

"Don't make…my mistakes. If you have the chance

to find happiness with someone special, grab hold…and don't let go. If you don't, you could end up like me…a shriveled, tired old woman…dying alone."

"You're not dying," Alex said automatically. "And you're not alone. We're here, right? We just got done watching a great movie and eating fabulous popcorn and laughing."

"Yes, and…I'm tired now. I need to sleep. Thank you, my dears. I shall…dream of…Matt Damon tonight."

As she settled Caroline into bed and turned off the light, Alex wondered if this would be her in fifty years, alone with her regrets.

CHAPTER SIXTEEN

CLAIRE WAS GOING TO PAY, and pay hard.

From her vantage point kneeling in the dirt around Caroline's south garden, where she had been hard at work yanking out annoying elm seedlings that had blown from the surrounding trees and rooted, Alex glowered at the pickup truck that had just pulled up behind her own SUV.

She knew that truck.

When a big, muscled figure climbed out, followed closely by a very adorable dark-haired boy, she wanted to cry. Or throw something, she wasn't sure which.

Of all the work projects going on all over town, why would Claire feel compelled to assign Sam *here,* where she knew full well Alex would be working all morning on the cleanup of Caroline's overgrown garden?

She didn't have to guess. It couldn't be a coincidence. Claire suspected she had feelings for Sam. Despite all her efforts the other day to avoid talking about him—or maybe *because* of them—Claire must have guessed her feelings for him ran deeper than she would admit.

For all she knew, her mother and sisters likely connived with Claire to force her together with Sam today. Matchmaking busybodies, the lot of them.

She sat back on her heels and watched him and Ethan grab matching tool belts out of the bed of the pickup.

Sam fastened his low on his hips but Ethan seemed to struggle with his. The boy's father reached down and pulled the ends around with care then guided the end through the loop.

Watching a big, tough ex-soldier help his son just about turned her heart and her brain to mush.

Claire was definitely going to suffer for this, even if it was a little tough to come up with creative ways to wreak vengeance against a pregnant woman.

She couldn't totally blame her, she supposed. Hope's Crossing was a small town. She couldn't avoid him indefinitely. If she couldn't figure out a way to deal with seeing him on a regular basis, she would quickly find herself miserable.

With that in mind, she decided to try the casual, friendly approach one more time, pretending everything between them didn't exist. She shoved her garden gloves into her pocket and headed over to the two of them.

He wasn't surprised to see her, she saw as she approached. Had Claire warned him or had he simply recognized her vehicle when he drove up?

He straightened up from helping Ethan and watched her walk toward them, heat smoldering in his brown eyes for just a moment before he quickly banked it.

To give her heart time to settle down, she chose to ignore him and turned instead to Ethan. "Hey, there. You're coming to work, I hope."

"Yes. I have my very own hammer. My dad gave it to me this morning. And I got two screwdrivers, a flat-head and a Phillips-head."

The tools gleamed on his belt, obviously new, and her heart squeezed at the thought of Sam picking them out for his son.

"Those are some impressive tools."

"I've been borrowing some from my dad but these are for my very own use. I don't have to give them back. We're going to build a tree house this summer. It's going to be the very best tree house in town, with four walls and a roof and windows that close and everything."

"Sounds perfect."

"You can come see it," he suggested. "Maybe you could bring Leo. And brownies, if you want to."

She smiled. How could she help it when this boy was so very open with his heart? "I just might want to do that. Thank you for the invitation. You give me the word when you're finished and I'll bring over the brownies."

Eventually she was going to have to meet Sam's gaze, she supposed. She couldn't avoid him forever. She gave a little sigh and straightened up.

The memory of that last, emotional kiss seemed to hover between them, fierce and intense, and she was amazed they didn't catch all the overgrown weeds on fire.

"My orders are to fix some porch steps and a railing. I think Claire also said something about an arbor that needed some work."

Those things did need attention but none was urgent. Even if they were, why did they have to be fixed by him? she wanted to whine.

"There's plenty of work to be done," she said instead. "Caroline hasn't been feeling well the last few years. But she's getting better now."

She waved at her friend, who sat on her porch wrapped in a blanket watching her work and offering the occasional helpful comment.

Caroline lifted her hand to wave back but didn't seem

to have the energy to raise it more than a few inches. She looked more pale out here in the June sunshine.

"I guess we should get started, right, Ethan?"

His son nodded, though he continued smiling up at Alex. "Guess what? I finished the first grade yesterday."

"Congratulations!"

"School is out for the summer and now I get to live with my dad here all the time. I don't even have to go back. I can't go back anyway because my uncle and aunt are in an entirely different country. We might go visit them sometime. Not soon, but sometime. It's in Europe."

"That's terrific!"

"And guess what else? My bedroom is all finished. We finished painting it last night. One whole wall is a chalkboard. My dad used a special kind of paint. I have colored chalk to write on it and a big eraser. I can draw artwork or do math or whatever I want."

"Awesome!" And the perfect touch for a boy who was scary-smart. *Nice work, Sam,* she wanted to say.

"Why don't you come see it? You wouldn't even have to bring brownies, really, if you didn't want to."

She glanced at Sam. Though she couldn't read anything in his expression, she could almost feel the tension and yearning radiating off him like heat waves.

I care about you, Alexandra. I think I could fall for you very easily, with a little encouragement....

"I'd like that sometime."

"How about tonight?"

She managed a smile, even as she was aware of Sam opening his mouth to say something. "I don't think I can tonight. I'm supposed to go to the big benefit gala and auction at the ski resort."

"What's a gala?"

"It's a big party where people dress up in fancy clothes and dance and sometimes have fancy food."

"That sounds boring to me."

She laughed. "You won't get an argument out of me, kiddo. But when you're a grown-up, you have to do boring stuff once in a while."

"My dad's going, too. He has a date. I have to have a babysitter. I think I'm too old for a babysitter, don't you?"

She had a sudden image of Sam with another woman, laughing with her, sharing those delicious kisses and his wry sense of humor. Pain clutched her gut, so raw it made her eyes water.

Through the shock slicing through her, she shifted her gaze to Sam. He gave her a cool look in response but she couldn't read his expression.

What else did she expect? She had shut him down in every conceivable way. She couldn't expect him to just sit around waiting for something they both knew wasn't going to happen.

She forced herself to smile, ignoring the pain that seemed like a living, breathing thing prowling through her. "Babysitters are a pain, yeah, but I'm afraid you've still probably got a few more years for them."

"I guess. I'm very responsible for my age, though. I think that should be taken into consideration."

Sam interjected before she could come up with a reply. "Come on, kid. We'd better get to work before Mrs. McKnight comes out here and cracks the whip."

It took her a minute to realize he meant Claire, not her mother.

"Right. You don't want to get on her bad side."

Or she might decide to send over the one person in town you wanted to avoid to spend the entire day with you.

Sam reached into the back of his pickup and handed Ethan some long boards to carry up to the house, and Alex turned back to the garden, grateful she had some convenient noxious weeds to vent her tangled emotions against.

It was hard, sweaty, backbreaking work but she found an undeniable satisfaction in cleaning up the mess so the bright, cheery perennials could thrive.

While she weeded and thinned and cleared out old growth, she did her very best to ignore both Delgado males.

It wasn't easy.

Every once in a while she would catch glimpses of Sam walking back out to his truck for something or measuring and cutting a board on the sawhorses he set up. Ethan's cheerful chatter rang out in the morning air and now and then he would yell out at her to admire a board he had just nailed or a cut he had made.

As the sun hit its apex after noon and began its slide toward the mountains, the morning clear skies gave way to a few gray-edged clouds. The more she cleared away the mess and brought order to Caroline's garden, the more tangled her own thoughts seemed to become.

How could she do this? How could she continue to live in Hope's Crossing, just down the street from Sam and Ethan, while Sam moved on with his life, dating, possibly marrying again at some point?

Just thinking about it left her feeling queasy, though she tried to tell herself it was the sunshine and the fact that she'd only had a banana to eat that day.

The alarm beeped on her phone about an hour after Sam and his son arrived, reminding her Caroline had been outside for quite some time and probably needed a change in position, if nothing else.

She walked up onto the porch. "Ready for a rest?" she asked.

"I'm doing fine," the other woman assured her with a smile that looked as if it took a great deal of energy. "But you could probably…use a break."

She could have put in a few more hours before stopping but she didn't want Caroline to push herself too hard.

"I had Helen make up some…lemonade when she was here yesterday. Maybe you could take some out to the nice man and his…little boy."

Call her cynical but she wouldn't have been surprised to learn Caroline was in on the matchmaking efforts. But maybe she was only being hypersensitive.

"Okay," she agreed. "Good idea. Why don't you come inside where it's cooler while I pour some."

"I'm…all right out here. It's the next thing to being in the garden myself. The sun feels good."

How many afternoons of June sunshine did Caroline have left? Alex's heart broke all over again.

"The sunshine feels nice after a long winter, doesn't it? I'll fix you a snack then, and bring you some lemonade."

"I hope there's enough. Helen can…make more. She was coming back today. Or was it…tomorrow? I can't remember."

Caroline's brow furrowed and she looked out at the garden as if she could find the answer there. Alex squeezed the fingers that rested on the curved rocking-chair arm. "I don't know how you keep everything straight, between all your appointments and your medications and the hot guys you have coming over all the time. We can find out easily enough. I can simply look at the hospice schedule on the refrigerator, my dear."

The woman's tension relaxed and she seemed to sink back into her chair. "Would you? Thank you."

She saw that Helen was indeed coming that day, and the next. In fact, the hospice had scheduled someone to come every day, indefinitely, which meant they knew Caroline was failing, too.

Fighting back the burn of tears, she busied herself with pouring several glasses of lemonade on the same tray she had served Caro's soup the other day. She found some of the cookies she had brought over as well and arranged them prettily on a plate.

When she carried the tray back out to the porch, she found Sam sitting in the rocking chair beside Caroline. Ethan was sprawled on his stomach on the sidewalk, watching something on the concrete with a peculiar intensity.

It seemed strange to have them here, in this place, with her friend.

"What have you found?" she asked Ethan as she set the tray on the small table at Caroline's elbow.

"A snail. He's all slimy. I read in a book that snails produce mucus to reduce friction so they can move better. Don't you think that's cool?"

Yeah, not really. The only thing she considered cool about snails was how very delicious the right kind could be cooked in butter and a good wine sauce.

"Sure," she answered anyway.

He smiled up at her just as the sun passed between

a couple of the clouds and a sunbeam landed directly on his head, bathing him in golden light.

Out of nowhere, she was suddenly overwhelmed with love for this boy who had suffered great loss but could still find joy in little things like a snail streaking slime across a sun-warmed sidewalk.

She wanted to sweep him into her arms and hold him close.

She couldn't. It wasn't her place. Someday Sam would probably marry again and that woman would have the right to smooch Ethan's cheek and straighten his collar and tuck him in at night.

She cleared her throat. "I brought you and your dad some lemonade. Do you want some?"

"In a minute," Ethan said absently, and she was forced to turn back to Sam.

He took a glass from the tray and sipped it and she found herself ridiculously fascinated by the slide of his throat up and down as he swallowed.

"I…appreciate you helping me out today," Caroline said in her garbled, thready voice. She was used to having to strain in order to understand. Sometimes people who didn't know Caro well grew frustrated with it but Sam only smiled with patience.

"You're welcome," he answered.

"Used to be, I could…take care of this place on my own. It's hard to watch…others handle what I…should be doing."

"We're happy to help, ma'am. You've got a beautiful place here. What a view! Have you lived here long?"

She wondered if Sam was purposely trying to distract Caroline from the reality of all she could no longer do. Yes. Of course he was. She had no doubt. Beneath that tough, masculine exterior, he was just that kind of man.

Wonderful.

"You could…say that," Caroline said. "Eighty-five years now. I…was born in this house and moved here as a…young bride, after my parents died."

For the few short months of her marriage, before her husband was killed, she must have been so happy here.

"I want to…die in this house."

"Not for a long time," Alex answered promptly.

"Humph" was Caroline's answer.

She asked Sam where he was living and the two of them engaged in a conversation about his house and the previous owners, all of whom Caroline had known from the time the house had been built when she was a girl.

Alex was tempted to go back out to the garden but she made herself stay. This was a test, of sorts. If she couldn't endure a few minutes of conversation with the man, how did she expect to spend the next several decades in the same town?

"You're going…to the gala tonight?" Caroline asked him.

He nodded.

"Make sure you dance with…my Alex. She's a good dancer, when she's not in the kitchen."

Alex could feel her face heat. "He has a date, Caro."

"Oh? Who?"

Sam was under no obligation to tell and he seemed reluctant to share but he finally did. "Charlotte Caine," he answered, gazing out at the garden.

So he had taken her advice from several weeks earlier and asked Charlotte out. It had been *her* idea. She had thought from the beginning that Charlotte would be perfect for him. She was sweet and kind, unlike Alex, and certainly deserved a great guy like Sam.

It was one thing to have the image of some nameless, faceless woman in Sam's arms playing through her head. But, oh, it was something else entirely when that woman was her good friend.

"She's a…nice girl," Caroline said. "Pretty as can be, even before…she lost all that weight."

She winced for Charlotte's sake but Sam didn't even seem to register the comment. "She is. Very nice."

"Charlotte is wonderful," Alex said. "I told you so. You should have a great time."

He gave her a long look over his glass. "I'm planning on it," he said, rather grimly, she thought.

"I hope you…dance all night," Caroline said.

Her voice seemed to catch on the last word and Alex gave her a closer look. Just in the past few moments, more color had leached away, leaving her features tight and pale as the sweet william growing along her porch.

"Perhaps it's time for you to go inside and lie down. You're in pain."

"Just a…twinge."

"Let's get you inside and I'll give Helen a call."

"That's not necessary. But…maybe I should lie down. Just for a bit."

"Can I help?" Sam asked.

Caroline summoned a smile for him. "No, no. I'm fine. Enjoy…your lemonade. Alex…can help me."

Sam stood and looked as if he wanted to sweep the frail old woman into his arms and carry her inside but Alex shook her head. Caroline would be embarrassed and flustered with his help, for all her talk about sexy men.

She tucked Caroline's arm through hers and helped her into the house and toward her bedroom, just off the living room.

It seemed to take all of her friend's energy to walk those few steps. Alex helped her out of her slippers and settle into bed.

"Now *he* is…hot," she declared after the blanket was tucked up and she had the pillows just so. "I…love a man with a few muscles."

Yes. She did, too. Unfortunately. That particular man.

"*That's* the sort of fellow…you should be spending some time with. Not those…snowballers and ski bums."

"Snowboarders, you mean?"

Caroline waved her blue-veined fingers. "Yes. You need a man."

A man like Sam. She sighed, feeling battered and achy.

"And that…boy of his. Charming, the both of them."

"Yes. They are. Utterly charming."

Something in her clipped tone must have tipped Caroline off—or maybe she had just been talking to Claire.

"He's the one…isn't he? The one you're…sweet on."

She shook her head at the old-fashioned terminology, even though it was an understatement. She had passed "sweet" a long time ago. "We're friends and neighbors, that's all, Caro. He finished the kitchen at my restaurant and now he's fixing up the old Larson place down the street. That's all there is to it."

"Too bad. I love…a man…who's good with his hands."

This saucy side of Caroline always made her smile. "Don't we all," Alex murmured, even though she was trying hard not to remember just *how* good Sam Delgado could be with those big, strong hands of his.

"Remember…what I said the other day. If you like the man, and his hands, you need…to let him know. A smart girl…would snap up a handsome widower like that in…two shakes."

She was *not* a smart girl. Hadn't she proved that again and again? "I will definitely keep that advice in mind."

"I mean it. Don't waste chances. Life is…gone in a moment."

She blinked back tears, refusing to show them to her friend. Caroline was dying and she couldn't fix this with chicken broth and fresh-baked cookies.

"I do…need to rest. Please tell everyone…thank you again for me."

She kissed Caroline's sunken cheek. "I will. Sweet dreams, darling."

She left the room and pressed a hand to her stomach for only a moment before she drew in a deep breath, squared her shoulders and walked outside into the sunshine.

"YOU CAN DO IT. I'll hold the board in place and you just nail where I showed you."

"What if I mess up?" Ethan asked, a glimmer of uncertainty in those clear, blue eyes.

"That's the great thing about nails. We can always pull them out and start over," Sam answered.

"Are you sure? I don't want to ruin it."

"You won't. Look. Just hold the nail in one hand and the hammer in the other. That's the way."

"I did it!" his son exclaimed a few moments later

when the support on the sagging arbor was firmly in place.

"Yes, you did. Now every time we come past this house, you can look at the arbor and the porch steps and remember how we fixed them."

Ethan glowed with satisfaction. He was very proud of himself when he accomplished something he had once deemed hard. Sam envied that in his son, his ability to celebrate his successes instead of looking for the next mountain to climb.

He loved spending time with Ethan while they worked together on various projects around this small, trim house. Being in this close proximity to Alexandra, on the other hand, was another story. All morning, he had been aware of her working in the garden, her hair in braids and a big straw hat shielding her lovely features.

Though he tried not to stare, his attention had been drawn back to her again and again. He liked looking at her, but this was bigger than simply finding a woman beautiful. He loved the way she smiled at her friend and went up frequently to check on her, the way she teased Ethan at every opportunity, the way she brushed her hair back with her forearm to keep from smudging dirt on her face.

He had almost run the nail gun through his finger when they had been working on the porch, simply because she had stood and stretched, her hands at the base of her spine.

She had been inside with her friend for the past twenty minutes. He hoped everything was okay. Caroline didn't look good. Before she sent him over here, Claire had told him the woman was dying from cancer.

After seeing Caroline, he recognized the signs from

Kelli's last days. She had the same pale cheeks, the same hollow eyes, and Sam knew she wouldn't be enjoying this arbor he was fixing or the garden Alexandra so diligently cleared for much longer.

Alexandra would hurt when the other woman died. He wished he could protect her from the pain, absorb it onto his own shoulders somehow.

That's what a man did when he loved a woman. Comfort her. Ease her sorrows.

He frowned. What good did it do him to be in love with her when she pushed him away at every turn?

"Can we have one of these arbors in our garden?" Ethan asked.

Right now they didn't have much of a garden, just a weed patch that had been neglected for years, along with the rest of the house. "Sure. Maybe not this summer but someday. We're going to be pretty busy with that awesome tree house."

Once that would have filled him with satisfaction, the idea that he could make plans to build something in the future. He would have loved nothing more than knowing he could plant a tree in his yard tomorrow and be around to enjoy it for years to come.

Now he didn't know what was happening to him. He was beginning to second-guess everything. He was very much afraid he wouldn't be able to enjoy the house he had planned for, saved for, worked for. Not when he knew she was so close but emotionally on the other side of the galaxy.

Alexandra walked out of the house while he and Ethan were cleaning up the construction mess around the arbor. Her hat still rested on the porch chair and he could see her features clearly. The pain in her eyes, the grim knowledge that her friend was dying, reached out and punched him in the gut.

She grabbed her hat and just stood there on the porch, staring out at the garden without moving. Finally he left his son and walked up the steps they had just repaired.

"How is she?" he asked quietly.

Alexandra turned to look at him, her expression haunted. "I'm sure she'll be just fine. She just needs a little rest. Being out in the sun was too much for her."

"That's probably it." He was lying and both of them knew it.

"I'm still calling the hospice nurse."

She sank down on the rocking chair where Caroline had been sitting and pulled out her cell phone. Sam knew he probably ought to finish up here and head over to the next job Claire had given him but he couldn't seem to make himself move. Alexandra needed him, whether she wanted to admit it or not.

"I don't know," she said into the phone. "Gut instinct, I guess. I can tell she's hurting but she wouldn't let me give her one of her pain pills."

She was quiet, listening to the other side of the conversation he couldn't hear. "Well, you know how stubborn she can be. Maybe you should come over a little earlier than you planned and see if you have better luck."

She paused. "Yes. I need to go check on the caterers and I'm supposed to be helping decorate but I can certainly wait until you get here. Oh, you're that close? Good. Thank you, Helen. You've been wonderful."

She hung up and gazed down at her hat, with its flowered ribbon around the base of the brim.

"What can I do?" he asked softly, reaching for her hand.

Her fingers trembled a little and he thought she would pull away from him but she turned her hand over and clasped his fingers while Ethan played in the dirt and the clouds continued to gather.

"Nothing," she finally whispered. "You've done plenty. It will make her happy to know her house and her garden are in fine shape again."

She held his hand for a moment longer and he wanted to think he was offering some small measure of comfort. They stayed that way until a small car pulled up and a plump woman in nursing scrubs climbed out.

"That's Helen," Alexandra said, unnecessarily.

As the nurse approached, she slid her hand away from his, much to his regret. Before the other woman could reach them, she touched his arm, her fingers cool.

"Thank you," she said simply with a small, strained smile, then walked down to greet the nurse.

CHAPTER SEVENTEEN

"EVERYTHING LOOKS spectacular," she said to Evie Thorne, head of the decorating committee for the gala a few hours later. "You've really outdone yourself this year."

"Thanks, Alex. I don't know what I would have done without your help. All of you." Evie's smile encompassed her committee: Maura, Mary Ella, Angie, Charlotte. Even Ruth Tatum, Claire's mother, was there, though she had grumped through the last hour of hanging tea-light lanterns throughout the ballroom.

Though she was crazy-worried about Caroline, Alex had done her best to put her concerns away for now and concentrate on the job at hand. Helen had assured her Caroline was sleeping peacefully after reluctantly agreeing to take pain medication.

At this point, Alex couldn't do anything to help and Helen had urged her to continue on with the rest of her Giving Hope Day responsibilities.

She had a sudden, fervent wish that Brodie hadn't decided to close the restaurant to give his employees the chance to participate in the day of service. She desperately needed the distraction and comfort she found in a kitchen.

"She wouldn't want you to miss the whole day, moping over her. Now go," Helen had insisted.

She hadn't known what else to do but obey. At least she was surrounded by dear friends, all of whom continued to cast worried looks her way.

"Is there anything else we need to do?" she asked Evie.

"Not a thing, except I'm ordering everybody to get out of here and go change for the benefit."

"I understand one of us here has a hot date." Maura grinned. "Charlotte's going out with your sexy carpenter."

"He's not my carpenter," Alex said sharply. Too sharply, she realized, when her mother and Maura both gave her careful looks.

"He finished the kitchen at the restaurant," Evie said with a teasing smile. "That makes him yours, doesn't it?"

"Technically, that makes him *Brodie's* carpenter," she muttered.

"I guess that's true," Evie said. "Brodie has so many projects going right now, he'd probably like to keep Sam on permanent salary. He's got several other jobs lined up once he finishes the work at the recreation center. That's what happens when you do good work. Everybody wants a piece of you."

Couldn't she go anywhere without the conversation coming back to Sam?

"I hope you have a fantastic time, Charlotte," she said firmly.

Her pretty features colored but her eyes sparkled and she somehow managed to look embarrassed and excited at the same time. Evie knew she was trying to reach out of her comfort zone socially. About time, she thought.

"It should be fun. Most of the guys in town still look

at me as, well, the way I used to be. It's refreshing to meet someone who has no preconceptions."

Charlotte was one of the nicest people Alex knew and she had worked so hard to remake herself over the past few years. Around their circle of friends, she was warm and bright and funny but she tended to draw into herself when others were around.

"I'm a little nervous, if you want the truth," Charlotte said.

"You'll have a great time," Alex said.

"Sam's really nice," Evie added. "He comes off as gruff sometimes but it's all bluster."

Sam? Gruff? She hadn't seen that side of him, she supposed. From the moment they had met, that painfully embarrassing encounter at the restaurant when she had thought he was breaking in, he had been wry and quick-witted and extremely sexy but not at all taciturn.

Did he show a different side to her than he did to everybody else?

She really didn't want to sit here and listen to her friends psych Charlotte up for her date with the man Alex was in lo—er, seriously lusted after.

"I should probably run. I'm going to swing by and check on Caroline."

"I'll walk out with you," Charlotte said. "I need to pick up the dress I'm wearing at the boutique. I had to go shopping. Nothing I had in my closet fit."

She received a round of high-fives for that, further evidence of how far she had come. Losing eighty pounds tended to completely change a person's outlook. Alex could remember when Charlotte used to hate shopping for clothes, but now it was one of her favorite things.

She was a terrible person, Alex thought, as they walked out of the Silver Strike Lodge to the parking lot some distance away.

Charlotte was a close friend and Alex ought to be jumping handsprings for her that she had a date with a great guy she liked.

She was the one who had suggested Charlotte was perfect for Sam, right? And she was. He and Ethan both needed somebody just like her—somebody giving and loving who could nurture them.

Instead, just the thought of them together made her want to cry.

She was only emotional because of Caroline, she told herself, but the explanation rang hollow.

"Are you sure you don't mind, Alex?" Charlotte asked when they walked outside the lodge. "That I'm going to the gala with Sam, I mean?"

Uh. She scrambled for some way to respond and tried to put on a suitably bewildered expression. "Mind? Why on earth would I mind?"

"I don't know. I just…" Charlotte's voice trailed off and she chewed her lip, one old habit she hadn't managed to break. "I heard Claire say something to Maura earlier today, that's all. About you and Sam. Going out a few times."

She could feel her face go hot. "We hung out a few times, that's all. You know how I am. Never happy for long with one guy."

As much as she hated that mostly unearned reputation and the jokes her friends sometimes made at her expense, in this case it came in handy.

Charlotte scrutinized her carefully and she wondered if she had been too quick, too hearty, with her answer. “Are you sure? I like Sam, of course, I mean, who wouldn’t? He’s a great father, a hard worker, a decorated war hero.”

“Yes. He is.” *And a fantastic kisser. Don’t forget that part.*

“That’s how we met, actually,” Charlotte went on. “I knew he used to be in the army and I thought maybe he could have some suggestions for how to deal with Dylan.”

“Oh. Of course. Good idea. How is Dylan lately? I haven’t seen him around.”

“Still struggling.” Charlotte’s eyes filled with sorrow. “He’s moved into that awful cabin in Snowflake Canyon. All he does is sit around collecting his veteran benefits and drinking and slamming the door on us when we try to go talk to him.”

“I’m sorry.” Today, with her emotions so close to the surface, she wanted to cry for all that wasted potential. Dylan had been smart and fun, a natural leader.

Why did there have to be so damn much pain in the world?

Life was so much easier when she could shut it all out, keep herself from caring.

“He just doesn’t seem to be getting better, you know? He needs some kind of purpose. I don’t know, I thought maybe Sam might have some advice for how to shake him out of it. Soldier to soldier, you know? He agreed to introduce himself.”

“Did he?”

She wanted to tell Charlotte right now to stop talking. She didn’t want to hear more about the wonderful Sam Delgado, but at the same time she wanted to know everything.

Charlotte nodded, her smile soft. “He managed to track him down at the liquor store and struck up a conversation. And, get this, he offered Dylan a job on his construction crew! Can you believe that? A one-armed, half-blind carpenter?”

“Of course he did.”

Alex began to laugh and once she started, she couldn’t seem to stop. Charlotte was giving her a very concerned look, probably ready to call for the paramedics and a straitjacket, but the laughter still bubbled out.

She couldn’t tell her friend she was only laughing to keep from bursting into sobs.

What could she do with a man like Sam Delgado except love him, whether she wanted to or not?

“Dylan turned him down, of course,” Charlotte said after a moment when Alex’s laughter subsided. “Quite rudely, from what I understand. I have a feeling that won’t stop Sam.”

“He’s all about persistence, isn’t he?”

“Yes.” Charlotte nibbled her lip again. “Just so you know, I’m the one who invited him to go to the gala tonight. Sort of my way of thanking him for going out of his way to reach out to Dylan and, I don’t know, maybe help Sam settle in to Hope’s Crossing. And, to be honest, because I like him.”

“What’s not to like? He’s a wonderful guy.”

Charlotte pushed a stray lock of hair from her face and Alex wondered at the self-control it must take for her friend to run the best handmade candy store in Colorado and still lose all that weight.

“I do like Sam but…the thing is, I care about our friendship more. I’m new to the whole dating world, yeah, but I'm pretty sure poaching a good friend's man is a no-no."

With a few words, she could break up this budding relationship. Charlotte would probably still keep her date for tonight—at this late hour, it would be too rude to break it—but she certainly wouldn't go out with Sam again.

She thought about it. For a few moments, she was unbelievably tempted. If she told Charlotte she had feelings for Sam, she knew her friend would back off and slip out of the picture without a second thought.

But because she *did* have feelings for Sam and loved Charlotte dearly, too, she couldn't do it. She cared about both of them. If they had a chance to find happiness together, she couldn't be the one to interfere. Even if it seared her insides.

"You're not poaching anything," she managed to say without a single quiver in her voice. "Sam is his own man, free to go out with anybody he wants. I'm just thrilled he has the good taste to recognize how fantastic you are."

"Are you sure?" Charlotte asked, her brow still furrowed with concern.

What more did she need, for crying out loud? A freaking lie detector test?

"Positive," she answered, with as much sincerity as she could muster. She was trying to come up with something else she could say that might convince Charlotte she had no claim on Sam when her cell phone rang.

Normally she wouldn't have considered answering it in the middle of an important conversation like this one, but sudden fear clutched at her.

Caroline.

"Hello?" she asked, her stomach suddenly roiling.

"Alex, it's Helen."

She had known. Somehow, she had known.

"Caroline is slipping in and out of consciousness," the hospice nurse said. "You need to come now if you want to say goodbye."

"ARE YOU SURE you're going to be okay to drive home? It's late."

Caroline's big grandfather clock had chimed 1:00 a.m. about ten minutes earlier. The time of death was actually ten-thirty but it had taken all this time to handle the formalities, first the doctor and then the funeral home director.

"I'm fine," Alex answered, squeezing the hand of the hospice nurse. "Thank you, for everything. You're a hero."

Helen managed a watery smile. She had known Caroline all her life, too, and cared for her deeply, especially these last few months of providing end-of-life treatment.

"Get some sleep," Alex said.

"You, too, dear."

She nodded, though she knew sleep would be a long time away. She felt scoured raw, like one of the pans in her kitchen.

She locked Caroline's door with the key, wishing her son had been able to make it back from Japan for the end, but it had happened so suddenly.

One moment Caroline was drinking lemonade on her porch, the next it seemed she was clasping Alex's hand to say a final goodbye.

At least Ross had spent several days with his mother

a few months earlier. It was probably better that way, so he could remember his mother as she had been most of his life instead of the frail shadow she had become at the end.

She walked toward her vehicle down from the porch steps Sam had only just fixed. The storm of the afternoon had blown away and the night was starry and bright, sweet with the promise of summer.

She wanted to walk. To just head off through the darkened streets of Hope's Crossing and walk and walk and walk until this pain eased, but her car was here and if she left it, she would have to arrange a way to pick it up.

And her dog had been alone far too long today, though she had called one of her neighbors to let him out a few hours ago.

Her eyes felt gritty and every muscle in her body throbbed with fatigue.

As hard as the long vigil had seemed, she was deeply grateful she had been there at the end.

Caroline's last words seemed to echo through her. "Go. Live." She had thought that was the last thing Caroline could say but she had added, barely audible, one word.

"Love."

Now, remembering, the tears she had fought back all evening burst through and trickled down her cheeks as she drove through the empty streets of Hope's Crossing.

Not completely empty. On Willow Creek Road, on her way to her house, she saw a pickup truck parked in front of Charlotte's house.

Sam.

A quick glance up on Charlotte's doorstep showed her two people, shadows, really, wrapped in an embrace.

She had to jerk her gaze back to the road before she drove into a telephone pole.

She didn't think it was possible but she still had room for fresh pain to slice through the grief.

Once when she had been eight, she had broken her arm riding her bike down the hilly street behind their house. Two weeks after the cast came off, she had been jumping on the trampoline in the backyard and had fallen on it, breaking it again. The pain the second time had been far worse because the bone and sinews had still been damaged from the first break.

Her heart had been broken once, so long ago she could now barely remember it.

This time, she knew, the pain would be worse. Much worse.

Charlotte and Sam were perfect for each other but seeing them together would hurt worse than breaking her arm again and again.

Sam kept one eye on the time while he navigated through summer traffic toward the community center where he was supposed to have picked up Ethan from his summer art camp ten minutes ago.

He pulled around an RV going about five miles an hour as its driver looked for an elusive parking space. Ahead of it was a minivan with a luggage carrier on the top, probably with the same goal.

The summer tourist season was in full swing, making him grateful he had spent a few months in town during the shoulder months. Though the big tourist draw was the winter snow, summer in the area still offered a bounty of recreational activities, from fishing and camping to mountain biking and kayaking.

So far he mostly had found the increasing crowds manageable, a few annoying moose jams aside. He wasn't particularly looking forward to the crush in winter and the inevitable invasion but he figured by then he might be able to approach it with the equanimity of the other locals—that the tourists poured money into the economy, which helped build roads and schools and community centers for the year-round residents.

He was now twelve minutes late. In three more minutes, the art camp organizers would probably start calling to look for him.

He had fully intended to leave work earlier but at the last minute, Harry Lange had dropped by the recreation-center site, nearly complete, and he hadn't been able to extricate himself until now.

He really had to get this whole child-care thing figured out. Finding full-time help with Ethan had turned into a bigger challenge than he had expected, mainly because his house still wasn't at all in optimal condition, though he wanted to think he had made progress.

Meantime, for the past two weeks since Ethan had come home, he had made do with this summer camp and a crowded day-care facility Ethan wasn't very crazy about.

A few times, he had ended up taking Ethan along with him if a job site was safe enough for a seven-year-old. The situation was reaching the critical stage, though.

He pulled up in front of the aging community center, just down the road from the high school. The new recreation center in the canyon wasn't really intended to replace this one but to augment the facilities. This one had a much more convenient location to town but his construction eye picked up various areas of the building that looked in need of attention, specifically the roof and new windows.

His vague worry that he would find Ethan sitting alone on the steps of the building, forlorn and afraid he had been forgotten, didn't materialize. Instead, he found his son deep in animated conversation with Claire McKnight and her son, Owen, a few years older than Ethan.

Ethan was telling a story, apparently, with broad hand gestures and exaggerated expressions. Both Owen and Claire were laughing at whatever he said, which warmed Sam's heart.

Even with the child-care chaos, his son had adapted remarkably well to their new situation here in Hope's Crossing.

Ethan missed Nick and Cheri and their children, who had played such an important part in their lives since Kelli's death, but he seemed to be embracing this new phase easily. Sam couldn't help being deeply relieved to know his huge gamble seemed to be paying off.

"Hi, Dad!" Ethan exclaimed when he spotted him. His son grinned and ran to him, wrapping his arms around Sam's waist, and the tension that came from dealing with contractors and job headaches and tourist traffic miraculously dissipated.

"Hey, there, kiddo. Did you have a good day?"

"Yes! I made a really cool bowl with a picture of a fish on it—I painted an Atlantic salmon—and it's going to be fired in a real kiln tonight."

"Wow. Very cool. Hi, Claire. Owen."

"Hi, Mr. Delgado," Owen said politely.

"Hi, Sam."

To his delight, Claire gave him a hug in greeting around the bulk of her pregnant belly. The warm, generous welcome of so many in town still took him by surprise.

"Tell me you're not running the art camp, along with everything else in town," he said.

She looked slightly aghast at the idea. "Oh, my word, no. I was just picking up Owen. He's been coming to the art camp every year since he was old enough and loves it."

"This year we've been doing some computer animation. It's very cool!"

"Great."

Seeing Claire made him automatically think of Alexandra and he wanted to ask how she was doing. He hadn't seen her since the memorial service for her friend Caroline the week before.

He had felt a little weird about going since he didn't really know the woman, had only met her the very day of her death, but he had decided to attend for Alexandra's sake, if nothing else.

She had looked pale and distant; her features that normally glowed with life had been tight and withdrawn. He had tried several times to talk to her, to convey his sympathies, but she had studiously avoided him.

Frustrated and, yes, rather hurt that she would turn away the comfort he wanted to offer, he had finally reminded himself everyone grieved differently. He certainly had learned that after Kelli's death.

On some days after his wife's funeral, he had wanted to sit on the couch and flip aimlessly through channels on the television so he didn't have to think. Others, he had to throw himself into frenzied work to keep the gnawing pain away.

He had a feeling Alexandra was in the last camp. She hadn't been around her house much, which meant she was probably working most of the time. Their disparate work schedules complicated the situation—he generally worked early in the morning until late afternoon and she went into work early afternoons until late at night at the restaurant, which made it difficult to connect, even if she had wanted to.

Which she plainly didn't.

The two boys were talking about some of the things they enjoyed in art camp. Because of their age difference, they were apparently on different tracks and Owen was telling Ethan about some of the activities he could look forward to in future years. He found it curious that Ethan had always been comfortable talking with adults or older peers, though he sometimes grew impatient and frustrated with children his own age.

The boys' conversation gave him the chance to speak more directly to Claire than he might have if Owen and Ethan had been paying attention to them.

"How is Alexandra doing?" he finally asked. "I've tried to talk to her since the memorial service for Mrs. Bybee but I can't seem to run her to ground."

Concern darkened her eyes. "She tries to hide it and go on like nothing is wrong but she's pretty broken up inside. She and Caroline were very close. Alex even lived in Caro's basement when she came back from Europe. I haven't seen her like this in a long time, maybe even since her dad left."

"Her dad left?" He frowned, feeling stupid for his

ignorance. Why hadn't she told him about such a crucial part of her life?

Claire also seemed surprised he didn't know. "She never told you the gory details?"

"No."

"Well, I suppose I should respect her decision not to share it."

She paused, her mouth twisted into a frown. "On the other hand, it's not exactly some kind of secret, since it affected the whole family, so why not?"

Yes. Why not? he wanted to say. Any tidbit of information he could find out about Alexandra might help him understand why she struggled so hard to keep him away.

"Alex and I were in high school when he left. Her dad was a high school science teacher and very well respected in town. One day, out of the blue, he just decided he didn't want to be tied down by a family anymore. Call it a midlife crisis or whatever but James McKnight decided he wanted to pursue his professional dreams and he didn't think he could do that while he was stuck in Hope's Crossing raising six children and teaching surly teenagers about protons and neutrons. He dropped everything and left to take a job on an archaeology dig near Mesa Verde. He never came back and was killed a few years later in a site accident."

He stared at Claire. He didn't think she would make up a story but he could hardly believe such a thing could be true. "How could someone as great as Mary Ella be married to such an ass?"

She laughed. "That is a darn good question, Sam. Actually, he was a good husband and great father through most of Alex's childhood. He was really funny and nice.

I used to love going to their house because it was so… different from my own. They were always laughing about something."

"What happened? Why would he just walk away from that?"

"What makes any man decide to make choices that end up hurting people he is supposed to care about? Ego? Narcissism? Who knows? I haven't ruled out a brain tumor, as crazy as that sounds."

Claire looked pensive and sad and her hand automatically went to her abdomen. Her husband, Alexandra's brother, had been affected by the same thing, he realized.

"Alex took it hard. All of them did, but Alex and James had been really close. She was the youngest daughter and was really a daddy's girl. For a long time, she shut everybody out. I'm not sure she's ever really gotten over it, if you want the truth."

That explained so very much about Alexandra. He had asked her once if she was blaming him for somebody else's sins. Her father's abandonment must have devastated her at such a crucial point in her adolescence when she had most needed the example of a good, strong man in her life.

"I love Alex dearly, don't get me wrong, but she can be the most stubborn person on the planet," Claire continued. "I mean, why can't she see that by running away now, she's only repeating her father's stupid mistakes?"

It took a moment for her words to penetrate his thick skull. "Whoa. Wait a minute. What did you say? Who's running away?"

Claire stared at him. "Alex. I'm sorry. I thought you

would have heard by now. She's all but accepted a job to run a restaurant in Park City."

The ground seemed to shift under his feet and he almost swayed with it. He couldn't have heard her right. She couldn't be leaving! "What about Brazen? She loves that place."

"She does," Claire agreed. "None of us can figure out what's going on. She's been so excited about the restaurant opening. Her whole life, all her years of preparation and training, have been devoted to that goal. And the restaurant is doing great, exceeding even Brodie's expectations, with almost universally glowing reviews. Now, just a month after it opened, all she will say is she's ready for the next challenge."

"You're not joking. She's really leaving." He couldn't comprehend it.

"She says she is. I don't know what she thinks she'll find in Utah that she can't have here in Hope's Crossing."

Once when he was in Afghanistan in a house-to-house raid for insurgents, a flash-bang grenade had gone off about three feet from him, leaving him nauseous and unable to see or hear or think for a good two minutes.

Yeah. This was worse.

Through his shock, he looked at his relaxed, happy son talking to Owen, at the town that had welcomed them with its clean streets, well-kept houses and historic streetlamps, all sheltered by the magnificent mountains.

"You don't know why?" he managed to ask.

"Not really. I don't know if it's because of Caroline's death or if something else happened. For all I know, it could be a combination of things. She won't say. I'm her best friend and she probably tells me more than anyone else but she still keeps part of herself separate. All I know is that she told Brodie she would work at Brazen for another month while she trains one of her sous-chefs to take over and then she's leaving. She's even started looking for a renter for her house."

She loved that house. She loved her restaurant, this town, her family. Why would she walk away from all of it?

He didn't want to be a narcissistic idiot like her father but he had to wonder if it had anything to do with him and the way he had pushed her so hard to open her heart to him.

He released a heavy breath.

He wouldn't be able to live with himself if he was responsible for driving her away. He had no idea how but he was going to have to find her and make her tell him the truth.

What, exactly, he would do then, he had no idea.

CHAPTER EIGHTEEN

SHE WOULD MISS these quiet walks along the creek, just her dog and her thoughts and the silvery water rippling in the moonlight.

Friday evening, nearly two weeks after Caroline's death, Alex headed out on her usual path to the fence where the Forest Service land began, with Leo sniffling along just ahead of her.

She no longer left him on the leash when they walked along this trail, confident now that he would return to her. He never moved far ahead of her and would circle back frequently, almost as if he felt the need to protect her.

If the trail curved in a way that took them out of sight of each other, she would round the bend and he would be there with his haunches planted in the dirt, waiting for her to catch up.

Tonight he seemed content to pad along beside her, probably as happy as she that she had managed to leave the restaurant before midnight, for once.

Nan, the sous-chef she intended to train as her replacement—though she didn't know that yet—wanted to practice closing the restaurant and Alex had left her to it. She had been able to leave before it was even 9:00 p.m., something of a miracle.

Nan would do fine, she told herself. She was creative and organized, a rare combination, and a natural leader. The staff already listened to her. Brazen would do well with her at the helm—assuming she agreed to take over. Alex had talked to Brodie about it and the two of them planned to approach her sometime mid-week about the transition.

Everything was coming together. She had a family interested in renting her house and was already scouting online to find a place in Park City that would allow her to have a dog.

Her family thought she was crazy to leave right now, just as the restaurant was taking off. Maybe she was. The thought of leaving everything she cared about behind terrified her but she knew she had to do it.

She wondered what Caroline would have said. She probably would have shook her head sadly and told Alex she couldn't escape herself, no matter how hard or how far she ran.

Caroline was gone and she had taken her wisdom and her strength with her. Alex missed her terribly. Without her guidance, Alex had to rely on her own decisions and this one seemed inevitable. She couldn't stay in Hope's Crossing while Sam was here, moving on with his life.

It sounded melodramatic, even to her, but it was easier to leave than to face everything she had turned her back on.

The moon was high overhead when she reached the Forest Service gate. She leaned on it, looking up at the wild mountains in the distance while Leo headed down to the bank to drink from the cold waters of the creek.

She would miss this splendor, but she reminded herself Utah had mountains, too. Beautiful peaks, alpine valleys, creeks. Park City wasn't all that different from Hope's Crossing, actually.

The restaurant she would be taking over was already well established and successful. She didn't expect to have any problems adjusting—other than missing her family and her friends and her home.

And Sam.

She rolled her eyes at herself. How could she miss someone who had barely been in her life a few months?

She hadn't talked to him in weeks, not since the Giving Hope Day, though she knew he had been trying to reach her.

She had seen him at Caroline's memorial service and had drawn undeniable comfort by just the sight of his big, solid strength, but she couldn't face him.

He had called a couple times and she had only listened about a dozen times to his messages asking her to call him before she forced herself to delete them. Once she had been at home when he rang the doorbell, and had hidden away in her home office with the door closed, feeling stupid and immature and weak. Finally he had given up and left.

She never did have a chance to see Ethan's bedroom finished or the tree house that had begun to take shape in their backyard. Things were probably better this way. Less messy. She would slip out of town and move on and he would continue dating Charlotte and maybe marry her someday.

They would move here to Currant Creek Valley and have a few more kids, easing seamlessly into the fabric of life in Hope's Crossing.

Leo returned to her side and stuck his wet muzzle

into her hand, sensing in that uncanny way of his that she needed a little love right then.

The dog had become a wonderful companion. She had cared for him for two months now, had put ads up everywhere she could think of, had checked regularly with the Humane Society shelter to see if anyone had come looking for him. So far, nothing.

Sometime in the last month, she had gone from thinking of him as a temporary guest to wondering what she had ever done without him. She loved him and refused to give him up.

"We belong together now, don't we?"

The dog gave her that wise look he wore sometimes, as if he understood everything she said and agreed with her.

He licked her hand and then moved back down the way they had come. After a few feet on the darkened trail, he turned back with a "hurry up" sort of look.

She smiled, despite the melancholy that clung to her like a dusting of flour after a long day of baking.

"All right, all right. I'm coming. Let's go home."

The dog gave a cheerful little bark and started off. She walked behind with the flashlight.

When the trail reached the houses on Currant Creek Road, the path ended and she moved onto the road. Sam's house was dark, she saw. Good. On the way past it earlier, she had seen lights and shadows moving around inside and had just about had to reach up a hand and physically yank her face around to keep from staring.

She quickened her pace and had just reached the edge of his lawn—neatly mowed now and beginning to green up—when his voice rang out.

"Alexandra!"

She closed her eyes. A few more seconds and she would have been safe. Damn it. She opened them and turned to find him trotting down his steps toward her.

Her heart gave one quick burst of joy at seeing him again, big and strong and wonderful, before her head reminded her how foolish a feeling that was since she wasn't the one for him.

She had a couple choices here, none of them pleasant. She could sprint to her house and slam the door or she could muster her nerve and talk to the man for a few minutes.

Sprinting won out by a long shot but he reached her before she could put that particular plan into action.

"Lovely night for a walk."

"It was. We're heading home now. And yes, I have bear spray." She held up the canister attached to her flashlight.

"Smart girl."

Oh, no. She was very, very foolish. "Is Ethan in bed?"

"Yeah. He has been for the past few hours. He runs pretty hard all day. By bedtime, he's ready to drop."

She forced a smile, ignoring the pang in her heart. She still owed Ethan some brownies. Maybe she could fix them for him before she left.

"Well, good night," she started to say, intending on a quick escape, but he spoke at the same moment and missed her words.

"I had a very interesting conversation with your friend Claire this afternoon," he said.

Her stomach clutched and she wondered what Claire might have told him. "Did you? She's an interesting person. You should ask her about the time Riley fished her out of Silver Strike Reservoir in the middle of a blizzard. He saved her life. The kids, too."

"Fascinating. We didn't cover that particular story but I'll be sure to ask her about it next time. No, today she was busy telling me some other disturbing news."

She couldn't meet his dark, intense gaze. "Oh?"

"She told me you're leaving."

Darn it. Why couldn't Claire have kept her big mouth shut? And why would she feel the need to discuss the subject with *Sam,* of all people?

She shifted her weight, wondering just how much of her feelings Claire might suspect. Probably all of them.

"Care to tell me why?"

She wanted to tell him it was none of his damn business. But a heated response like that would only make him suspect that perhaps it was.

"I was handed an unbelievable opportunity. One of those chances you have no choice but to grab when they spin your way." She tried to make her voice cheerful and excited, though it took all her limited acting skills.

"My sister Rose has a friend who owns one of the top-rated restaurants in Deer Valley, with great visibility," she went on. "He's looking for a new chef, heard about Brazen from Rose and stopped by to check things out when he was in Colorado a few weeks ago. He was impressed enough to ask me if I would consider moving."

"And you said yes."

Not at first. She had initially turned him down flat. After taking a few hours to think about it, she had realized this was her best chance to leave Hope's Crossing. Maybe it was a sign, coming as it did at this particular juncture in her life.

Though it scared her to death and she was very much afraid she was making a terrible mistake, the alternative—staying here with the status quo—was worse.

"How could I say no?"

"I don't know. It shouldn't be that tough for you. You've had plenty of practice saying it to me."

She blinked but his expression was unreadable in the light from the moon and the streetlights.

"I can't believe you're leaving only weeks after opening Brazen. Shouldn't you be savoring the challenge of making your own restaurant top rated, not taking over what somebody else has already accomplished?"

His words sliced right to the bone. It was ridiculous, really. She knew it was. Giving up her hopes, her dreams, her *life,* because of a man.

Why did he have to come to her town and ruin *everything?*

"This way has a great deal less pressure. Brazen is doing well right now—"

"Amazingly well, from what I've heard. People are driving up from Denver just to say they ate there."

Pleasure spiked through her but she tamped it down. "That could change in a moment. The dining public can be capricious. In the early days of a restaurant, one bad night or one bad review can be disastrous. The Park City restaurant has a track record and a fan base. All the glory with none of the pressure."

She said the words with a flippancy she didn't feel.

"So that's why you're leaving. Because this was an opportunity you couldn't pass up."

She forced a smile. "What other reason would there be?"

"I don't know. You tell me. Two weeks ago, you were

the damn poster girl for the Chamber of Commerce, full of all the reasons why Hope's Crossing is the perfect town. Utopia with a ski lift. Now you're ready to just walk away from all of that."

She didn't owe him any explanations. She should tell him good-night and walk the few hundred yards to her own house, just take her dog and go. As tempting as that was, she didn't want him to think she was running away—from this discussion or from anything else.

"Just because I love Hope's Crossing doesn't mean I can't be happy in Park City. Maybe I just need a change. Plenty of people start over somewhere new. You did."

"And that's the whole point, isn't it?"

She frowned. "What do you mean by that?"

He fell silent, his gaze troubled as he absently patted Leo. "I've been running this through my head ever since talking to Claire today," he finally said. "It sounds crazy. Completely crazy. But I have to ask. If I weren't here, living down the street, would you still be all ready to throw your life away, everything you've worked so hard to build here, and move to another state? Away from your family, the home you just bought, the restaurant you've always wanted?"

Those nerves in her stomach now clutched so tightly she couldn't seem to draw a breath. No. Oh, no. She couldn't let him think that. While she managed a shaky little laugh, she was very much afraid she didn't fool him for a second.

"Wow. Talk about unbridled conceit."

"Yeah, maybe. But right now, listening to you talk about opportunities you couldn't pass up and taking the easy route to success, my bullshit meter is spinning off the charts."

"Maybe you ought to have somebody take a look at that."

She couldn't do this, lie to him, with any hopes of convincing either of them. And the truth was, she didn't owe him any explanation. Why should she bother to try? She gripped Leo's leash and took off blindly in the direction of her house but only made a few steps before he caught her, reaching for her arm.

"Alexandra." The troubled sincerity in his voice stopped her progress more effectively than the fact that he was a six-foot, one-hundred-eighty-pound former Army Ranger, and she froze.

"Tell me the truth. Please. Does your decision to leave have anything at all to do with me?"

He still had his hand on her arm and she could feel the heat of him radiating through her muscles, her nerves, straight to her center. How could she flat-out lie to him? Her decision to leave had *everything* to do with him, but she certainly couldn't tell him that.

"Don't be ridiculous." She tried to sound dismissive and composed, hoping he didn't hear the shaky note to her voice. "You really think I'm the kind of woman who would completely change my life because of a man?"

"Classic diversionary tactic. Answer a question with a question. Which was really no answer at all. If you can look me in the eyes and tell me straight up that your decision to leave has nothing to do with me, I'll back off."

She gazed at him solemnly, drawing on every ounce of deception and subterfuge she might possess while she prayed he couldn't see the truth in her eyes. "My decision to leave has nothing to do with you."

"Liar." He said the single word softly, damningly.

She shrugged her arm away. "I'm too tired for this

right now. Go to bed, Sam. Why don't you take that colossal ego with you?"

She took a few more steps down the street, Leo beside her, trotting obediently along. Poor, confused dog.

Again Sam followed after her. This time he moved in front of her to block her way. They were now directly under the streetlight in front of Mr. Phillips's house and she could easily see his expression. For once it was open and clear. He didn't look angry. He looked upset, his eyes dark with concern and with something else. A soft, warm tenderness that terrified the hell out of her.

"What if I were the one to leave? Would you stay then?"

She stared at him, oddly aware of the light glowing around him and the bright spangle of stars above that. "You're not leaving."

"But what if I did? Ethan and I have only been here a few months. It would be easy enough for us to make a new start somewhere else. Easier than it would be for you."

She felt cold, suddenly, as if all the heat in the world had been sucked away, and then it rushed back, scorching through her like a brush fire. He would do that, for her? Pick up his son and walk away from the life he had spent these past months building so carefully?

She didn't know what to say, what to do. Suddenly she was angry at him, furious that he would even make such an offer.

"You…you can't just leave. You have a business here. A house."

"You have a restaurant. And also a house," he pointed out. "That's not stopping *you* from running away."

"It's not the same. I don't need you to be some kind of martyr for me. How pathetic do you think I am?"

He stared at her. "Where the hell did that come from? I don't think you're pathetic at all, but I do think you're running from me, from what we could have together."

How could he know that? She closed her eyes, gripping Leo's leash to keep from bursting into tears. "We don't have anything together, Sam. We kissed a handful of times. That's it. For heaven's sake! You really think I would pack up and change my whole life because of a few kisses?"

"Maybe not. Maybe I'm crazy."

He was silent and she thought for one blessed moment he was going to give up and return to his house and his son and his life, but he shoved his hands in his back pockets, a funny little smile playing around that expressive mouth.

"No maybe about it. I'm definitely crazy. By the way," he added, almost as an afterthought, "I'm in love with you. Does that make any kind of a difference?"

All her bluster and bluff seeped away and she could do nothing but stare at him, feeling as if the street beneath her feet had just sunk into Currant Creek. "You are not."

He laughed roughly. "I'm pretty sure I know my own mind, after thirty-eight years on the planet. I've known I loved you for some time now. I'm sorry if it comes as a shock to you."

Just for a moment, joy bloomed through her like Caroline's flowers, bright and sunny and glowing with color and life, but harsh reality was a chilling wind that shriveled it like frost-kill.

"You're not in love with me," she said through lips

that felt as frozen as the rest of her and didn't seem to want to cooperate. "You might think you are but it's all part of this fantasy you've built up in your head, that once you move to this perfect little town, you'll have everything you ever wanted."

"Oh. Is that what it is?"

"Yes! But you're wrong. Hope's Crossing isn't perfect. People leave. They cheat on each other, they lie, they drink and steal and walk out on their families. They die."

To her horror, her voice broke on the last word and the tears she had been fighting forever threatened to burst free.

"Oh, baby. I'm sorry." He looked so wonderful there in the streetlight, big and strong and steady, and she wanted to sink into his arms and never leave. Instead, she forced herself to straighten shoulders that ached with strain.

"It's not real. You're not in love with me, Sam."

"Will you stop saying that? I love you, and I'm not about to stand here in the street and argue about it with you! If I were going to daydream about the perfect woman to fit into this Hope's Crossing fantasy you think I have, you really think I'd pick a smart-ass chef who fights me at every step and who's too damn stubborn to see what's right in front of her?"

He was angry. Heat flared in his eyes, and his jaw had hardened. He looked every inch a soldier—big, tough, scary.

"I love you," he said once more, and she could see he was fighting to tamp down his temper. "Maybe if I say it enough times you'll finally believe me."

She had no choice, she realized, gripping Leo's leash

so tightly she could feel the imprint of it on her palm. She had to tell him. Everything. Every terrible detail. Then he would finally see she wasn't the kind of woman who deserved him.

"You can't love me, Sam. You don't even know me."

"I think I know you better than anybody."

"Not this."

She drew in a ragged breath that seemed to slice her lungs and blurted out the words she had never spoken aloud.

"I had a baby. I had a baby and he died. Because of me."

THROUGH THE EDGES of the temper he rarely let get away from him, Sam heard her words as if from a long distance away. A baby. She had given birth to a baby who had died.

He hadn't expected that one. Shock froze him for just a moment but then he forced himself to speak.

"What happened?"

"I don't… It's ugly. So ugly."

He didn't need to hear—didn't *want* to hear, but he sensed she needed to tell him, for reasons he didn't quite understand.

He glanced back at his house and then at her. "Ethan could wake up. I need to be there. Will you come back and tell me? We can sit on the porch."

"I don't talk about it. Ever. To anyone. Not even… My family doesn't even know."

How could she have kept something like that a secret from her big, boisterous, loving family? His heart ached that she had carried that burden alone.

"It's your choice. Tell me or don't. Nothing you have to say will change the way I feel about you anyway."

"You can't know that."

"Not unless you tell me."

This was the reason she didn't let him close. Somehow he knew it. Just that afternoon, Claire had told him Alex kept part of herself separate. This. This was the part she didn't share with anyone.

He wanted to scoop her up and hold her close and tell her his shoulders were strong enough to help her carry any burden.

"Come on up to the porch, so I can hear my son if he wakes up. I can keep the light off if you want."

Confidences always seemed easier in the dark, something he had learned in some pretty dark and ugly places in the desert.

She drew in a breath that sounded shaky and hollow, as if she wasn't drawing air deeply enough into her lungs. "Yes. I…need to tell you."

They walked up his sidewalk without talking or touching, her dog leading the way. She stood for a moment on the porch, her hands tightly clasping the dog's leash.

"Can I get you something to drink?'"

She shook her head, her features in shadow. She didn't seem to quite know what to do, what to say, so he made the first move, taking the ladder-back chair and leaving her free to sit on the porch swing.

After a moment's hesitation, she sat stiffly. The chains rattled a little with the shift in weight then stilled.

She unhooked the dog's leash and Leo immediately moved to Sam for affection. He petted him for just a moment then surreptitiously pushed him to Alex, sensing she needed the dog more than he did right now.

"This must have happened during your time in Europe," he finally prodded.

In the dim light, her eyes were huge against her shadowy features as she stared at him. "How did you know that?"

"You said you hadn't told your family. The way I see it, as close as you all are, as much as they love you, the only way you could have kept something like a pregnancy from them would be by living across the world."

"Yes. I…I was in culinary school."

She was quiet for another moment and then she pulled her knees up onto the swing and wrapped her arms around them, drawing into herself. "I was so stupid. From the very beginning."

He let the silence linger. When she spoke, her voice was crisp, almost as if she had detached herself from the story.

"As part of my training, I worked in various restaurants in France and then Italy, learning different techniques. It was a wonderful adventure and I loved every minute of it. About a year into it, I started work at a restaurant near Florence when I…fell in love. Or thought I did. Marco was the chef and he was…brilliant. In the kitchen and out of it. Just this…irresistible force."

She drew in another breath. "We had to keep our growing relationship a secret, of course. It would cause friction among the staff if people knew about us. Resentment, petty jealousies, that sort of thing. The political games played in a fine kitchen are as complicated and cutthroat as the Borgias."

"I've heard that."

"Maybe that was part of the excitement, the forbidden aspect of it. For several months we lived that way, with him sneaking into my little flat in the middle of the night or taking me away for weekends in the countryside."

She paused. "And then I discovered I was pregnant."

She was silent for a long moment while a breeze blew through, rustling the leaves of the tree beside the porch.

"I was thrilled," she finally said. "Beyond thrilled. I had all these ideas that we would marry, I would move to Italy permanently and we could run this wonderful restaurant together. It was a magical time. In my head, anyway. I didn't tell him right away. Even then maybe I sensed something wasn't quite right between us, but I told myself I wanted to wait until the moment was perfect. He could…have these moods sometimes, which I told myself was all part of his passionate, creative genius."

Sam figured he had left his violent days behind him when he took his discharge, but right now he was struck by a fierce urge to rip a certain passionate genius into tiny, creative little parts.

"Finally, when I was three months along and starting to show—six or seven months after we began seeing each other—I set the stage. I cooked him my very best meal, I spent a week's salary on a new dress, I even had the pastry chef at the restaurant prepare Marco's favorite dessert. *Semifreddo* with grappa-poached apricots. You'll never see that in my restaurant, by the way."

An owl hooted somewhere on the Currant Creek but other than that, it felt as if they were alone in the night.

"You can probably guess what happened next. I finally told him about the pregnancy over dessert. He…

wasn't happy. Said I was a stupid American girl and why did I have to ruin everything. He said all manner of things about me, worst of all that my *alla bolognese* was bland."

This would have made him laugh under other circumstances but right now he couldn't find anything about this story funny.

"Only then did I realize he was right. I had been incredibly stupid. As he finally so clearly pointed out, we would never be together. All this time while I had been dreaming of the time we could make our relationship public—when we could start our happily-ever-after together—he had been going home every night when he left my bed to sleep beside his wife. The wife I had no idea existed until that night."

He remembered that first day he had met her at Brazen, when she had grilled him so intently about whether he was married or not before she would consider dating him. The pain of that treachery and how she had unknowingly betrayed another woman must be etched deeply inside her.

"I have no excuse. I should have seen it a million times over, I just… I guess I didn't want to see. I wanted to blame the language barrier, since my Italian was terrible and he refused to speak English, but really it was my own stupidity."

"You were a young woman living in a foreign country and you made a mistake."

"I wasn't that young. Twenty-five. Not some naive teenager. I was certainly old enough to suspect something when the man who claimed to love me would only see me in secret."

He was willing to bet the charming Italian son of a

bitch was probably older, with worlds' more experience. She had probably transferred all her pain over losing her father to him, but he wasn't sure she would appreciate that insight right now.

"That's not the worst of it," she said, her voice small.

"What happened?"

"He fired me. Well, technically I quit before he could, but he told me he didn't want me to come back to his *ristorante* ever, with much dramatic gesturing and throwing things around. And since the apartment was owned by the *ristorante,* of course I had to leave there *immediatamente.*"

Now he *really* wanted to find the bastard. Anybody who could throw a pregnant young woman out into the street deserved the full force of an angry ex-Ranger trained in hand-to-hand combat.

"I couldn't see any other choice in the matter so I packed my things and I left Florence. What else could I do?"

"You didn't come home to Hope's Crossing, though."

"No. I couldn't. I… My older sister Maura had had a baby on her own when she was a teenager, my niece Sage, and I saw how hard that was for her. I heard the whispers and the way certain people looked down on her for it. Call me selfish, but I didn't want to go through that or put my family through it. I didn't want to tell my family what an idiot I had been and I certainly didn't want the baby. My heart was broken and I didn't want any part of Marco in my life."

"Completely understandable."

"I had some vague idea of giving the baby up for adoption, maybe, but I needed to work to survive, so I took a job at a restaurant near Bologna. A terrible place, with a horrible little man for a chef."

The breeze sighed through the treetops and she sighed along with it. "I worked sixteen-hour days, six days a week. Some days I forgot to eat. I didn't go to a doctor. I just wanted to pretend the whole thing hadn't happened. I had loved him so much and I still couldn't believe he didn't want me. That he could hurt me like my…" Her voice trailed off abruptly.

"Like your father did," he finished, wishing he could reach out and touch her. An arm around her shoulder, a hand on her arm. Anything.

"Claire *does* have a big mouth," she said after a moment.

"She cares about you."

"Yes. I couldn't believe he could hurt me like my father. He abandoned us, and Marco basically did the same."

This was why she was so careful to keep her relationships light and casual. The men in her life had been assholes, all of them, and she wanted to remain in control so she didn't have to risk being hurt.

He had no idea how he could heal a lifetime of disappointments.

"You should know," he said carefully, "nothing you've told me makes me suddenly discover I can't possibly be in love with you."

She looked at him, her face pale and lovely against the shadows around her and completely solemn. "Oh, just wait."

The dog moved closer to her, resting his chin on her leg, and her hands absently moved through his fur.

"When I was about six months along, still working

sixteen-hour days on my feet in a hot, crowded restaurant kitchen and not taking any kind of care of myself or the baby, I started having pain under my rib cage. Severe pain."

He ached for her, for what he sensed was coming.

"It went on for two days. I didn't go to a doctor. In fact, I continued working and told myself it would pass. On the second day, I fainted just before the dinner rush while I was slicing tomatoes for the *insalata caprese* and I started hemorrhaging all over the floor."

His own blood ran cold thinking of her, a young woman alone in a foreign country where she didn't speak the language well in dire need of medical attention.

"I was rushed to the hospital where it turned out the pain I had been so stubbornly ignoring had been a placental abruption. The baby didn't survive. I nearly didn't."

He could feel his insides tremble at the thought of how close she might have come. "But you did."

"Yes. More or less intact. Well, less, actually. They had to take out everything to save my life. All the girly parts, I mean."

She said the words as if they had some great significance, but he was just a big dumb carpenter and didn't understand why she thought that would matter to him.

"And where is the part where you killed your baby?" he asked.

She stared. "Haven't you been listening? If I had taken proper care of myself, seen a doctor, stayed off my feet for five minutes, maybe, the baby might have survived. Instead, I was so busy hating myself for my stupidity and naïveté and hating Marco for being an ass and even hating the baby for ruining everything that I let an innocent child die because of it."

Again he chose his words carefully. Everything—*everything*—hinged on him not screwing this up. "Sorry, but I'm not seeing it. You made poor choices, but you didn't kill your child."

She made a strangled noise as if gearing up to argue and he purposely hardened his voice. "I served three tours in Afghanistan and Iraq. I know what it means to kill someone, defending myself or my platoon or the mission. I also know the difference between that and an emotionally battered young woman alone in a foreign country neglecting her health while she tries to survive. Trust me, there's no comparison."

CHAPTER NINETEEN

DESPITE THE SUMMER EVENING, she shivered at his blunt words.

He had killed people. She probably shouldn't have been surprised. He had been a Ranger, after all, but it was hard to reconcile the soldier he had once been with the man who talked to Ethan with such patient gentleness and taught him to use a hammer and was building the world's best tree house for him.

You made poor choices but you didn't kill your child.

The words seemed to seep inside her, finding all the dark, ugly corners she didn't want to explore. She *had* been young, not nearly as sophisticated and urbane as she had wanted to pretend when she took off alone to Europe. She had grown up in a tight-knit family, in a small, conservative town. She had made really stupid choices but she didn't know anybody who couldn't say the same.

The doctors afterward had told her that even with the proper medical care and attention, the placenta had been weak and might have abrupted anyway. She hadn't wanted to believe them. It was easier to blame herself but now, a dozen years later, she could view that young woman she had been with a little more compassion.

"In the end," she whispered now, "when I woke up after the surgery and the doctors told me what had happened and that the baby was dead, I…finally I wanted him again. So much."

The tears began to fall and she couldn't seem to stop them and she stopped trying. She hadn't cried in forever and now, here in the darkness with Sam, she cried for her empty arms and a young woman's shattered dreams and all the chances she had lost along the way.

Sam swore and rose from his chair. Before she could protest, he sat beside her on the porch swing he had hung and pulled her into his arms.

In some corner of her mind, she knew she should protest but he felt so wonderful—strong, steady, solid—and she couldn't resist. He held her for a long time while she wept and she was vaguely aware of a light pressure as he kissed the top of her head softly, as he might a child who had come to him with a bad dream.

The moment was almost unbearably tender.

"You need to forgive yourself, Alexandra," he said, his voice low. "Take it from a man who went through a pretty rough time after a few missions, where I second-guessed decisions, my own and others. People make mistakes. You can either let it eat away at you from the inside until you're hollowed out and have nothing good left. Or you can learn to accept that none of us can change our past. All we can do is move forward and make something better out of the rest of our days."

His words resonated with truth. She had blamed herself for too long. It was time to let go, to embrace what she had done with her life in the years since and the person she had become.

Sam had moved forward. He had come from a rough childhood and had made something of his life by serving his country. He had fallen in love, married, then had lost his wife tragically.

Many men might have become bitter and railed at fate, yet Sam had this core of goodness in him that made him push past the disappointments and sadness and seek out something better for his son than he had experienced.

To a man like him who had known both the horrors of war and a tumultuous personal life, the quiet streets and quaint houses of Hope's Crossing must represent unimaginable peace.

She couldn't let him leave this place he already loved. She didn't want to go, either, but how could she stay?

"For a long time, I thought the fact that I can't have more children was punishment for my mistakes."

"I hope you know better now."

"I think some things just happen. Not for a reason, not as some punishment from a higher power, not as part of some master plan. They just are."

"You can still be a mother, you know."

With his arms still around her, he shifted so she could see his face, and in the pale light on the porch, he looked serious and intense. "I know a certain seven-year-old boy who could use someone like you in his life."

"Sam." She clamped down hard on the wild joy fighting to flutter through her again at the implication behind his words.

"No. Listen to me. You keep telling me how you're not what I need, what Ethan needs. Let me tell you all the reasons I think you're wrong."

She couldn't bear this. How could she possibly push

him away again when everything within her wanted to stay right here in his arms?

"You make me laugh," he said. "I haven't laughed in so long. Even before Kelli got sick, I was so busy being a husband and father and a good soldier that I didn't often pause to just savor each moment. When I touch you, when I see you, when I simply *think* about you, I'm happy."

She wanted to block out his words, knowing they would only make this harder, but each one seemed to imprint itself on her heart.

"You treat my son with respect and affection and see beyond that brain of his to the reality that despite it, he's still just a boy who loves brownies and dogs and having fun."

"He's a wonderful boy, Sam. How can anyone who meets him help but love him?"

"He doesn't respond to everyone the way he has to you, believe me. He can be stiff, awkward, even downright rude. But when you talk to him, he knows your interest is genuine."

He paused and his hand caressed her cheek with such sweetness she almost cried again. "You care about everyone like that. You tell me how prickly and difficult you are. I see a woman who gives her love freely and generously. Who prepares food for people who can't take care of themselves, who helps a dying friend with her garden, who takes in a dirty, bedraggled stray dog because that's just the kind of person she is."

Leo, curled up at their feet, slapped his tail against the floor of the porch, almost as if he understood Sam was talking about him.

"I love you, Alexandra. Nothing you've told me tonight changes that. I love you in spite of all the reasons you think I shouldn't. In part, maybe, *because* of those reasons. You're the person you are today because of everything that has happened to you."

She gazed at him in the slanted moonlight as his words and the tenderness in his eyes seemed to slide through her, shining the brilliant beacon of hope in all those dark corners.

He loved her. He knew the very worst about her but somehow he loved her anyway. This man, who understood all about pain and loss and regret, was offering her a miraculous chance to move beyond the hurt.

She had been stupid when she was twenty-five, yes. She wasn't twenty-five anymore and she wanted to think she had learned a little something along the way.

If she walked away from this, from Sam and Ethan and the chance he was offering her to embrace a future with them, she deserved to spend the rest of her days miserable and alone.

Love, bright and joyful, bloomed in those once-dark corners like the most brilliant flower garden, like a perfect, crisp-on-the-outside, springy-and-light-on-the-inside soufflé.

It was so big, so sweet and lovely as it swelled and burst inside her, she couldn't contain it. She did the only thing she could. She reached up and kissed the corner of his mouth, this man who had seen beneath her sharp, thorny edges to the woman she wanted to become.

She felt the sharp inhalation of his breath against her cheek but beyond that, he didn't move for several long moments and then finally his mouth moved on hers and he returned the kiss with dazzling sweetness.

His familiar Sam-smell of laundry soup and cedar

shavings filled her senses and she had to fight down a bubble of laughter, of pure happiness. She kissed him fiercely, arms tightly around his neck as if she feared the swing would topple them both to the floor.

When she finally broke the kiss and eased away long moments later, his dazed eyes reflected the starlight.

"Just so you know," he said, his voice gruff, "I don't think I will ever understand the way that mind of yours works."

"You do understand me. Better than anyone ever has."

He smiled that slow, sexy smile she loved so much and she had to kiss him all over again.

"Does this mean you're not going to be taking a job in Park City?" he asked sometime later.

She thought of all she had been willing to give up—and, more importantly, what she would gain now if she stayed. But first, she needed to be completely clear.

"What about Charlotte?" she had to ask.

He stared. "Charlotte Caine? There's a non sequitur for you. What does she have to do with any of this?"

"I saw the two of you. The night of the gala. You were at her house on the porch. She was in your arms."

He looked shocked first, then his features lit up with as close to a grin as she had ever seen there. "You were jealous!"

"No, I wasn't…." Her voice trailed off and she sighed. "Okay. Yes, I was. Insanely jealous. But only because I thought she was so perfect for you. I love Charlotte but, right at that moment, I wanted her to choke on some of her own blackberry fudge. Which is fantastic, I must admit."

He blinked. "Wow."

"What? I would have done the Heimlich. Eventually."

He laughed and she didn't think she had ever heard a more beautiful sound. How could she have moved so abruptly from utter despair to this sweet, bubbling joy?

She thought of Caroline's advice to her. This was what she meant. *Take a chance. Embrace life.*

Caroline had been afraid to risk being hurt again so she had spent most of her life alone. Alex was afraid, she would be lying if she didn't admit that, but she also knew with all her soul that Sam was a man she could count on.

"So," she said lightly. "Back to Charlotte and the gala."

"You might have seen us embracing," Sam said, a little cautiously.

She could be jealous here but she wasn't. She had complete trust in him, which she found breathtaking.

"That was probably right around the time I told her that I happened to be in love with someone else. You, for the record."

"You did not."

"Ask her. She mentioned, by the way, that she thought you just might share those feelings. Something about you being entirely too quick to assure her how wonderful I was."

She blushed, remembering that scene with Charlotte after they had decorated the ballroom together.

"There's that ego again," she teased.

"Was she right? About your feelings?"

She heard a thread of uncertainty in his voice and realized this big, tough soldier could be as vulnerable as she was when it came to laying his heart bare.

She was overwhelmed, consumed, with love for him.

He was such a good man and she knew she didn't deserve him, but in that moment, she didn't care. She wanted him, whether she deserved him or not.

Maybe that was the very best part of loving someone. Wanting to do anything she could to become the kind of woman who could feel worthy of a man like him.

"Charlotte can be an amazingly astute person," she finally said, her voice prim.

His laugh held joy and a trace of relief. He kissed her, his mouth warm against the cooling air.

"Say it," he ordered against her skin. She wanted to respond in some light, teasing way but sensed he needed the words as much as she did.

She eased away and slid a hand to the curve of his cheek. "Yes, I love you, Sam. I loved you then, I love you now. I probably fell in love that very first night we spent together at the Lizard. I flirted and teased and joked but I think I was tumbling hard, even then."

"Yet you wouldn't even agree to see me again."

"Because you scared me to death! You were so… well, you."

"I'm afraid I can't do much about that."

Her hand curled into a fist and she trailed it down to his hard chest, where she could feel each pulse of his heart. "I don't want you to change anything. I love you exactly as you are. Big, tough, scary. Wonderful. I love you more than I ever imagined possible. You're everything I never knew I needed."

He smiled with pure joy and wrapped his arms around her, then he kissed her there on his porch swing while the creek rippled past and his son slept peacefully inside and the lights of their town twinkled in the moonlight.

EPILOGUE

"ARE YOU COMPLETELY exhausted yet?"

"Who, me? You must be joking?" Alex grinned at her mother across the work island in Harry Lange's gleaming, gorgeous kitchen, with its gourmet appliances and extravagant cookware. "I'm in heaven. Who wouldn't be?"

"Oh, I don't know. Maybe somebody who's been on her feet since 5:00 a.m."

Actually, the clock beside her bed had read four-thirty when she tumbled out to take care of the turkey, but she wasn't about to admit that to her mom. "Not me. I'm full of energy. Why wouldn't I be? I'm surrounded by two of my favorite things, food and family."

She was completely in her element, even if she did feel a little odd and off-kilter to be cooking somewhere besides her mother's small kitchen, where she had helped prepare dozens of Thanksgiving dinners.

She had always believed traditions were meant to shift and morph to meet new circumstances, though, and this wasn't such a bad change. Harry's spacious kitchen was tricked out better than her own place at Brazen, with all the very best culinary toys.

Just now, the kitchen was lushly redolent of delicious things cooking: her garlic smashed potatoes, her grandmother McKnight's famous stuffing recipe, with her own twist of using venison sausage instead of pork, and of course the huge tom turkey resting on the sideboard, ready to be carved in a few moments.

"Well, everything looks and smells divine," Mary Ella said, leaning in to kiss her cheek and tuck a stray blond strand of hair behind her ear. "But of course, you already knew that."

"I did quite outdo myself, didn't I?" she preened.

"The modesty of my daughters is always so heartwarming."

She grinned. "Okay, okay. We both know I can't take all the credit. This is a team effort, as always. I'm just the traffic cop, telling everybody what to do. Anyway, I have a feeling the pies Claire and Rose made last night are going to steal all my poor turkey's thunder."

She gestured to a nearby counter where pumpkin, blackberry and pecan pies waited in all their glory, golden crusts and all.

"The crowd is growing restless out there. How much longer, do you think?"

She added one more shake of coarse ground sea salt to her potatoes. "That does it for my part. The only thing left is the gravy."

"I guess that's my cue."

Alex made a mean turkey gravy, but she was also honest enough to admit it couldn't compare to her mother's.

"I've already transferred the drippings for you." She pointed to the Wolf range.

"Perfect. You'd probably like a minute to freshen up while I finish up here and then we can let everyone know we're ready."

"Thanks, Mom."

She took off her apron, hung it on a hook inside the pantry and headed for the powder room conveniently located just off the kitchen. Her dressy white blouse glimmered in the tasteful lighting of the bathroom, accented by a necklace she had made in one of Evie's classes a few months earlier. It was made of semiprecious stones and Czech glass beads floating at intervals on a nearly invisible fragile silver wire.

Hidden beneath it, she pulled out another length of chain nestled between her breasts. Threaded along it was an exuberantly beautiful emerald ring, so lovely it stole her breath every time she saw it.

She couldn't wait to wear the bling all the time—except when she was cooking, of course.

But not yet.

Three days from now, Harry and Mary Ella would be marrying in this very house. All her family was already in town for the big event, including Rose and her family and Lila from California.

As silly as it might seem, she figured her mother deserved to have these magical three days of attention without Alex intruding with her own news, stealing a little of her thunder. When things calmed down a little, maybe at Christmas, she and Sam would announce their engagement—though she doubted anyone in the family would be particularly surprised, since they had become inseparable these past months.

Since that far-distant summer night when she had hovered on the edge of despair and had yanked herself back to find a shining future waiting, everything with Sam and Ethan had come together perfectly. They were like a new recipe with disparate elements that somehow seemed to meld and complement each other to breathtaking effect.

Who would ever have guessed she could be so utterly, completely, outrageously happy?

She studied the ring for a moment more, then tucked it back against her heart and walked out into the great room of Harry's estate. The room was vast and high-ceilinged but the McKnight brood still managed to fill the space.

Lila and Rose, the twins, were chattering in the corner while Sage seemed to be chiding her grandfather about something as Harry's son, Jack, looked on with an amused smile. Her oldest sister, Angie, was deep in conversation with her two daughters and Maura, and several of the men were loudly protesting a ref's call in the football game showing on Harry's retractable big-screen television.

Sam was in the middle of the action, of course, on the sofa watching the game. He looked big, hard, tough—and completely adorable cradling a little pink-wrapped bundle in his arms.

By some unerring sense, he seemed to know when she started to head in his direction. He looked up from his game-related conversation and smiled at her over the head of three-month-old Emma, daughter to Claire and Riley, and the most beautiful little cherub around.

Her insides did a long, slow melt and she was suddenly awash with love for him and so happy she didn't quite know what to do with it.

"Give," she ordered when she reached him.

"Do I have to?" he asked. When she nodded he complied, reluctantly handing over her goddaughter, who smelled of baby lotion, milk and heaven.

He slid over on the sofa to make room and she plopped down beside him, savoring this perfect, crystalline moment—surrounded by family, with a baby on her lap and Sam's arm across her shoulders.

A moment later, a herd of the younger children came galloping through with many squeals and much laughter as they chased Owen, who seemed to be holding a sought-after toy just out of their reach.

One of the laughing children broke away from the pack and veered in their direction.

Ethan leaned against her knees, looking down at Emma with that slightly fascinated, slightly terrified expression only a seven-year-old boy can wear while looking at such a tiny creature.

"I'm starving, Alex," he announced dramatically. "When are we eating?"

She smiled and rested her free hand on his sweaty curls. "It shouldn't be long now. My mom is finishing up the gravy and then I think we're good."

"Yay! If I don't eat something soon, my blood sugar is going to plummet and I'm seriously going to fall over!"

She laughed. "We wouldn't want that to happen. Can your blood sugar hang on a few more moments?"

"I suppose."

He raced off after the other kids, apparently staving off his impending collapse by force of will.

Alex watched him go, crazy for him. He had accepted her in his life with a sweet willingness that still made her want to cry sometimes.

In a way, Ethan had actually been the first to propose to her the night before.

He and Sam had set the stage beautifully. They

had all gone for an evening walk, bundled against the cold and with Leo leading the way, to enjoy some of the twinkly holiday lights that had begun peeking out around town.

She had known something was up, since Ethan had just about been bursting with excitement, as what had appeared to be a casual, random walk had eventually led to Sam's latest renovation site, a decrepit old warehouse he was working to turn into a small indoor mall a few blocks off Main Street.

Sam said he had to check something and suggested they all come inside to warm up a little.

When he flipped the lights on, she saw a huge message across the length of one wall, two-foot-high letters written in chalk in childish handwriting: *Will you marry us?*

"I love you, Alex. I want to spend forever with you," Sam had said.

"I really, really, really want you to be my second mom," Ethan had added.

Her heart bursting with joy, she had sniffled and laughed and hugged them.

She sighed with contentment now, and Sam caught her gaze with that secret, sexy little smile she loved, before he turned back to argue with Riley about a call.

She considered one of the very best things about her relationship with Sam was how seamlessly he and Ethan had merged into her family. They all loved him, from her mother to her sisters and even the brothers-in-law. He, in turn, loved them all back. While her big, loud, boisterous family sometimes drove her bonkers, Sam reveled in all of them.

If she wasn't completely convinced he loved her—

much to her constant joy and wonderment—she might have thought he had only proposed to her so he could become a permanent part of the McKnight clan.

Mary Ella suddenly appeared in the doorway and Harry immediately muted the football game with the remote that he probably wouldn't relinquish to anyone.

"All right, gang. I think everything's ready."

Alex probably should have been helping set everything out but she figured she had done her part by cooking most of the food.

The kids cheered.

"Finally!" Ethan exclaimed in that dramatic tone again.

"Agreed," Harry said with a chuckle and led the way to his dining room, with its sweeping views up the canyon to the Silver Strike Resort.

She reluctantly relinquished Emma to Claire and followed Sam and Ethan to find a spot at the table.

Harry was probably the only one in town with a house big enough to comfortably contain all her siblings and their respective families. Even so, it was a squeeze around his massive dining table to accommodate everyone.

As host, Harry stood at the head of the table until everyone was settled.

"It's been quite a few years, hasn't it?"

Alex looked around at her family and thought of the many changes they had seen—tragedies and joys, heartaches and second chances.

"We have much to be grateful for," Harry said. "New opportunities. New life. New marriages."

He reached for her mother's hand and, with a courtly sort of gesture quite incongruous to his bluff personality, he kissed the back of her fingers. Mary Ella blushed and a few of the younger kids made exclamations of disgust.

Beneath the table, she felt Sam's hand on her knee, strong, firm, comfortable. On her other side, Ethan nudged her arm with his shoulder and tried his best to wink at her over their little secret, though he hadn't quite perfected the expression and it came out more as a funny little spasm of half his face.

"Despite the past," Harry went on, "you have all welcomed me into your family and I must thank you for that."

He paused, looking around at them, and in any other man she might have thought he was a little choked up. Not Harry, of course. He had probably just swallowed an olive the wrong way or something.

"Life is a strange thing," he said quietly. "We make our choices, pick our course and usually have to live with the consequences. But sometimes we're given the rare and precious chance to take a different path. When that happens, we often can discover what truly matters. Not money, power, land. Not grand houses. It's this."

He cleared his throat, the old coot, beaming at all of them but especially at his son, Jack, from whom he had spent so many years estranged.

"This," he repeated. "Family. Friends. Love."

"Don't forget food," Alex added.

"Hear, hear," came a chorus around her.

Harry was right, she thought after grace had been eloquently offered by Angie's husband and they all began to fill their plates with her delicious food.

Until Sam came into her world, she had been certain

her course was set, that she was on her way to grabbing everything she needed.

She had convinced herself she had all she could ever want. Sam and Ethan had given her the chance to venture onto another path, one filled with laughter and joy and life.

Now she refused to have it any other way.

* * * * *

Revisit the enchanting Donovan clan from
#1 *New York Times* bestselling author

NORA ROBERTS

These fascinating cousins share a secret that's been handed down through generations—a secret that sets them apart...

CHARMED

Her legacy had been as much a curse as a blessing, so Anastasia Donovan had learned to keep it hidden. But when single dad Boone Sawyer swept into her heart, she longed to reveal everything despite her fear of the consequences. Then fate stepped in...

ENCHANTED

Lovely, guileless Rowan Murray was drawn to darkly enigmatic Liam Donovan with a force she'd never imagined could exist. But before Liam could give Rowan his love, he first had to trust her with the incredible truth about himself...and his family.

Available wherever books are sold!

PSNR167

#1 *New York Times* bestselling author Linda Lael Miller returns to Stone Creek with a sweeping tale of two strangers running from dangerous secrets.

LINDA LAEL MILLER

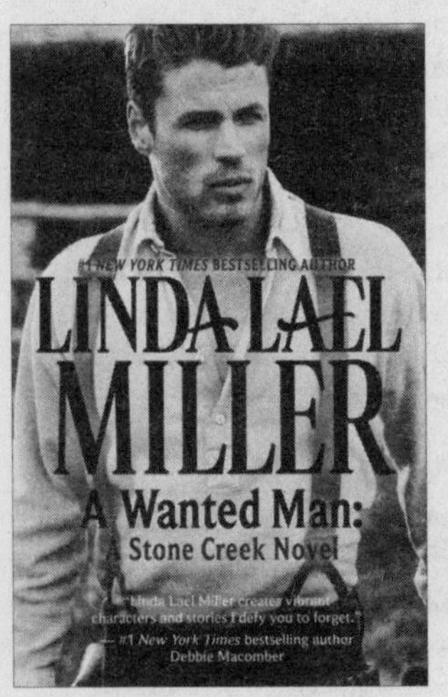

The past has a way of catching up with folks in Stone Creek, Arizona. But schoolmarm Lark Morgan and Marshal Rowdy Rhodes are determined to hide their secrets—and deny their instant attraction. That should be easy, since each suspects the other of living a lie…

Yet Rowdy and Lark share one truth: both face real dangers, such as the gang of train robbers heading their way, men Ranger Sam O'Ballivan expects Rowdy to nab. As past and current troubles collide, Rowdy and Lark must surrender their pride to the greatest power of all—undying love.

Available wherever books are sold!

Be sure to connect with us at:

Harlequin.com/Newsletters

Facebook.com/HarlequinBooks

Twitter.com/HarlequinBooks

PHLLM722

SHEILA ROBERTS

Jonathan Templar and his poker buddies can't figure women out. When Jonathan stumbles on a romance novel at the Icicle Falls library sale, he knows he's found the love expert he's been seeking—Vanessa Valentine, top-selling romance author. At first his buddies laugh at him for reading romance novels, but soon they, too, realize that these stories are the world's best textbooks on love. Poker night becomes book club night…and when all is *read* and done, they're going to be the kind of men women want!

"At last! An author who writes her way straight to the heart of every woman." —Susan Wiggs, #1 *New York Times* bestselling author

Available wherever books are sold.

Be sure to connect with us at:

Harlequin.com/Newsletters

Facebook.com/HarlequinBooks

Twitter.com/HarlequinBooks

MSR1432

RaeAnne Thayne

77637	WOODROSE MOUNTAIN	___$7.99 U.S.	___$9.99 CAN.
77593	BLACKBERRY SUMMER	___$7.99 U.S.	___$9.99 CAN.

(limited quantities available)

TOTAL AMOUNT $______
POSTAGE & HANDLING $______
($1.00 FOR 1 BOOK, 50¢ for each additional)
APPLICABLE TAXES* $______
TOTAL PAYABLE $______
(check or money order—please do not send cash)

To order, complete this form and send it, along with a check or money order for the total above, payable to Harlequin HQN, to: **In the U.S.:** 3010 Walden Avenue, P.O. Box 9077, Buffalo, NY 14269-9077; **In Canada:** P.O. Box 636, Fort Erie, Ontario, L2A 5X3.

Name: ______
Address: ______ City: ______
State/Prov.: ______ Zip/Postal Code: ______
Account Number (if applicable): ______

075 CSAS

*New York residents remit applicable sales taxes.
*Canadian residents remit applicable GST and provincial taxes.

PHRT1012BL